MASINISSA: ALLY OF CARTHAGE

D1422080

ROB EDMUNDS

Copyright © 2020 Rob Edmunds

The moral right of the author has been asserted.

Apart from any fair dealing for the purposes of research or private study,
or criticism or review, as permitted under the Copyright, Designs and Patents
Act 1988, this publication may only be reproduced, stored or transmitted, in
any form or by any means, with the prior permission in writing of the
publishers, or in the case of reprographic reproduction in accordance with
the terms of licences issued by the Copyright Licensing Agency. Enquiries
concerning reproduction outside those terms should be sent to the publishers.

Whilst some of the characters in this story were real and influential,
and some of the events described are documented, this is a work of
fiction drawn from historical sources.

Matador
9 Priory Business Park,
Wistow Road, Kibworth Beauchamp,
Leicestershire. LE8 0RX
Tel: 0116 279 2299
Email: books@troubador.co.uk
Web: www.troubador.co.uk/matador
Twitter: @matadorbooks

ISBN 978 1838594 282

British Library Cataloguing in Publication Data.
A catalogue record for this book is available from the British Library.

Printed and bound in the UK by TJ International, Padstow, Cornwall
Typeset in 11pt Adobe Jenson Pro by Troubador Publishing Ltd, Leicester, UK

Matador is an imprint of Troubador Publishing Ltd

For the J's

CONTENTS

HISTORICAL CONTEXT

The story begins in 213 BC in Carthage, which has been Masinissa's home for several years. He is the heir to the throne of the neighbouring Numidian kingdom of Massyli. His father, Gala, is an ambivalent ally of Carthage and bitter rival of Syphax, the king of the rival western Numidian kingdom of Masaesyli. Masinissa has been trained for war and tutored by the finest Greek scholars, and is widely regarded as an exceptional young man. He has also fallen in love with Sophonisba, the beautiful daughter of one of the most senior Carthaginian generals, Hasdrubal Gisco.

In terms of the wider world, Rome and Carthage – the most powerful nations of the time – have been at war for five years, ever since Hannibal crossed the Alpine passes and inflicted catastrophic and crippling defeats on the Roman armies at the battles of Trebia, Lake Trasimene and, most devastatingly, at Cannae, where an army of nearly 90,000 Romans was completely destroyed.

The war in Italy has subsequently petered out due initially to the evasive tactics of the senior Roman consul and occasional dictator – Fabius Maximus – who refused to engage Hannibal in open warfare, and later to a revival in their military fortunes, partially due to their excellence in siege tactics and the failure of the Carthaginians to forge extensive alliances with other Italian cities and territories.

The main theatres of war at this moment are the Roman siege of the Greek city of Syracuse in Sicily – which is being innovatively and belligerently defended, not least by the philosopher and scientist Archimedes – and the war in Iberia, which is being prosecuted from the Carthaginian side by Hannibal's brother Hasdrubal Barca and from the Roman side by the Scipio brothers, who are successfully preventing Hasdrubal sending reinforcements to Italy via the same route Hannibal had taken, and – in their turn – are threatening to attack North Africa with the support of Syphax.

THE PROMISES
WE MAKE TO LOVERS

Masinissa had met Sophonisba at a banquet a couple of years earlier. He had been aware of the fact that she was a Carthaginian noble and from one of the most prominent families, but this had played no part in his attraction towards her. He had also been sensitive to his own place in society, and to the fact that his status as the heir to an important strategic ally would allow him greater access to her company and perhaps even her hand. His feelings for her, however, were entirely romantic and completely detached from her station in life. His heart still retained the simple impulses of his youth, and the moment he had set his eyes on her something was released, fluttered up to his throat, and he knew that this was the girl for him.

He had heard and read many love stories, and often wondered when he might experience those depths of devotion. He knew, more usually from the older men and especially those who had returned from campaigns, of their yearning for their companions or wives. He knew he too would leave for the war at some point, and having the consolation of memories of shared moments with someone and the comfort of knowing that his well-being was in their thoughts and prayers was something he had long hoped for. He wanted the daydream to be there when that time came, to keep him going through the drudgery of long hours on horseback, and the imprinted face of a loved one to provide some kind of antidote to the horrors that he might see or inflict. The softness of Sophonisba's face and the smile that would light up her eyes he hoped would have the power to wipe away the cries of the fallen.

He knew she was a virgin. How could she be anything else but there was plenty about her to suggest that she had received all the necessary knowledge she required from her handmaidens. She moved with grace, but with an awareness of the most alluring parts of her body. She was naturally coquettish and in a way that suggested she had passed from being a mischievous, playful child to a woman of similar tendencies. Nothing appealed to Masinissa more in terms of a woman's qualities, and he relished her company for the fun it provided, as well as the passionate charge her company immediately triggered. A woman who appealed to his manhood as well as his sense of mischief was, in his eyes, perfection itself. Every time she saw him, she would greet him with a misty and willing expression, knowing that she was instantly dazzling him with her mere presence.

When he had first met her, he had trouble composing his body in ways that were unexpected for him. He was always controlled in his thoughts and movements, but her company had played havoc with his self-possession. His legs would betray him and feel as if they were treading in quicksand, and he would often break into a sweat that he would pass off as the after-effects of exercise. The most noticeable and embarrassing thing for him, though, had been an involuntary tremor in his hand. This was harder to conceal or explain, but Sophonisba had shown quickly her solicitous nature. Her touch would always immediately allay his anxiety. Most often, she would cup her hand or arm under his, and his tension would evaporate on the air. His blood and his breathing would restore themselves, and he became like a lion under a tree, lolling contentedly in his own power and affection.

He recognised the extent of the spell he had fallen under by how preoccupied he was by her and how sharply defined certain moments became for him. It was often so pronounced that he could recall partial glimpses that had made his heart sing. He remembered a spring morning earlier in the year when he had spied her from a distance from a window overlooking a courtyard. He had looked at her back and her neck, and the light and shade that played through her hair as she walked further from the building where he furtively admired her. She was idly wandering between palm trees, carelessly swinging her arms, and he concentrated hard on her every movement trying to imprint it on his memory. He had succeeded. Sometimes, memories that become indelible are determined by fate and accident, and you come by them because of the ways they have impacted on you, usually in either very happy or sad ways. There are others, though, over which you are the director or you know at the time to hold still all your senses, to mark the moment as clearly as possible. It was as if his heart and mind were conspiring to let in what they wanted, and to keep the precious moment there and to cherish it.

He had looked at her, not knowing anything other than his desires and his hopes were at that moment completely encapsulated by her receding form. Time had seemed to slow for him. The movements of her body and the expressions on her face were no different from those he had seen before and which would have been replicated very closely by any other woman of her age walking along the same avenue. However, the intentness of his gaze raised them to a different level for him. He was trying to preserve them somehow. It may have been a residual need of the youth that was falling away from him quickly or just a pessimistic realisation that he would not be able to look at her so easily in the future. The demands of the war that raged around them and an end to their innocence, both his as well as hers, made him aware of the transience of this perfection. He knew this blend of emotion, beauty and insouciance, at least on her part as she casually strolled away, was only ever fleeting. It was like a dance or a play by actors. Enjoy it for that moment but don't expect an encore.

There was also an element of mystery and anticipation in the memory and still in his evolving relationship with her. He knew that if they ever consummated their passion, the coquettish frisson that this and other moments held for him might be lost or changed. It was tied a little by her being separated from him. At the point when their courtship became fully consummated this distance would be shattered. It would be replaced then by more intimate memories, some of which would probably not be so easy to distil. The sexual moment is more urgent, and he couldn't frame it so easily as he could from his window.

Unlike many other women he encountered, who could often be quite bold in their manners, Sophonisba rationed her feminine wiles, with Masinissa never being quite sure whether her relative demureness was artful, ingenuous or some blend of the two. Regardless of her motivation, he did not feel the least compromised or emasculated by her. It was not as if her kisses were chaste. They were passionate and full, and, in those moments when she was in his arms, she devoured him to the extent to which she felt she was allowed. She wrapped him as tightly as anyone had. It seemed to Masinissa that she was very conscious of her own tipping points, and therefore the parcels of her body accessible to him were surrendered to him incrementally, with the implicit understanding that her most responsive parts would only be his fleetingly, enough to raise their excitement but not enough to break her virginal resolution.

It was a comical anatomical journey. It had started with her hands, and then her mouth and neck. Her ears were unexpectedly delicate triggers, which he began to revel in increasingly. He felt that perhaps this sensitivity was a little due to the fact that, to shield herself from the sun Sophonisba, in common with most women of her class, wore a light veil most of the time, which framed her face but concealed her ears.

Masinissa was a glutton for her responses. He loved her body for its shape and form, but he also treated it as a musician would treat his instrument. The way she would coo, and her muscles ease and contract, or her breathing or laughter alter were all part of the enjoyment for him. In his ardour, he was not of a mind to take from her but to give. If she was not responsive to his touch and kisses, his own passion would dissipate. Fortunately, for all her apparent chastity, Sophonisba was always pretty amenable to his embraces.

In her own amorous arsenal, she had been blessed with the most exuberant mouth, possibly the most voluptuous part of her, which was, in itself, quite a statement to make. Around her mouth and in her eyes, it was easy to detect the absence of care or worries. The smoothness around both showed that the lines that stresses and exhaustion had etched into others had not blemished her. Not around her mouth were there signs of the worries or creases that were easy to notice in the faces of young widows, who found work where they could in the fields or the in the arcades of the marketplaces.

Her eyes were simultaneously the most revealing and inscrutable part of her. Her eyelids had a prodigious range, capable when tired or thoughtful to be quite narrow, like those of some Bactrians he had seen. When excited, amused or inquisitive, however, her eyes would widen into saucers and gain a childlike quality which captivated him. He became highly attuned to this adjustment in her expression. He would treat it like an open door or a permission. He had her attention and interest then.

At a distance, her eyes seemed like pools of obsidian which always drew him towards her. When he was closer or when the light shone directly on her eyes, it was possible to detect a very dark green colour in her irises, which was unusual for Carthaginians, but more common in Greek or Celtic people. She invariably drew attention to this feature through cosmetics, an art which she was obviously extremely proficient in. Masinissa enjoyed the fact that she would make frequent cosmetic alterations in her appearance, which was deliberate and enjoyable for them both. Some women he knew dressed purely for themselves, and others did so clearly to garner male attention. Sophonisba did both. She was livelier in her dress than most women he had encountered, and adorned herself, with her powders and her jewellery, in ways that showed her beauty and innate vivacity very well. She was also quite unapologetic about it, to the point of vanity. Some women insisted that wearing kohl was for the purpose of cleansing the eyes or protecting them from the sun's harmful rays. Sophonisba was quite frank about the fact that, for her, it was all about lengthening her eyelashes and adding beauty to her eyes. She often went even further and wore a slight dab of malachite under her eyes, which drew out their deep green colour very attractively.

Masinissa teased her whenever she went with this look. "Here comes my little Egyptian princess!" he would cry as she approached. This mild insult would rarely go unacknowledged, and he knew to brace himself for a little thump to his bicep, and a little mock flash of anger and scorn. Depending on his mood, he had often continued with the game and made a theatrical yelp or grimace, pretending that she had caused him the most painful injury, saying, "Oh Sophonisba, what are you doing? I think you may have broken my arm."

He soon realised the pointlessness of his protests. It only encouraged her to be more irrepressible with her blows. There was no way she would ever be cool or aloof with him. Her thumps were a part of their physical intimacy. Anyone passing or in their company would often smile, laugh or look at them knowingly or conspiratorially. A six-and-a-half-foot Adonis being pummelled and berated by a gamine, young girl was an incongruous sight, and one only explainable by the fact that the two must, in some way, be lovers. Neither minded such an exposure. As long as form and protocols were not breached, then it was likely that no one would interfere with them, beyond casting jealous looks at them, or talking about them in their villas and bathing houses.

*

That day, they were going to meet in the Byrsa, but neither had told the other where. It was part of a game they frequently played and their favourite spot to play it was within the cramped and narrow arcades of the citadel. It was a hide-and-seek game that they had refined over a period of months. The beach had proven a poor spot to hide at, even though, once discovered, it was a pleasant place to enjoy each other's company. The port and harbour had been flawed as a location too.

It was not the greatest location for play. There was constant loading of men and materials, and the general ambience of the place was not conducive to their intentions. The stevedores, soldiers and sailors were often short-tempered and envious of a happy, blithe couple cavorting around their workplace. Besides, hiding alone whilst waiting for your beau in a dockyard where there may be men alighting who had not seen an attractive woman for some time posed some serious dangers. They hadn't really thought it through. The potential for mistaken identity for a painted, alluring woman at the port of Carthage was almost overwhelming.

Sophonisba had to deflect quite a few suggestive and ribald comments from the dockers before she had been found by Masinissa, and they were able to make their reasonably hasty retreat. There was a suspicion on the part of Masinissa that Sophonisba hadn't minded this lewd attention one bit. It would have been much more probable for him to have found her in a state of distress or even tears. Instead, he found her holding her ground quite well. In fact, it might even have been said that the half a dozen men who had gathered around her and who were making quite indiscreet overtures towards her were, to a man, entranced by her and that she was savouring their attention as much as they would her breasts, in the implausible scenario that they could have agreed a price for her ravishment.

The Byrsa it was, then. Besides its natural advantages for playing hide-and-seek, it also benefitted from being a location with a proximity to a host of sellers and merchants, who paraded goods from throughout the Carthaginian Empire and often from far beyond. Masinissa knew well, from his serendipitous discovery of silk, the exotic wares that could be procured by the persistent and lucky shopper. There was always a prize and a forfeit in his and Sophonisba's games, and one that could be decided by another round of exploration added another degree of excitement to their adventure. Sophonisba, in particular, liked to be spoilt, and if he could contrive to lose the game, all the better. He knew that the real prize of the game was her gratitude.

Within the Byrsa, there were so many places of concealment, and they both were well acquainted with enough of these to make discovery a prolonged affair. Both, too, ordinarily would spend a great deal of their time within its enormous fortified walls. The Carthaginians had taken care to ensure that everything they needed had been situated within their pretty-impregnable stronghold in the unlikely event of an attack or siege. The whole gamut of social and public life was to be found within it. The most prestigious school in the city was just off the small, central square, and Masinissa had spent many hours perfecting his Latin and Greek tenses there. There was a produce market, with particularly well-appointed vintners, whom Masinissa had become very familiar with; a warren of a bazaar that occupied a large precinct of its own; an amphitheatre where many of the most urgent debates of the day were voiced; a sumptuous spa and baths where Masinissa had enjoyed soaking away many of his post-exercise aches and pains; the senate buildings themselves; extensive stables for horses and elephants; and barracks, mostly unoccupied, for troops who would be charged with defending this last fortress of Carthage. There were also towers and defensive fortifications along many of the walls, particularly those facing the ocean, and many of these had ballistas and other siege equipment *in situ*. Five years of war and fluctuating fortunes had made for a pessimistic preparedness in the heart of the city. Finally, there were the gold-inlaid temples to Baal Hammon, Tanit and Melqart, the last of which was an occasional refuge for Masinissa in those moments when he sought consolation or guidance.

Masinissa was very much fond of the story of the founding of the Byrsa and, subsequently, the city of Carthage itself. It was a very important point of identity for all the people there who traced their personal histories back to the Phoenician and Tyrian settlers. It was also relevant to him as a Numidian, and as a descendant of the king who had ceded territory to Dido and her Phoenician exiles when they had fled Tyre and Pygmalion's wrath. It was funny, Masinissa thought, how such an apparently minor concession, which could even be regarded as an act of mercy, could have such enormous ramifications centuries later. If Dido had been rebuffed, would she have continued on and made landfall elsewhere, perhaps in Mauritania or Iberia? Maybe they could have found shelter beyond Mons Calpe and made their colony close to the Temple of Melqart, near Gades.

For Masinissa, the story was also potentially a salutary lesson in so far as it gave him a reminder of Phoenician cunning and duplicity. He would only ever have to remind himself of the actions of Dido to realise that the Carthaginians were not to be trusted. Dido had asked the Numidian king Iarbas only for a tiny and temporary parcel of land for a brief refuge. In appearance, if the country were represented by the king's body, the land she asked for would be merely the tip of the king's fingernail. Once granted, Dido proceeded, figuratively, to devour the rest of his arm. The covenant that was agreed upon granted Dido as much land as could be covered by an ox hide. Wandering the alleyways of the Byrsa, it was clear that this could not have been achieved literally. Dido had craftily torn the ox hide into thin strips, which when laid together were – so it was told – sufficient to encircle the entire hill on which they stood, and that had developed into the citadel of Carthage. Its name was even taken, a little scornfully, from that legend: the meaning of Byrsa being "hide". It was also the Phoenician word for citadel, so perhaps its future purpose may have been ordained by the gods.

Masinissa was excited by the prospect of spending time with Sophonisba, and it was the first moments with her that he always looked forward to the most. It was a mixture of the pleasurable thoughts of reunion after their absence in which he could reform her beauty outside of his imagination and also share her delight at seeing him again. She provided him with a sort of reflection of himself, as if he were looking at her in a sort of pellucid emotional mirror. She exhibited immediately and guilelessly the emotions he felt, and she quickly released him from any social strictures he may have felt, and he was the giddy, besotted fool he longed to be.

The one thing that Masinissa tried to ensure in their hide-and-seek-play was that he would lose. Aside from the enjoyment both he and Sophonisba would gain by him having to pay the tribute and buy the gift for her, he found thrilling the notion of being stalked and the way in which Sophonisba would declare his capture and defeat. It had become almost a form of greeting, and one that he certainly preferred to the formal bow or the informal kiss. His peripheral vision and sixth senses were pretty acute, and he always knew when she was sneaking up on him. However, rather than turning around and exposing her, he simply would become quiet and still, and await his seizure by her. He had been told by some animal keepers once that the best response to being mauled by certain creatures, bears in particular, was to lay still and play dead. Sophonisba wasn't going to treat him so roughly, but the ploy of stillness was one he certainly enjoyed using.

The way in which she did it, after carefully shadowing her prey was to reach her hands over his face from behind and cup his eyes, so that he was blinded by his assailant. Of course, he knew exactly who it was, but the sport in the game was for him to guess. It was as if he were playing a game with a child, and he made sure that he faked a little confusion and maybe even threw out a wild guess, which usually would only make Sophonisba clasp his face even tighter. The sport would conclude with him placing his hands on hers and, suddenly and theatrically, realising it was her all along. At which point, he would turn, give her the broadest smile and wrap his arms around her, whilst she yelped her delight at his happiness and cooperation.

In order to facilitate such an easy kill, Masinissa had made the most abject attempt at concealment and tracking. He had positioned himself at the edge of a wall leading into the lane that headed to the chambers of the Council of Elders, and he just waited. One way of looking at such a move would be that he was in a position to ambush her if she were to approach from that direction. Another would be that most of the rest of the Byrsa was behind him, and his location could be spied easily by people coming from most directions. He had given himself effectively a one-in-five or one-in-six chance of victory in this game. He liked those odds very much.

Inevitably, it was only a matter of time before she pounced, and he was blinded and temporarily paralysed. When she first started to play this trick on him, this incapacity was almost real as he was so overwhelmed by her presence. He soon learnt to control his love daze, though, even though the thrill always remained the same as ever. The complement to this sensory deprivation of light was the sensory overload of scent. If Sophonisba could be regarded as an expert at anything, it would be at the art of the perfumer. She always wore the most alluring and feminine scents, and always applied them just before she was leaving her home, so that their intensity was at their greatest. If they were to play their game for real, she would stand no chance of winning, as her presence would be as detectable on the air as a cavalry unit being tracked through a woodland after rain.

Masinissa knew she had anointed herself in several of the most obvious places, locations that she had amended marginally in his honour. Not that he needed any cues, but they were given to him, nevertheless. As the cloud of flesh, scent and joy had enveloped him, he had no need for his eyes, and as soon as he had given Sophonisba that first squeeze of greeting, he buried himself as deeply into her throat, neck and breasts as he could. His face could not have been better signposted. She could have done no better if she had left pieces of cake at those spots and lured the nearest starving glutton.

It may have been better for him that his eyes were closed, and his mouth and nose were buried in his beloved's cleavage. For despite their disregard for their surroundings and preoccupation with one another, this indifference was not reciprocated. To those around him – be they nobles, scholars, merchants or slaves – he and Sophonisba were objects of much interest, some of which was simple curiosity, but some of this attention was of a more vicious and jealous kind. They were both well known, and consorting with each other so openly could be offensive to the more patrician elements within Carthaginian society.

Masinissa, though, was carefree, and oblivious to the condescension or hostility of some of the passers-by as he was engulfed by the sensory pleasures Sophonisba had gifted him. He wrapped one of his arms low around her hips, and the other he held higher, tracing the line of her spine with his thumb and forefinger. His hands were flat at first, spread as wide as they could be to accommodate as much of her body and flesh as possible. It was a mix of possession, sensual ardour and also an automatic response her musk had compelled in him.

Holding her, he inhaled and, as deliberately as he had from his secretive vantage point when he spied her, he tried to fix her scent in his mind, both to enjoy it for the moment and to save it as an imprint for the future. He wondered if, in the coming months, he might be able to open a bottle of this perfume, and recall her body and this moment as a result. He doubted his olfactory senses could be relied upon to conjure such a vision, but it was worth the effort, he was sure. He wanted a bottle of that scent quite badly, in truth. He wanted to be able to drizzle tiny amounts of it on a cloth and smother his face in it as a comfort, in the same way as a baby would seek out a blanket. It is funny how some passions, even in their delirium, could have premeditated elements.

It was impossible for him to analyse her smell properly, but he ardently sought the most conspicuous notes that he could. As there was only one Sophonisba, there would only ever be one scent that he wanted to associate with her, despite the frequency with which she might alter the blend. This essence of her would always be the most recent one, as the most recent could always be the last. Masinissa held to the romantic absolutism of the desperate and the beguiled.

He knew that there was an element of practicality to her scent as well, and that it offered her a modest protection from the sun, which – in tandem with her veil – helped shield her complexion from the fierceness of the daylight. That benefit was incidental to the moment, as he savoured the symphony of cedar, myrrh, frankincense and cypress, and tugged gently at her hair so that more of her throat and bosom was exposed to his greedy senses.

There was only so long he could submerge himself in her cleavage, and, as he rose for air, he breathed out compliments as avidly as he had inhaled her sweetness.

"Ah, my Aphroditeeee," he purred. "It always seems too long."

It was a compliment that was sure to find its target; Sophonisba sighed slightly in approval, and her diaphragm dropped momentarily, as if the deflation in her lungs gave an accompanying inflation of her ego. "Oh, my Melqart. I've missed you too. It's only been a few days, but I've suffered. Tanit help me when you start campaigning. I need an artist to draw your likeness to keep me going, I think. Sometimes I wonder if I would have been better off if I hadn't known you."

Masinissa looked at her a little ruefully and tried to put a little commiseration into his words and eyes. "Oh sweetheart, it is the nature of the world for us, for everyone, to know departures and reunions. Savour the moments we have and see me as much as you can in your dreams; well, when the time comes and I'm away in Numidia, Iberia or Rome even, wherever the tides of war wash me up. I will do my best to come back to you in one piece and with enough of a reputation to hold you in the night as I do in the day."

Sophonisba put both her hands on her hips, accentuating that region considerably in the process, and looked at him in mock seriousness. It was another of their games that they played to indicate annoyance or the semblance of it in most cases. One hand on her hip was, in their lover's lexicon, a single humph, and two hands on her hips was a double humph. A single humph was a very rare sighting in Sophonisba's play. "Do your best? You will do your best to return to me as I pine and yearn and pray for you my every waking moment? You can't lay that one at my feet and expect me to do anything other than kick it away. I need more, Masinissa. I need everything." She raised her hand and pointed two fingers at him, which she waved slightly in front of him to indicate that she was disapproving of his lacklustre commitment. The gesture retained a little of the comedy of the pose, but it was clear that she was genuine in her pique.

Masinissa realised his error. This girl was all or nothing, and he'd given her uncertainty and the prospect of failure. He backtracked sharply. "You have it. I'm sorry. I don't mean to offer weakness or doubt. You need my strength and my conviction, and I'll give it to you. I will be back, and I will claim you as my own with all my mind and body intact. I will evade my enemies and make my way through this mad world of conflicts. Your heart will be my beacon, and I will follow it and race back to you as soon as I am able." Masinissa could see that had left a better mark on her. She needed his reassurance as she had about her portions of the realist as well as the romantic, and he needed to steer her towards the later.

She lowered her voice a little and spoke more earnestly. "I hope it is easy for you to love me when I become a memory. I hope I do not fade away like a cheap dye as you march on your conquests."

"No, my darling, you must trust me as I do you. My feelings for you are as indelible as the scars I bear." He pointed at one on his forearm from a dagger swipe, which once had been livid and crimson, but now was like a furtive worm, curling between the hairs of his arm.

"I'm not sure I want to be compared to a scar you know."

The sensitivity of his woman never ceased to surprise Masinissa, but he had enough wits about him to realise his metaphor had held some substance for Sophonisba. Nevertheless, he knew she needed more, and it was time for his feelings to pour out. *I'm going to have to keep laying this on*, Masinissa thought, channelling a little masculine bravura, although in a measure that couldn't hope to dilute the intensity of his true feelings.

"I believe in fate," he said quietly whilst focussing his gaze directly at Sophonisba, "and the interventions of the gods, and we are fated by them to be together. I believe in the all-consuming nature of love as the most intense expression of our beings. Without that emotion, we are no better than the animals who live out their short existences listlessly and mechanically. Knowing you has lifted me out of that drudgery, and given me purpose and fearlessness."

He saw that Sophonisba was quietly being moved by his words but held a little self-possession to her core to prevent herself from embracing him and curtailing his lover's monologue.

He continued, "You know each day alters me a little; little parts of my soul are exhausted and fade, whilst other parts are awakened.

Maybe I mature, shed a little innocence and gain a little wisdom, but certain emotions and attitudes abide and are constant. My first thoughts of the day and my final ones are of you. I cannot imagine a moment in the hopefully long chain of my days that will change that fact, even when my mutable being rewrites my story a little every day." He held her hand, almost as a gesture of formal commitment. "I am yours now, as is obvious to see, but I will be yours forever too, which is a claim I know is harder to believe or trust. I know the war will lay waste to large parts of me, and little deaths will afflict me even if I am spared a final blow, but – regardless of the trials ahead, and the new days when I will awake with new eyes and changed feelings – you will always be there as my joined soul, in the part of me that is inviolable. I love you. In all the complexities of our universe, I hold to that simple truth."

Masinissa knew that this was the natural point to stop. He had made his confessions and his claims, and it was for Sophonisba now to absorb what he had given her. There was an inevitable pause as she let his words embed themselves into her memory and heart.

"A promise is a promise, sweetheart," Sophonisba murmured with her eyes slightly shadowed and downcast, and with a tone of obvious doubt and uncertainty, as if she wanted to believe him and trust the conviction and certainty he had packed into his words. She continued, "I know words are not as solid as rock or as certain as the march of waves on a shore, but when they are spoken by the man whom you have sworn to believe in, then they should carry weight and obligation. Don't say words to me just to fill the air, to make me smile or to even give you the belief that you don't completely possess in silence. I know that, whilst we are masters of our souls, we are not masters of our destinies, especially people like us who could be flung to all parts, all suitors and all causes in this terrible, endless war. We may both fail in all our hopes and dreams, but stick to your promise, my darling, until the point where it is torn from you, so that you can be comforted by the knowledge that you stayed true to your noblest and most sincere emotions."

Masinissa buckled visibly with the force of her words. She was full of surprises and the wisdom and apprehension in her words shook him. "The fates will push us like the fiercest gales will rock the flimsiest sailboat, but the promises I make to you are filled with certainty. Every portion of my being pledges fealty to you, to what we have and to what we could have if our destinies are allowed to entwine. This is not an idle promise that I, or any of my soldiers or vassals, might make in a moment of passion, or as thoughtfulness or deceit to please or trick a curious girl. This is not even a promise made to lovers, as these can be shared and transient. This is more a promise made to love itself; that is, the emotion that can only be exclusive and mutual, and that can only be discovered once in its purest form. I love you, Sophonisba."

For a second time, she dropped her gaze to the earth and closed her eyes; although, this time, it appeared to Masinissa as if it was to savour, in a momentary stillness, an ecstasy that his words had given her. She breathed deeply, then exploded into his arms, and held him as tightly and possessively as she ever had.

GAMES WITHOUT FRONTIERS

Conon stood over his desk, with a compass in one hand and a hunk of bread in the other. He had dipped the bread in honey so he took care to perform his drawings with his uncontaminated hand. Whatever his design, it would appear to be a preliminary effort. Breakfast looked as if it at least had equal call on his attention. When he noticed that it was Masinissa at the door, he beamed and ushered him in with his sticky baton.

The scholar had developed a great affection for Masinissa, initially as one of his Greek tutors, but latterly as a friend and confidante. It was a fondness that could be traced to a number of origins. There was Masinissa's natural charm, impressive stature and amiability, but it was also related somewhat to his status as a Numidian and a Massylian. As a Greek, Conon regarded him as a fellow minority and the fact that Masinissa retained a detachment from the Carthaginian nobility and his freedom of thought, if not always his freedom to act impressed him. This was not a trivial attribute in Carthage, where there was an increasing deference to the Barcid clan, following the victories Hannibal had made in his Italian campaigns.

For his part, Conon subscribed to a view that was broadly neutral and detached. He would not be part of any levy or military recruitment – due to his engineering and medical prowess – so he, perhaps naively, felt a little immune from the war. He could serve any master, and they were likely to be equally as bad as each other. He was ambivalent about both Rome and Carthage, and his understanding of the behaviour of both made him wary and distrustful. He could prosper in both cities, but he had chosen Carthage as he felt it more resembled the city states of Greece. He shared Aristotle's view of his hosts in that they had constructed a state and a cluster of governing institutions that matched the best in the world; Sparta and Crete in particular.

He looked at Masinissa a little more attentively as he came through the atrium, and the sharp light of the low morning sun highlighted the tensions in his friend. Masinissa's shoulders, hands and eyes were rigid and strained, and it required little intuition to realise that this was more than a social call.

"Relax Mas, you can drop your guard. We Greeks are known for our oaths and confidentialities, and maybe a few other things besides,"

Masinissa released his hands a little, clutched them tightly together and then splayed them wide again with a cephalopodic thrust. It was as obvious an indicator that he had shifted his mental state as there could be. Conon had come to recognise and appreciate that Masinissa was as agile emotionally as he was physically. Anger, agitation and amusement all moved swiftly across him. Only sadness appeared to linger with his giant Numidian friend.

"OK, Conon, I'm sorry. I don't mean to meet you with a glower on my face; not all ground is as safe as your home for me, you know! Sometimes, I need a moment to switch down."

"Well, I hope it's off now," Conon replied in as reassuring a manner as he could manage. "I'm not going to run to Himilco or any of the Barcid faction to tell them of any views you may have. You are as free to talk with me as if you possessed the licence and authority to do so of a senator or *suffete*. I would listen to you as if you were Hanno himself, who, for me, may just be the only voice of reason we can count on at the moment."

Even though they were both broadly aware of each other's opinions, Masinissa was a little surprised by Conon's political reference. "Ah, you are in the appeaser camp then, Con?" he asked, more out of curiosity than to know whether he needed to realign his relationship a little. He knew he wouldn't need to.

Conon bridled slightly. "Hanno is no appeaser. He just sees weaknesses as well as strengths. He learnt the hard way during the mercenary war about the dangers of complacency. Carthage's foundations are not as solid as Rome's my friend."

The reference to the mercenary war interested Masinissa. The war had created a powerful legacy for Carthage. It had made the city wary of its paid legions being too close to itself. For an incipient general, it held other lessons too. Hanno's actions were not to be emulated. He had taken his soldiers for granted, and they had mutinied and attacked their hosts. For Masinissa, it was a reminder that you should never undervalue your own soldiers and you should never lose their trust. In truth, most of the mercenary army had served under Hamilcar, who had assumed joint command of the army as the tensions worsened, and they surely would have shown him greater loyalty, but neither he nor Hanno sensed the mood very perceptively. Presenting yourself in person would also have reaffirmed the bond, and Hamilcar's failure to do so was a final insult to a restive army.

Masinissa was far closer to the military elite than Conon, and viewed the Carthaginian generals more in generational terms. He regarded the younger Hannibal, his brothers and Hasdrubal Gisco as the leaders of consequence, and the older figures as increasingly peripheral and irrelevant. He explained, "Hanno is old. His influence fades and his reputation is not as unblemished as his followers would make out. He has cost Carthage dearly, and his own failures make him cautious now."

Conon sensed a little exasperation in his friend's tone and steered the conversation accordingly, "Maybe. Anyway, is it history you want to talk about or what?"

It wasn't. History had always interested Masinissa. He was an avid student in fact, and knew far more than even his tutors suspected, but he was looking for company and wanted impartial views and easy company. "Archimedes?" Masinissa ventured.

Conon rolled his eyes and shrugged his shoulders simultaneously. "As the resident engineer and scientist in this part of town, you think I am an expert on him?"

Masinissa knew the body language signalled resigned amusement and ploughed on. "How much will his inventions and strategies keep Rome from Syracuse? You must have an opinion."

"Don't you mean how long? It's a siege. The stronger party is preying on the weaker, and unless Carthage relieves them or the Roman forces are redirected then it should just be a matter of time."

Masinissa was surprised by his friend's pessimism. "But Archimedes has created miraculous weapons that can pick ships out of the sea and overturn them. The Roman fleet is being dragged out of the sea by Archimedes cranes. Then there are his mirrors too, which harness the sun and burn the sails of the besiegers."

"I know they're fascinating inventions. Syracuse has a genius at its disposal, but even a genius cannot make food out of air. The claws of Archimedes can smash the hulls of Roman ships, and the ballistas on the city walls can rain down rock and fire on their attackers, but their commanders learn quickly, and if the Syracusans cannot break out, then the pressure will just increase. Marcellus is in no hurry and has his own siege engines to counter Archimedes. Look at the Sambuca. They have engineers who have made their siege towers float."

None of this was new to Masinissa. Syracuse was a major theatre of the war, but not the most important one. If Hannibal were to regain his momentum, and the war in Iberia went favourably for Hasdrubal and Mago, then Syracuse, Sicily and all of Magna Gracia would be a sideshow. When the war was waged so widely, then it was inevitable that some places would be stalemates and reversals, and others frantic and devastating victories. Hannibal needed more of the latter. His lightning war through Northern Italy, and the blows delivered at Ticinus, Trebia and Cannae were spearheads right at the most vulnerable and complacent territories of Rome, which demoralised and dislocated their forces, but his momentum had slowed, and surprise and speed were no longer assets he brought to the battleground.

Masinissa thought he would express some wonderment at Archimedes, and hoped some of his awe might rub off on Conon, who had a flair for similar devices. "You know, Con, surely you can see how all these contraptions – pulleys and levers, onagers and ballistas, and mirrors to concentrate the sun's rays – can bewilder a cavalry officer? They impress me. Controlling the sun is a grander feat than controlling a horse!"

"Not really, once you have the tool it is just a matter of pointing. A horse is much more capricious. You cannot plot its movements so precisely, however much mastery you have."

Masinissa raised his fingers and tapped his head, acknowledging his friend's wisdom and kindness. Defending each other's talents was a habit that they shared. Conon would praise Masinissa's skills, and, in turn, Masinissa would do the same and applaud Conon's intellectual achievements. Neither could aspire to the other's gifts, and their mutual admiration made them even fonder of one another.

"Come on, let me challenge this general-in-waiting. Do you fancy playing some petteia?" asked Conon.

Masinissa clapped his hands in approval. "You are such a Greek! Let's do it." *Petteia* was a game that Masinissa enjoyed immensely. He realised that it was almost a vanity of his to take pride in the game, but it took strategic dexterity, logic and even sacrifice; all talents he nurtured and knew he needed.

Regardless of one's class or station in life, *petteia* was popular. It was often played in camps by idle soldiers, and bets were frequent. Everyone fancied themselves good at the game. The square *petteia* board – composed usually of black and white pieces, most commonly in stone but sometimes in marble or even silver – was often seen dotted around campfires. It was ostensibly a simple game, but casual players would be routed quickly by an experienced opponent. The essence of the game was to move your pieces, or "dogs" as they were frequently referred to, in horizontal and vertical lines along a board divided into squares, eight by eight. Each player took their turn, and the object was to trap an opponent's piece or pieces between two of your own. When this was achieved, the opponent's piece would be removed.

The Greeks took particular delight in the game, and some of their most eminent figures were known to have been aficionados. Aristotle had used a *petteia* metaphor of an isolated piece to describe a stateless person. If the tutor of Alexander the Great had been a fan, then it was almost incumbent on Masinissa to follow suit and become an expert in the game himself. Those were the kind of role models he could respect. Plato, in his *Republic*, had also elevated *petteia* onto a pedestal. He went as far as to refer to Socrates's victims as poor players who had finally been trapped and isolated by more-accomplished opponents. He had also pointed out that it took long hours of training before someone could regard themselves as an expert. It was a pleasure to play, but it also required dedication to master, which was a combination that suited Masinissa's temper well.

Conon had set up the board or "city" as everyone called it, and placed out their respective dogs. He turned to Masinissa, in quite a canine way, and looked at him expectantly. "Do you want to go first?"

Masinissa was never sure whether the game granted a particular advantage to the opening player; he was doubtful that it did, but there was always something about a virgin board that made him want to plot out an opening gambit. He was the same with coin tosses, although he was always predictable on those occasions. He would wait until the coin was in the air and always pick the side featuring the unbridled horse. He wondered if his continual snub of Tanit's head would one day start to irritate the god. He thought it would probably be OK. "Of course, I have to make a few traps don't I?"

As Conon sat down and let his friend lead, Masinissa observed him and realised how much a man of science and scholarship he was. Despite Conon's learning, or perhaps because of it, his innocence was easy to detect. His studies had absolved him of any military training or service, and – when regarded by someone who was familiar with the most Spartan forms of training – his softness was transparent. Masinissa wondered if it was too much of a leniency of the state to have granted him such immunity, especially in this time of worldwide conflict, when even the safest havens and strongest cities could be threatened. Pity Conon's peer Archimedes in Syracuse, who was using all of his genius to keep the Roman swords from his throat.

For all our shared amusements and fellowship, how different we are, thought Masinissa. In appearance, they couldn't have been more different. Conon had narrow, slumped shoulders; little strength in either his arms or legs; a very flat chest; and even a slight paunch, which was almost criminal in someone of such relative youth. He also appeared to take only a passing interest in his appearance. His tunic was drab and ill-fitting, and he was otherwise unadorned. Even his hair seemed to reflect his disinterest in his physical appearance. It was lank and had grown to look more like one of the woollen hats that he had sometimes seen on some of the mercenary Gauls in the docks than a proper head of hair.

Masinissa stood in quite imposing contrast. He stood several inches higher than his friend, and his shoulders and arms were twice the circumference of his friend's. With his arms folded, the curves of his muscular upper body were apparent and would draw attention from his face if he held the pose for any time. They could no doubt indicate quite specific body language in other circumstances. They could offer a barrier, hostility or even authority, although on this occasion it was merely that he was clearing his mind before starting the game.

His face was as impressive as his physique. He was a few shades darker than most Greeks or Carthaginians, but lighter than most Libyans and other Africans. He was evidently of Numidian stock. His eyes shone with a piercing inquisitiveness. Rarely did they cloud over with a daydream or a moment of absent mindedness. For the most part, to look at him directly would be to notice his alertness and attention. His eyes were as dark as he was, but seemed to draw you into his gaze, revealing a little of the openness of the man. His nose was straight and flat, in contrast to the aquiline features of many Greeks and certainly Romans. It resembled the nose of a man who had been in many fights and had endured his nose squashed down, but it had none of the detours of bone and cartilage that betrayed a brawler. His hair and beard were short to medium length, with the hint of a heavy curl, and his mouth was full and prone to wide articulation. Masinissa had a wide range of expressions and an inability to disguise his emotions very well. He also had the widest yawn when tired, which women tended to find quite endearing, and some men felt gave him a momentary and incongruous resemblance to an infant. His mouth also made some emotions even more pronounced, particularly disdain or sorrow. It was an unfortunate feature to possess in conversations with some senior Carthaginian figures, and he was painfully self-conscious of his efforts at concealment. He consoled himself with the fact that his expressions, for the most part, were benign, and showed his affable and personable nature.

His clothing indicated a man of rank as well as action. Sometimes, he was happy to wear just a simple tunic, especially in the heat of the summer, but it was his habit to dress as he would with his men. Dressing casually in his position would show a slovenliness that could easily be viewed negatively. That day, he wore his tunic as his first layer. It ran to a little below his knee, and had a slit up to that point on either side to give him a better range of movement. It was sleeveless, being cut to just over his shoulder, and was light sand in colour. If ever he was in need of camouflage in the desert, then this would be the outfit to be in. Over this and to the point of his groin, he wore a chain-mail hauberk or *lorica hamata* as it was called by the Romans. As it probably had been worn originally by a Roman officer before his corpse had been plucked of any valuable items, it was in keeping for him to refer to it occasionally as his *lorica*. It was relatively light and comfortable for this type of armour, and he had grown accustomed to it as a second and largely unobtrusive skin.

Unlike many Carthaginian nobles, he was barefooted and barelegged. He had no time for the leg greaves that had become fairly standard infantry equipment. The only time he would be willing to relent was on the eve of battle, where they would give him a degree of protection against the slashing blades of those who had the bravery to meet any charge he made.

Across his shoulders and in the manner of a cloak, Masinissa wore a pallium. He had wrapped it around his throat and let the bulk of it trail behind his back. It was a practical item for him, but he liked the fact that it was a style of clothing most favoured by philosophers and teachers. He enjoyed the sensation of it when he was on horseback, as it lifted behind him giving the pace he generated a rising eddy and counterpoint. Its colour also drew the eye, especially in crowds, where the ordinary citizens usually wore quite uniform and drab hues. It was a bold Tyrian purple, which was a colour much coveted by many Carthaginians. Their Phoenician forebears had even been named after it. The literal translation of Phoenicia means "Land of Purple". He had bought the garment several years ago, but, as the merchant had promised, it had retained all its original depth of colour, and age and the elements hadn't faded any of the dye. It was a good thing that it hadn't either. Purple-dyed textiles were expensive, costing many silver pieces for some of the finer cloth. He knew he was parading his wealth a little when he wore it, which was pretty much all the time, but he didn't mind appearing a little dashing and flamboyant. He quite revelled in giving that impression, in truth.

It was held by a clasp on his right shoulder, which he prized very highly, both for its ornamental value and its sentimental one. It had been given to him by his father, and there was an element of solemnity about the gift. It was a solid-gold circle and within it was depicted the silhouette of a horse in flight, with a tall palm behind it. The bar that affixed it to his cloak was hidden neatly behind it. Two such clasps had been made by the most capable artisan that Massylian Numidia could call upon. One was in his possession and one in his father's. It was meant to represent the crown of Numidia and would instantaneously show his kinsman who he was. He could be a bloodied, starving mess, but he knew there would be countrymen who would brave any danger to save him so long as his clasp was still in his possession. To him, it was the most potent symbol of his succession and his nation. It was also poignant, as it was a constant indicator of his father's love and regard for him. He remembered vividly the emotion and even the tremor in his father's voice when he had given it to him and closed his hand around it. "Never forget who you are or the loyalties you command," Gala had told him.

Masinissa wore two belts, or, more precisely, a belt and a sash. His practical belt was narrow and made of leather, with some minor gold trim for decoration. This was buckled over a wide and bold cummerbund, which was perhaps the boldest and most idiosyncratic part of his attire. It was also the most expensive and rare. An advantage of living in Carthage was that it was the centre of so much trade in the world, and items found their way to the bazaars from the farthest corners of the world. His sash was one such item. It was the boldest and most azure shade of blue, with a luxury and lustre only to be found in the finest silk. It was always admired, and people often even stared at his waist, as so few of even the nobility had ever seen such a fabric.

He had come across some traders who had a small roll of silk, and he had bought the lot. The fabric would fade a little, unlike his cloak, and he rotated the sashes he had made out of the roll: a worn one was used for most days, and another was reserved for special occasions or days away from the horses and the sun. According to the traders, the silk had come to them via Parthians who, in turn, had bought it off some Bactrians, who had travelled from a market close to the great stone tower in the middle of their territory. Masinissa wondered somewhat if this was just a little fanciful sales talk on the part of the trader, as such vast distances made everything a little vague. Maybe this great tower was nothing more than a flag in the earth, or maybe even a fiction or totem meant to mark the midpoint between the Mediterranean civilisations and the lands of the Seres. He couldn't really properly make sense of this mysterious land of Serica, with its peculiar people, but there had been several traders he had spoken to who had attested to coming across them, and their wares were as unique in appearance as they were. He had seen a ceramic pot in the parlour of one of the *suffetes* once, and had been mesmerised by its beauty. It shared a little of the colour of his cummerbund. There must be a great liking for blue amongst the Seres.

Hooked into his belt was his sword. Masinissa never left home without it. The sword he usually preferred was a *xiphos*, a short, double-edged weapon much favoured by the Greeks. It was a secondary weapon for them, as it was for the Numidians, with both having the javelin as their main weapon of choice. That day, though, he had opted for an alternative weapon, which he was favouring increasingly. It was an Iberian *falcata*, which was gaining popularity amongst many of the infantrymen he came across. Even the sound of the word had a forceful ring to it. It was a heavy, curved blade, almost always made of the finest and strongest metal, and it was much feared on the battlefield as it could crush most armour with ease. The trade in them between the Iberians, Numidians and Carthaginians was widespread. Many Iberians had developed quite a lucrative arms trade in the weapon.

"Snap out of it, Mas," Conon said sharply.

At rest, Masinissa could let his mind wander, and the ease of the company and the prospect of the game had given him a moment of reflection that had stretched to the point that it was starting to irritate his friend. He needed movement to jolt him sometimes. Horses and exercises always kept him focussed. Physical stillness often allowed his interior reflections to occupy him.

"I'm sorry, it's my go. I'm going to get you this time for sure." Masinissa employed different tactics in *petteia*, according to the ability he detected in his opponent. For most people, he felt he had an edge and let the game take its natural course, but with Conon he knew he was overmatched when the board was full and more congested, and when the variables were more numerous. His chances were best served by making as many exchanges and sacrifices as he could, reducing the board to a few pieces and then trying to scratch an advantage. Even a slight advantage in *petteia* could be crucial, and he knew how to maintain it once he had it. He was more likely to slip up in the beginning, but he felt more confident with the board pared down to just a few pieces.

He kept Conon as distracted as possible too, with jokes and anecdotes, especially at moments when Conon was concentrating hard, and his diversionary tactics did seem to unbalance his opponent. After a series of exchanges, he nipped in and took Conon's fifth dog without sacrifice and gained himself the advantage he sought in the process.

From there, he coasted to victory, thwarting Conon's determined attempts to regain parity. It was a rare victory and one that didn't sting Conon in the slightest.

Conon knew he could get his revenge without too much trouble. He declared, "You've done me, my friend. I didn't think you'd do it, but that was some good play. As a prize, I've got wine and a fable. Are you OK with that?"

Masinissa replied, "A fable? I'll take that, but wine first and some olives if you have some. If you're going to get all smart on me, I want to get a little woolly. You never know, you might even sound even more profound after a few cups!"

Conon agreed and fetched the wine. "Well, I'm going to test your knowledge of Latin now. You're meant to be good at languages, and this is one of the main ones. *'Licat volare si super tergum aquila volat.'* Translate that for me, Mas?"

"That's easy; do you think I waste my time with my language tutors? Speaking Latin is almost as second nature to me as speaking Numidian, or the Massylian version anyway. The Masaesylian version is a little more guttural, and I just can't figure out what they're saying sometimes. It means 'A man can fly where he will, if he rides on the back of an eagle.' Where are you going with this proverb, Con? It seems slightly cryptic. Are you saying that I can fly and need some kind of eagle to do so? There is an obvious association I can make. The Aquila is one of the main standards of the Roman legions. Each legion even has a specific eagle bearer, who carries and protects the standard. It's a point of great pride for them."

"I know about the *aquilifers*, but don't assume that the eagle is the exclusive symbol of the legions or of Rome. It is certainly favoured, but so is the wolf, the bear and even the Minotaur. The *signum* standard is less dramatic, but is far more commonly used by them when on the march. You have a point though. I'm trying to hint as subtly or perhaps as bluntly as I can that your destiny is as much determined by whom you associate with as by your own actions. Do you know the proverb anyway? It's a very simple Greek one. Basically, the gods decided that they would elect the noblest bird of them all by having a race around Mount Olympus. All the birds agreed, and, after commencing, the race looked like it was being dominated by the eagle. The eagle, though, had not realised that a tiny sparrow had been resting on its back the whole time, and, when the finishing line was in sight, it popped off the eagle's back and beat it to the finish line."

"So I'm the tiny sparrow, am I?" Masinissa scoffed, a little hurt by the derogatory comparison.

"No, not at all; only in the sense of scale of the world around you. Rome could be an eagle, as could Carthage, and Syphax is maybe some kind of falcon, but knowing your relative strength, my little warrior sparrow, will aid you greatly. Sometimes, it's expedient to be taken under another's wings to preserve strength and gain advantage."

"Sometimes you use a cudgel to make a point you know," Masinissa scolded, upset by his friend's comments.

Conon realised that he may have been a little condescending to his friend. Despite himself, he kept falling into the trap of assuming Masinissa was just a warrior with only a thin veneer of an education. His powerful appearance belied the sharpest intelligence. "I'm sorry, I just feel the need to guide you sometimes, and that may make me a little overprotective. I'm also getting far too used to having to make allusions rather than making a direct point. I am as mistrusted as you."

"For a smart guy, you can be pretty simple at times, but I appreciate you for all your lessons. I have few points where I can take my bearings and you are certainly one of those; you're a beacon or a star for my soul! You keep me sane. I am kept at a safe distance by some and by necessity I have to keep myself at a distance from others so to be able to be properly sociable and at my ease is very important."

Conon was impressed by his friend's openness and reflection. He was such an uncommon blend. Men were not meant to be blessed in all ways, but, clearly, through the gifts of the gods and his own endeavours, Masinissa had achieved mastery of most. He still felt the need for cautionary advice, however, or a guiding hand. There remained an aspect of the pedagogue about Conon, or perhaps the overzealous mother. *I should carry a stick or a scroll*, Conon thought. At least he recognised this flaw and it may even have been part of his appeal to Masinissa.

Despite himself, Conon continued with his advice, hoping to avoid platitudes but recognising that he was getting pretty close to crossing that particular line. "Don't be afraid to make mistakes or look foolish, OK, as long as it doesn't cost you your life. Confound people. So many of our leaders are remote and uncommunicative, probably out of their own fear and uncertainty. Be yourself as much as you can, and be your foolish self. Avoiding foolishness is a fault of youth. Do not take pride in it as a man. Be heedless in those areas where you can. Of course, be meticulous in your strategies, but be a little reckless with your habits. Give your spirit some room to sing. Here's some more Latin for you, Mas: 'Gratia dei sum quod sum.' Meaning 'thanks be to god that I am what I am' – whichever god you're most fond of, gratia Heracles or Melqart in your case, no doubt."

Masinissa paused for a moment. His friend was well-intentioned, but, for him, he was stating the obvious. He had a robust love of life, and a degree of self-awareness and self-deprecation that certainly included mischief and error. Sometimes his friend's learning and care was exhausting and bordered on being patronising. "I am what I am, eh, Con? Life's just not worth a damn until you can shout that, huh?"

"Exactly, shout that out, at the empty sky or the empty ocean, to Baal Hammon, Tanit or Melqart. Sometimes you just have to affirm yourself, your own being."

"On that note, my merry songbird, I'd better get going. I have books to study, spears to fling and armies to subdue."

"Go then, my unconquerable hero. You know that's a good nickname for you: unconquerable. I can't see your spirit bending to any trial. You just look too tough. Maybe the Latin version is better; yeah, actually, that suits you. See you Invictus. Masinissa Invictus! See you knocking every challenger around in the next *pankration* tournament."

Masinissa gave a short but theatrical bow and followed it up with a comical growl, in deference to the *pankration* comment. It was a nice way to end a pleasant morning. Conon did help give a good balance to his emotions and a focus for his thoughts. He also knew his friend cared for him very deeply. The sensitive guy going to the trouble of parting with an invented pet name was typical of his nature. Conon admired him without envy or agenda, and that meant a lot to Masinissa. "That's just between us, OK, Con? That name. I can't let that be adopted into common usage. It would be pretty bad form to be known by a Latin nickname in a Carthaginian city. For us though, it's nice. I appreciate the compliment. I'll add it my secret names. You're the first man to give me one! I'll try to be worthy of it too. I will try to remain in possession of myself and my father's kingdom, and remain master of my fate. Invictus. I'll remember that, to be the master of my soul; you know what I mean."

"I do, brother," replied Conon, who was thinking that he may have done his friend a small service with his flattery.

THE ART OF THROWING

Masinissa had agreed to meet Massiva at the stables. Both were keen horseman and felt most at home with their steeds. As he expected, Massiva was already there waiting for him.

His nephew leant over the gate and threw him a fig. "Hey Mas, where we headed today?" he asked as he tossed the fruit.

"Do you want to mix it up? Head into the mountains and then down to the beach to cool off—" Masinissa began.

"And clean up! I get so dusty when I go into the mountains with you. If we're going to do that kinda trek I'm going to need to thrash in the sea for a bit."

"Sounds good; maybe we can eat by the harbour too then, if that's OK? I saw a big catch coming in earlier and there should be plenty of choice today. I fancy some squid, although a little bit of everything would do me fine."

"OK, I'm up for sharing a few plates of fish with you," Massiva replied enthusiastically. "I'm sure they'll have any fish you wish today," he joked, with a comical, lisping accent on the "wish" and the "fish".

Masinissa was feeling in a really good mood. The morning was fresh, and he was well rested, which was a great combination for lifting his spirits and giving his mood an effervescence that was quite in tune with his younger nephew, who seemed as frisky as his mount. Neither of them looked as if they were in the mood for training, target practice or any of the military duties that they had been drilling relentlessly. They just wanted to enjoy themselves, and that's what they were going to do. They would savour a rare day out of the grind. He didn't really need the bonus inducement of a beach gallop, but he liked the idea, nonetheless. One of his earliest experiences on a horse was riding through the surf just east of Russicada on the smallest pony his father could find, and it was a playful thrill he always relished. It had to be kept till the end though, like the tastiest morsel in a banquet. Both men and horses would appreciate the refreshment of the ocean later.

Unlike the Iberians and the Romans, Masinissa and Massiva concerned themselves only with grooming in their preparations. They, like most Numidian cavalrymen, had no need for saddle or bridle. Perhaps if one were injured or new to a horse one might take advantage of such tack, but, for most circumstances, all accessories – even down to stirrups, reins and bits – were discouraged. They encumbered the horse, making it more difficult for it to move in its most natural way and distanced the rider from it. To a Numidian, the horse was more than a possession or a beast of burden. It was almost like a woman in that it was to be treated with a degree of intimacy, and the better the rider could sense the mood and movement of his horse, the closer the tie he would have with it. "You don't dress a woman when you mount her and nor should you a horse" was the bawdy motto that always raised a smile.

Masinissa enjoyed watching the care that Massiva took with his horse. It was a task both easily could have entrusted to a slave, but they both knew the bond between horse and rider was important and not to be neglected, particularly in a horse that you regarded as a favourite and one you were going to take out regularly. These animals would go with you into battle, and face the darts, spears and blades of your enemies, so they deserved the pampering. If it helped them be braver and more loyal, so much the better.

They both also took great pride in their horses. A glance at a horse could often tell you a lot about the rider. Just as you could often tell the state of a slave from their teeth or their eyes, you could tell much about a horse from its skin and its gait. Nothing repelled Masinissa more than a horse that had been neglected. You wouldn't take blunted javelins into battle, so why let a horse succumb to wounds or diseases. When your life depended on it, you and your steed were one. Cavalrymen who forgot this were always the first to fall. The agility and power of your animal was the greatest protection a soldier could call on. Dressing your horse's wounds was as important, probably even more important, than dressing your own. There was a symbiosis between man and beast; the one depended on the other, and it was right to pay attention to your animal when you were off it.

There was a point where this care crossed the line into vanity and indulgence, and Massiva invariably crossed it. Masinissa considered it sufficient to brush his mount thoroughly. Massiva, in contrast, pampered his beast like a new lover. He even cut patterns on her rump. He was always talking and whispering to his horse, which he had called Lilybaion, after the Carthaginian city across the straits in Sicily. This was strictly for formal purposes, though, as he abbreviated it at all times and was forever cooing to Lily. She was a fine, black mare and quick as lightning but highly strung. She suited Massiva well, as he was much smaller and slighter than Masinissa, who would have worn out the animal's racing frame on a long day.

Masinissa also rode a mare. He'd had her for a few years by then, and she was entering her prime years. She was extremely compliant, and he had broken her easily as a wild pony. She was slightly heavier and slower than Massiva's horse, but was agile, revelled in the mountains, and charged through thickets and over rough ground with ease. As far as horses go, she gave the impression of being indefatigable and was not skittish in the least. Massiva had ridden her on the longest daily rides, and she had always comported herself well. She was well made for journeys or for battle, and many Numidians who he had ridden alongside failed to disguise their envy in a few of their comments about her.

He grabbed her mane, leapt onto her back in a smooth, effortless motion and goaded her with a bouncy thrust. He'd called her Napla after one of his elderly aunts, who had looked after him for chunks of his infancy, and who had told him fairy stories and legends to lull him to sleep. He cooed to his mount as his aunt had cooed to him in his cot, and Napla responded with a lusty snort.

"Come on, Seev, get your act together," he cajoled Massiva, and, for good measure, caused Napla to rear, who added a little flourish of her own with a slight kick of her airborne forelegs.

"Take it easy, cuz; there's no impatient widow waiting for you today. You're not on a promise!" responded Massiva. He gave Masinissa a smirk, which suggested both a mild chide and a deeper masculine admiration.

It was clear that Massiva was very conscious of Masinissa's ease with women, and there was an element of helpless envy in his esteem. Masinissa had even started to note traces of mimicry in his manner when they were in the company of ladies or courtesans.

"Yeah, yeah, some reputations can be a little inaccurate, you know," Masinissa offered somewhat defensively. Massiva looked at him skeptically and gave him a plausibly equine snort. "Please, Mas, save that for the maidens you ain't met yet and see if they buy it. I'm not!"

Masinissa gave him a shrug, not wishing to add an acknowledgement or further details to his nephews' presumption, but recognising that such a view of him only burnished his reputation for the boy. He put his hands together in a gesture of mock meekness and capture. "It was just a phase. I'm not like that anymore."

"Sure, sure!" came the quick, sceptical reply. Massiva was clearly dubious of the claim that a man such as Masinissa could switch off his charms so easily.

"No it's true. I've only got eyes for Sophonisba now. And you can help me out a little by keeping your scurrilous mouth shut, OK? Gisco would ban me from his villa if he heard any of your out-of-date banter." The truth – or the relatively recently expired truth at any rate, which Massiva was largely aware of and a little too careless in discussing – was the fact that, for the last few years, ever since the calamitous Battle of Dertosa had compelled far more forces to head to Iberia both from

Carthage and Numidia, Masinissa had found himself at greater liberty. This was a freedom that he had enjoyed considerably.

All the brothers of the Barcid clan – Hannibal, Hasdrubal and Mago – were now gone from Carthage and campaigning elsewhere, and, whilst Masinissa lacked a little of their cachet within Carthaginian circles, he was the heir to its key ally and the guarantor of its western border, which was contributing huge numbers of skilled cavalry troops to the Punic forces. This gave him a certain status in the parlours and banquets he often frequented. Moreover, he more than compensated for his perceived junior position by his appearance. He was well aware of the admiring glances directed towards him when he arrived at an event. There was a palpable frisson of excitement, as if he were a dancer or performer, particularly amongst the younger women and girls.

War was known to sharpen passions, of course, and there were numerous widows or women who hadn't cared to wait for news of their widowhood before finding some form of solace in Masinissa's arms. He often found himself inadequate as a romantic analgesic however as many of these despondent ladies found their passions turning to sorrows and their heartbreak would often overtake them in paroxysms of guilt and despair. It was at those moments when he revealed his consolatory qualities both to himself and to his companion. He knew he allowed these ladies to forget and then to remember, and they were grateful for both. He was also grateful to them. He thought wisdom and judgement were best nourished at a woman's breast. He needed to see beyond the perspective of the scheming warlord or mercenary soldier, who could be preoccupied with their own survival and the subjugation of their enemies. He needed to focus more widely on further ways of being, and develop a wider emotional range than ones dominated by fear, hatred, greed and lust.

His experiences, the example of his father, and the philosophical and ethical guidance of his Greek teachers had taught him much. For him, the closed mind was an ending, even a death. He promised himself that he would keep his heart open and his mind curious. He liked to compare his outlook to the cavalry units he commanded or allied with. He believed his actions should echo the movements of a horse in battle; well, one ridden by a Numidian at any rate. They could whirl and change direction with ease, attacking, retreating, probing and ready to change according to the shifting fortunes on the battlefield. The alternative would be to attack like an elephant. These creatures were formidable but capable only of crashing charges. They had none of the deftness that a horse possessed. The Romans had learnt, to their cost, how these beasts could scythe through their massed ranks and trample anything in their path. They were also, by the accounts of convalescing soldiers, starting to learn about their deficiencies and weaknesses too. They simply charged, and these charges were indiscriminate. If one allowed them channels to blunder through, they could be easily attacked from the rear. A wounded or terrified elephant was as much a danger to its own forces as to its enemies. The horse, in contrast, offered loyalty and agility. That is how he would be. He would reward any faith and manoeuvre according to circumstances.

He shook himself. How did a compliment about his sexual prowess end up with thoughts about charging elephants? Well, there were times when the similarities might not have been too out of place! He blamed Massiva for his distraction. The obsessive kid needed to hurry up with his grooming. He'd have to bring something to read next time whilst he waited, to stop himself from daydreaming. He'd been reading a Socratic dialogue, the *Apology of Socrates to the Jury* by Xenophon, and he could have finished it in the time he took to wait for Massiva. He was at the point where Socrates was making the case for dying before the onset of senility. *You take the crumbs of comfort you can,* he thought. Masinissa did wonder a little about the relationship between the author and Socrates. Xenophon was clearly a devoted acolyte. He even owed Socrates his life. It was well known that, during the Battle of Delium, Socrates had showed his courage and rescued Xenophon when he had fallen from his horse. According to Diogenes Laertius, Socrates had saved Xenophon's life. Masinissa wondered whether someone might do the same for him one day, perhaps even his fussy cousin. The image of someone riding back into battle to rescue a fallen comrade who was at the mercy of enemy spears seemed the noblest act to Masinissa. Stories from battles, and even songs, commemorated these sorts of acts of heroism. One of the most emotive was about two brothers, one of whom had ridden right into the teeth of the enemy's assault to haul his brother onto his pony. It never failed to touch Masinissa.

With a final flourish of the brush to Lily's rump, Massiva finished his equine ablutions, threw his brush casually towards the nearest attendant, swigged some water, tossed the empty water skin just as casually in the same direction and mounted Lily even more smoothly than Masinissa had Napla. "Let's go, bro," he called out as he spurred the horse out of the stables. He waved at Masinissa, sweeping his arm in front of him, in effect asking for directions.

Masinissa gave him a bearing, and he directed his mount accordingly. Massiva kicked Lily into a gallop, which Masinissa knew from previous form would last a while, and he settled into keeping within reasonable touch without frothing Napla too much.

They rode roughly south-west, in the general direction of Sicca, which was the highest settlement in the region, and a formidable stronghold, well placed between Cirta and Carthage. Gala had always instructed Masinissa to be particularly considerate of the elders and chieftains there. With the volatile forces that vied for Numidian tribal loyalties, it was crucial to have such an important citadel supporting you. No doubt Syphax would love to undermine the Massyli by gaining the favour of the Siccans. Fortunately, the people were kinsman, and their loyalties were fierce and unwavering.

"Mountain people see things in more binary ways than coastal folk" was a dictum that had been inculcated into Masinissa from an early age. The deeper one went into the mountain ranges of the High-Tell, the more rigid, and usually more conservative, the views became. "Party by the sea, pray in the hills" was another credo his father was quite fond of.

As they rode, the landscape unravelled and altered, sometimes subtly and sometimes dramatically. It kept one's attention with its abundant natural contrasts. The rock formations, in particular, went from soft, weather-worn undulations to jagged ridges, and then back again. This was far from a uniform landscape, until you reached the desert fringes, of course, where the colour and textures fizzled into myriad shifting grains.

The hues of brown and green, and the limited shades between, dominated the landscape. There were few flowers or flora, which might have infused some more vivid splashes of colour into the landscape, other than the resilient shrubs and trees that had anchored themselves where the earth's waters allowed. He wondered if the interiors of Iberia would be similar. Would the scrub be the same? Would the lands be more cultivated? There would be fewer date palms that was for sure.

Napla finally made up the distance that Lily had put between them with her early spurt, and the two horses broke into a more relaxed stride. Masinissa could see signs of the terrain on both her and Massiva. *So much for all that pampering,* he thought to himself. Clearly, his nephew had been meditating a little whilst on horseback, as Massiva looked at him quite thoughtfully when he drew alongside.

Masinissa knew there were moments in their relationship when he had to play the wise, nurturing mentor, and Massiva became the hesitant-but-willing pupil. Sometimes, finding the right theme or tone wasn't easy, but there was a touch of apprehension in his nephew's look and his concerns were pretty transparent.

"You know, Massiva, we are such privileged men," stated Masinissa.

Massiva's uncertainty deepened. "We have our freedoms and our luxuries, but how does that make us more privileged than others of our class?"

"War," Masinissa replied. "It gives no opportunities to the common soldier, but it gives us opportunities for heroism and change. Look at Hannibal. He is barely much older than us, and yet his name is on the lips of every man alive, and he is changing the world."

Massiva's mouth pursed and his eyebrows furrowed, a little comically. "Well, let us see how much he changes the world. He is killing a lot of Romans, that is for sure, but he yet may lead Carthage to disaster. His boldness has stalled with his supplies, it appears."

Untypically, Masinissa rushed to Hannibal's defence, choosing the divine as his support, "He is fulfilling the prophecy he received at the Temple of Melqart. The snake is leaving destruction in its wake. The countryside of Etruria and Apulia must be barely able to sustain his rampage."

The reference failed to blunt his nephew's criticism. "It needs to, though, doesn't it? We have so many men there. There are the Samnites and Gauls too. If they start to grow hungry or disillusioned, Rome may turn the chase around on Hannibal's armies. They must be growing tired of the attritional tactics of Fabius Maximus."

This was a possibility that Masinissa had certainly entertained, but he still admired the tactical acumen of Hannibal. "I'm not so exalted or deluded as to compare myself to the finest general on earth. I'm merely suggesting that our lives have opportunities others lack, and our guile, bravery and good fortune can create glorious fates for us, and for Numidia, of course. You see, Massiva, the vast majority of people just man the oars; only the most fortunate can rest his hand on the rudder. So many people – be they Carthaginians, Numidians, Romans, Libyans, Iberians or whoever – live to satisfy their immediate needs. They are always, especially our soldiers, living on the edge of the void and living lives without real substance. Their aspirations are no better than hallucinations that will never be realised. To wake the next morning, and to be free of pain and hunger is the best they can hope for. Can they plan more than a few days ahead? Even if they do, it is only the smallest and most trivial matters they can influence. They cannot even gain control over which direction they march in. That is a decision for you or me, or whichever legate or tribune they are assigned to. We may as well attach strings to them and animate them like the fools of the puppet theatres."

"Free will is it, Mas? Don't waste your time pondering that. It will get you nowhere. I would be more practical. A general should always be mindful of the views and feelings of his troops. Look at the forces of Carthage. How many of the men who fight for her do so with steadfast loyalty? No doubt the citizens of the Sacred Band will never break, but how many of those men march on foreign soil? They are a privileged militia who do not hold the centre in any battles Hannibal or Hasdrubal are going to wage. The forces of Carthage are dominated by mercenaries and opportunists, and if the tide turns and flows against them, they will be as reliable as sand running through your fingers." For dramatic effect, Massiva waved his fingers together as if passing a handful of dust through them.

Masinissa's eyes rolled. "You are as crude in your analysis as you are in your symbolism, nephew. Gold and promises. Dangle those in front of the average soldier and lubricate him with a modest amount of wine, and he will hold. What is his alternative? Slavery? Death? Is not Hannibal still in a good position? Whose army marches closer to their enemies' city? Maybe he could have pressed his momentum. Should he have listened to Maharbal and seized the moment when he had it and pitted his forces straight at the Roman heart?"

This was the debate that raged throughout the Numidian and Carthaginian ranks, and it always seemed to follow a circular route back on itself. Preservation, glory or destruction? So tantalisingly close had Hannibal been, so should he have thrown his dice and his elephants at the gates of Rome?

Massiva saw the futility of this line. "Let us save that one for the comfort and idleness of a banquet. I will lie on the most comfortable couch, perhaps in the most opulent triclinium we can find on our conquests, and bat about the wisdom or folly of Carthaginian hesitation with you till my goblet falls from my hands."

"You know Seev, Maharbal did make an excellent observation, and it is a criticism that you can lay at the feet of even the most triumphant generals. Hannibal knows how to conquer. That much is obvious, but does he know how to make use of his victory? Time will tell. For me, I think reinforcements are critical. This is a long war. A direct assault with depleted forces would have brought ruin to his army. The upper hand remains with Carthage as it is."

Massiva sighed. "We are too distant to know for sure the morale or predicament of the advance forces. They have fought many battles and now seem to be trotting around the Italian countryside, as far as we are told in the news of the campaign that reaches us, anyway."

"Yeah, it's funny how war can be just a story for those not engaged in it. I'm sure the reality is more tedium than adventure for those troops at the moment."

"Well, let's not let the monotony of the northern camps intrude on our day. Race you to that hill!"

"Give me a start then, you boy racer!" Masinissa entreated, knowing that he would be chewing on dust if Massiva didn't give him a sporting lead.

"OK, I'll give you a minute, but that's all."

Masinissa agreed and stirred Napla into a sprint. There was no way Massiva would give him that amount of time. He probably was weighing up a spot from which he could comfortably reel him in whilst making it look like a reasonably well-handicapped race. Still, he might misjudge the terrain as the hill kicked up sharply, which would suit Masinissa's animal and his style of riding a little better, and might give him a chance. He could hold him off on the plain, and trust to Napla's strength and his horsemanship to do the rest.

Massiva's whoops and taunts were in his ears from the beginning, and they offered Masinissa a good estimate as to how well his nephew was closing in on him. It also gave him the spur to reach the steeper incline with a lead, which he managed. He zigzagged up the slope expertly, with Napla's shoulders and crest punching forwards on the harsher gradients. Massiva's taunts lost a little conviction when he realised he would be eating them shortly.

As Masinissa reached the ridge line, he turned back to see how close Massiva was and let his imagination race to find the funniest riposte. His pursuer was only a little further down the slope and cantering briskly, and he had only a moment or two to get his phrase just right. The quip got as far as, "So much for…" before the alarm on the braking Massiva's face checked him. His eyes were wide with shock and darting at whatever activity Masinissa had his back to.

Masinissa spun Napla like a top and surveyed the scene in the valley below, which his triumphant victory had excluded. There was much to take in, although a fair number of the protagonists in the tableau lay motionless, so their arrival clearly coincided with the last struggles of the fight. A caravan of heavily burdened camels and horses had been ambushed and, for the most part, cut to pieces by marauders. They could be bandits, Libyans or Masaesylians; it was difficult to determine. Naturally, the camels had been spared, but were bolting in all directions. The raiders, for their part, were not too bothered that their booty was absconding, being fairly safe in the knowledge that they wouldn't go far and would be retrieved easily. They were, like vultures, more preoccupied with their static prey. About eight men lay dead or motionless, two of whom – from where they were lying and what they were wearing – could have been with the assailants. Another nine riders were scattered around the lone surviving defender, who was wedged against the belly of a camel, with what appeared to be two others of uncertain mortality. Protruding from the camel and the ground around the defender were a number of javelins; there was at least one for each of the attackers, suggesting that either the riders had poor aim, for which there was ample contradictory evidence, or the last man had a rare agility and skill at evasion.

The two men watched mesmerised as the figure gestured to the riders and shouted something, which was only a sound of rage and defiance by the time it reached them. Encircling their putative victim, two of the riders, who were at opposite ends of the wide circle, broke and charged. Both held javelins ready to fling and *falcatas* twinkled in their robes, ready to finish the job. They were quick, but the boy – and Masinissa could by then see that was what he was – was quicker.

The boy looked like he had some kind of short sword or dagger in his robe, but it was not to that he reached in his defence. He was holding a sling by his side and he quickly put a stone bullet in its leather cradle. The presumption of the onlookers up to that point was that the bandits would pierce their victim with ease or lop chunks off him as he tried piteously to fend them away. They knew better than to discount his chances, though, once they knew he had a range weapon. Some of these shepherd boys were deadly. The trouble was that the horsemen were a bit quicker and deadlier than a hungry jackal.

Masinissa realised that his view of the scene beneath him was becoming far from detached, and that, for all the fact that the shepherd boy's demise appeared imminent and the odds of him surviving an attempt at rescue far from assured, he was picking out his own targets and plotting how his own ambush might unfold.

His resolve was confirmed by two things. The first was the fact that the boy's odds improved quickly as his first projectile found the forehead of one of the charging riders, whose head recoiled and his body slumped off his mount, either unconscious or dead. The slinger's skill was clear from the accuracy of the throw, but Masinissa had observed much more in the poise and balance of the boy prior to unleashing it. He was very familiar with slingers – both mercenary Balearics, and his own and Carthage's auxiliaries – and none had looked as fluid and easy in their action as this young herder. His target had been small, moving rapidly and was still about a hundred yards away, but he had looked as if he could not miss as he made one slow rotation to seat the projectile and then a rapid overhand whip, which exploded the stone into his attacker's face. There is training, and then there is instinct and natural ability, and the boy's calmly coordinated motion was a special talent. A special talent that Masinissa suddenly was keen to harness. The boy had even managed to put a little leap into his swing to give it greater elevation and velocity.

The second prompting came with the curse that managed to reach them from the valley. The boy's enraged shriek contradicted the composure of his movements, but, importantly, showed Masinissa conclusively where his loyalties lay.

"Have that, Syphax dog!" the boy yelled in a momentary pause before reaching into his pouch and loading another bullet into its cradle. Whether that meant he was a fellow Massyli was moot at that point, but it certainly was clear that they had a shared enemy in the Masaesylian king. His second release, which exploded in the face of the other rider, was just as spectacular and appeared to hit the second man right between the eyes. There was a thud and a red gush, and then a solitary horse lost its urgency and occupant.

"That's it; let's go," Masinissa instructed Massiva, who looked at him puzzled and uncertain, as if the directive was unclear or absurd.

"Are you kidding? Why risk our necks for a lone shepherd?

The reply struck Masinissa as dismissive and cowardly, and he felt the bile of contempt rise towards his own kinsman, which he had never felt before. He grabbed Massiva by the hair roughly, as if it was the mane of a horse and barked, "We're going if I have to drag you behind me. If that were you down there, would you expect me to go, 'Feh, it's not worth the risk,' and slink off back towards the coast?"

"Well, no, of course not, but it's a different situation."

"Look, there are seven left. That's two each, more or less, even if we have to kill them all. How do those figures look in terms of your personal risk assessment? Your time is ordained, son, and it's not now. Your pouch of luck is still pretty full. Move, unless you want me to slice your nuts off here and now, and send you to the priesthood."

Masinissa didn't wait for an answer and slapped his javelin forcefully against Lily's rump, and men and beasts charged down the slope towards an uncertain opposition. The resolution of their targets may well have been waning anyway, as – in the moments Masinissa had taken to upbraid his nephew – the slinger had performed the same precise throw and despatched another charging rider just as expertly. The remaining six started yelling at each other as if they needed the playwright of the scene to revise the picture that was unfolding, to switch the locations of the dying. Their cries rose an octave when they spotted the approaching riders.

It was strange to describe it as such, but the solitary slinger and two riders were performing a flanking manoeuvre on the hapless bandits. The three choices before them – attack one or the other, or flee – seemed to confuse them, and the hesitation was fatal. Neither Masinissa nor Massiva raised their javelin until they were clearly in range, so their enemies were unsure whether they were threats. At the point when their raised arms confirmed the danger, the two javelins were heading at two still-beating hearts. The remaining beats of those hearts could, however, by then be counted on the fingers of the throwers.

The slinger had also noted the changing conditions in the field, but, clearly, it did not give him cause to pause his own defence and reconsider the urgency of his self-preservation. As the two javelins did their work, another of his bullets hit another skull, although in the temple of an uncertain enemy this time, rather than between the eyes.

In an instant, the brigands remaining numbers had dropped from seven to four, and those were scattered and in a state of panic. Their easy pickings had turned into a deadly calamity, and, at almost even odds, their courage was evaporating visibly. It was not unexpected of bandits. They only preyed on the weakest targets with guaranteed success. They hadn't counted on the fates and a deadly boy intervening. None of the men managed to muster any kind of charge and were at a massive disadvantage from the galloping Numidian riders.

Massiva's resolve had been buoyed by his accurate javelin, and he peeled off from Masinissa, seeking his transfixed opponent. Masinissa switched his focus similarly, loosened his *falcata* from its scabbard, took it in his left hand and attacked the weak flank of the nearest bandit.

As Masinissa was aiming for the throat, his adversary had the presence of mind to duck. In doing so, he managed only to meet a slower and more agonising demise, as Masinissa's blade found the bridge of his nose and eye sockets rather than his neck. The scream that an accurate strike would have stifled erupted from his larynx. Napla barely checked her stride as Masinissa urged her into a shallow turn and bore down on the next rider, who had started to turn and flee. His horse was clearly no match for Napla; it was a thickset quasi-donkey that bounced comically at a full trot in a way that juxtaposed pathetically with Napla's punchy charge. Masinissa was on his prey as quickly as a fox on a hen. With his peripheral vision, he could see that Massiva had killed another bandit and was bearing down upon the last rider, who had turned for the hills on his own woefully underpowered ass, and the slinger was reloading with the last rider in his sights too. One way or another, that final opponent was doomed. That realisation allowed Masinissa to reconsider his method of dealing with his own pursuit.

In reality, his enemy, who was showing his back on a slow pony, stood no chance, but he held a javelin that he might prove accurate with over a short distance. He may have possessed a weaker side, but Masinissa could not speculate whether this was the case. As Napla drew closer, he freed himself a little by grabbing her mane tighter and jumping onto her back, so that one foot was on her withers and the other close to her croup. He was ready to parry and dive. When the rider turned and saw the position Masinissa had taken, he realised his only chance was an immediate and accurate throw. A wiser foe would have thrown at the horse, but the man threw at Masinissa. Given the angle of his body, it was a fair effort, hard and at the chest.

Nevertheless, Masinissa anticipated it as if he were catching a slowly tossed ball, and deflected its trajectory harmlessly with his *falcata*. The man was now left with only his limbs to fend off his enemy. These proved useless, as Masinissa leapt acrobatically over them. His target was the man's head, and he wrapped both hands around it in mid-air, dragging the man off the horse as his momentum carried him beyond it. He twisted in the air, yanking the man over and under him, and he landed, cushioned by his enemy's body, on the dry earth. It was a jolt that sucked the air out of him a little, but he had no need to ready himself for a struggle on the ground, as the man's neck was broken and he was dead before he had absorbed the impact of the fall.

As Masinissa rose, he had enough time to witness the demise of the last rider. His own duel had lasted only seconds, and Massiva still had not reached the remaining brigand. He didn't need to as the slinger had a final act of revenge ready to be released. This time, the boy did not fire the bullet from the top of his swing, rather he executed a much harder underhand throw. He took a step forwards, and whipped shoulder, elbow and wrist in concert. The rider looked clear of the weapon's normal range, but the boy's aim was as true as before, and, from a very acute angle, he crushed his stone into the back of the man's head. For a second, Masinissa's mouth stood agape. This type of throw was very common in warfare and in training, but accuracy was much less when compared with an overhand throw, and, more often than not, they were intended as wild sprays into an opposing army. This boy had hit the skull of a moving target at about a hundred yards. Not even the most skilful slingers he had encountered could have performed such a deadly accurate throw.

Massiva rode to the fallen figure and confirmed the kill to the others by making a slicing gesture to his throat. The skirmish was done. Incongruously then, the boy gave Masinissa a nonchalant wave with his free hand, and then balled his fist and drew his elbow into his torso in a gesture of triumph. In response, Masinissa performed the same action; the small muscular contraction felt good, and punctuated the moment between mortal danger and fresh curiosity.

ARI'S DOLL

Masinissa took in the stillness as he jogged over to where Napla had pulled up and begun to graze on some brown tufts of grass. His eye was drawn to a vulture above him, which seemed keen to become flirtatious with the corpses. There was something serene and beautiful about the bird in the air. Its spread wings were elegant, with a natural grace permeating every quivering feather. He knew that this show was reserved for the sky only. The creature would show a much more grotesque aspect when it landed. Its placid spirals would turn into ugly, avaricious hops as it tore into the meat these dead men had become. The sky would soon be full off these duplicitous avians, and they would be falling on their free lunches without much ceremony if the bodies were left exposed. Masinissa had neither the time nor the interest in sparing these men from entering the food chain of the desert. He was sure the boy would wish to bury his own dead, and he would help him, but the others could be consumed. By the next day, the marrow of their bones would be being gnawed over a range of several miles as the wild things took advantage of their unexpected human meal.

Looking at the bundles of goods that littered the ground, he could see why these bandits had launched their fatal assault. There was fine cloth, spices, dyes and some jewellery. Masinissa doubted whether all of it had been acquired legitimately. Either way, as far as he was concerned, it had become his reward. He wasn't covetous enough to take it all, but he and Massiva would have their cut, particularly of the precious stones and metals, which they both knew could brighten the moods of the ladies of Carthage, Cirta and Russicada.

Napla seemed unfazed when he reached her, which was a good sign, and he mounted her and spun her back towards the boy, who appeared to be waiting patiently for him. The sling remained in his grasp, but it could have been a length of worry beads for all the aggressive intent the boy now evinced. Masinissa wondered whether the term "boy" ought to be discarded when describing or thinking of him. That vestigial term of youth did not sit well on someone who had just killed several people. Whether he had just grown up fast or had experience of dealing out death previously didn't really matter. He was a man now, with the memories and sins to prove it.

Masinissa could see that Massiva was as reluctant and unsure of himself at the end of the battle as he had been at the beginning, and, although he was much closer to the slinger, he stood hesitantly at a distance from the boy, as if they had not yet forged any kind of bond by fighting for each other's lives. Maybe the "boy" designation suited Massiva much better. There were no protocols on a battlefield or need to stand on ceremony. Embrace your life and salvation, or at least greet your comrade and rejoice in your mutual survival. He certainly intended to express a little of that relief. However, whilst the euphoria of deliverance still coursed through his veins, his mind still posed questions.

As Masinissa approached the young man, his curiosity grew even further. The blur of motion that he'd been – leather, projectile, swirling rope and cloth – presented an entirely different aspect when still and attentive. He was moderately slight and very poised, balanced as if on his toes, but with a gait that appeared to rock sideways rather than forwards. It looked as if he was ready to anticipate any movement and evade it. There was something feline about it, but also something a little pugilistic. Whilst not in the least threatening, Masinissa had the sense that the boy could hit him first should it ever come to that.

Whether his power would be commensurate with Masinissa's was highly doubtful, but his reflexes certainly appeared to be sharper. His shoulders had the merest hint of sway and his attention was fixed on one object; in this case, that object was Masinissa.

His expression offered a further contrast. There was something guileless in the easy smile he offered Masinissa, which spread to his eyes but still managed somehow to leave traces of a flintier coldness in them. Maybe it was a little harsh to judge the boy's expression. He had just killed a few people, and who knows how close his relationships had been with the corpses littering the tracks of the decimated caravan.

There was an incongruous neatness to him too, adding a shade of femininity or perhaps more like a formality to a young man who must be living the harshest possible life. He expected a more chaotically attired figure, for sure. His clothing was more fitting than the usual Bedouin garb, as if he insisted on wearing robes that he'd just outgrown. His scarf, though it billowed like a flag, evidently had been used wisely, as his skin retained a smoothness that would usually long have been surrendered to the abrasions of the sun, even for youths of his age. The most striking of his features was a small, circular mole or birthmark located right in the middle of his forehead, a little crown to his procerus muscle. He had seen some women of Eastern origin decorate themselves with cosmetic markers at almost that exact point on the face, and Masinissa was unsure if such marks were intended to be alluring, a sign of spiritual devotion or both.

As with any distinctive feature, be it appealing or grotesque, it was best not to stare or linger on it, and Masinissa instead offered his hand and arm as a greeting, and reciprocated the smile, just as naturally. As the two gripped palms, Masinissa noticed something he hadn't seen before that made him pause. Tucked into his new associate's belt was a painted wooden doll. Where you might expect to see a sword or a blade of some kind ordinarily, the youth had chosen to hold on to something of his childhood. Masinissa had witnessed similar behaviour before, usually in captured young slaves, who had been pressed into military service before their innocence had faded properly from them and who retained an obsessive compulsion for childhood remnants. It was a sign of trauma, but one that held more pathos than others. Clinging to the hope of an obliterated childhood or trying to deny the adult realities couldn't help but engender a little pity. You couldn't help but feel a little complicit too in not having shielded these young boys. Once it's gone, childhood is unredeemable. Everyone knows that.

It would seem that, despite the evidence of his own eyes, Masinissa had underestimated this very adept killer before him. He had assumed that his actions may have been spontaneous, fortuitous reactions, but that was clearly a naive assessment. It takes a little bit more than an instinct to survive, and natural gifts of accuracy and athleticism to accomplish what he had just witnessed. There must be a bit of history, and sometimes, as he knew from wiser heads, that history needs to be forgotten or submerged. He wasn't going to ask this boy what he had seen or done, or, especially, what might have been done to him. He would stick to the basics and the future. The past was the carved object, with the ragged hair and painted smile, that hung at the young man's waist, and he didn't want to go there.

Where was he to begin then? The boy seemed bothered by the delay, the scrutiny or perhaps both. His smile became a little more wan, and, in his impatience, he flexed shoulders and hips into something that would have turned into a swagger if he broke into stride.

A swagger can be good, Masinissa thought, with an eye to the qualities that would be appealing in a potential recruit. Any type of command needs an air of confidence, and that has to be visible in your body and gestures, and be explicit for all to see, especially to those who are about to ride into a hail of javelins behind you.

Masinissa started his introduction light-heartedly, "You're some shot."

Nothing breaks the ice better than a compliment; the boy's beam returned, and his restored assurance reached his face as he cocked out his chin, twisted his head a little, and gave a slow, deliberate and intentionally comic nod, which he repeated as he saw Masinissa's ease improve by the gesture. "I sure am!" he replied with an accentuated rural twang. "You fling a javelin pretty good yourself, and, as for breaking a man's neck in mid-air, I ain't seen that done before."

"Well, I don't do it competitively or anything. Maybe I should," Masinissa replied, in the unexpectedly jovial spirit in which the conversation had begun. "I'm not sure if it's a career path with much longevity, mind."

"Too right!" came the rapid assent. "I'm Ari." He paused and became more sober. "And I owe you my life. There were too many of them, and they would have killed me if you hadn't intervened. I can't make sense of things now, but I know I owe you and I will serve you as best I can. I can see you are noble in your appearance as well as your actions, and I will pay my debt to you in the ways I am able."

"You certainly seem able enough to me, and I will hold you to your vow. A blood debt ought to be the surest loyalty anyone could have. This world is always shifting like the sands, but nothing stakes something more firmly into the ground than gratitude."

"I've got a load of that, sir."

"Forget the 'sir'; that's a word for people who don't know me. We have… a bond." The comment, when spoken, surprised Masinissa because he was not usually so quick to jettison formalities, particularly with subordinates, but he was instinctively at his ease with this impressive survivor of an ambushed caravanserai, and he had a quick sense that he could rely upon him. *Trust those first impressions!* he thought to himself. "Next time, we'll find danger together, if it doesn't find us. I need a bodyguard. With a ranged weapon, you couldn't be better suited. Bulk up a bit and practise with the knife. If you can cook a little too, that would be good. I'm pretty hopeless. I've relied on taverns too much. My manners! I'm Masinissa, and the slouching guy over there is Massiva."

He was meaning to leave the introduction there, but a little bit of mischief grabbed hold of him and wouldn't let him go, and he fired out a line of mock conceit. Preening a little and arching an eyebrow for comic effect he added, "You may have heard of me." He half-regretted his cocky adjunct.

However, he needn't have, as, immediately, Ari roared with laughter and clapped his hands. "Ah, so I have the honour of meeting the new incarnation of Hercules. Hercules! Hercules! I've heard of you, dreamboat. The girls I know yearn for you and put up with me. You really put a crimp in my action sometimes, big guy."

For a moment, Masinissa stood there stunned. He was used to a little banter from time to time, but this definitely exceeded the usual boundaries. A stiffer personality would no doubt have considered it gross impertinence, but Masinissa didn't and learnt something about himself in the process.

He smiled, accepting the backhanded compliment in its intended spirit. "Sorry, mate, I really didn't mean to mess with your lady business, but how can you dumb this down?" He swept his hands from the top of his head to his toes, topping it off as he brought his hands back to his hips with an elongated, "*Aaaaall this!*"

He tried to hold the pause, but the joke's reaction took over, and Ari and Massiva, who had seen a few versions of the self-parody before, both gave him wincing looks and raced each other to get the first pin in his pomposity. Massiva was the first, with an imitation of the "*Aaaaall this!*" top-to-toe gesture, and then Ari, stumped for a better riposte, doubled down with an even more extravagant version of his own. Masinissa cracked too, and a little fraternity was formed with its first shared catchphrase.

It was one of those comic interludes, however, that didn't have much momentum. The opportunity to bond and purge was there, and they took it and would remember the moment as much as anything on that day, but more sober matters needed attention.

Awkwardly, all the men turned a little quiet and still, until, finally, Ari asked the others, "Will you help me?" as he glanced towards the dead man closest to him, and the others who were at various points in the inadequate barricades they had erected hastily.

Masinissa and Massiva did their part of the digging, but let Ari take care of the removal of the bodies and the parts that were detached. It was harrowing for the observers, and Masinissa wondered how such a young man could cope with such a distressing undertaking. He felt a little voyeuristic watching Ari as he looked at the empty heads, cradled the skulls and ruffled the hair of some of the corpses. He saw Ari nuzzle and whisper into the face of one of the dead men, then take his knife and cut a lock of his hair before wrapping him in one of the sheets he had taken from the pack of the closest camel.

When the earth was piled over the graves they had made for the bodies, all three joined in prayers to Baal Hammon, Tanit and Melqart; the shrieks of the griffon vultures defied the peace of their short vigil. During the moment when their movements were limited to the quiet murmurs of their lips, Masinissa thought of the expression that he had seen on Ari's face when he held the corpse of the last man. The slightly glazed expression, and the mingle of love, confusion and grief was very moving. He wondered if the man had ever witnessed any of those emotions on Ari's face whilst he was alive. Masinissa knew we can condition even our eyes to conceal our feelings, and being able to see right through to the soul's emotions was such a luxury. He remembered a woman, a very young woman really, whom he had spent a few months with; she would burrow into him and look up at him as he held her after he had taken her, and the expression on her face was searingly sweet. He could tell that she loved him without the need to hear the words or feel the touch. Her eyes shone with affection and devotion. It kept him with her longer than he had really wanted, but it was hard to abandon such an obvious love. No doubt they would have been a happy couple, as she was also funny, mischievous and mature for her age, but his loving gaze was reserved for another. She could see it too, despite herself. He gave her no mirror to her emotions, and she understood, through tears, that her look and him as her lover had no future.

Almost unconsciously, Masinissa and Massiva moved away from Ari, leaving him to a few moments of private grief.

Massiva whispered to Masinissa, "Well, you've picked up a stray there. Now you've got to look after him, and he's gonna need a little looking after."

Moving his face into his cousin's ear Masinissa replied, "That'll go both ways; the looking after, that is."

"Sure, but that kid's trauma hasn't started yet."

The forceful opinion irritated Masinissa. "I wouldn't bet on that. You saw the doll. The kid's got history. If he hadn't, he'd be dead or quivering in a pathetic heap right now. He's got grit." He looked hard at Massiva. "More than you have!"

Massiva bridled, knowing that Masinissa's scorn held other consequences for him.

Masinissa continued, but he stopped looking at Massiva, and it was more as if he was working it out for himself. "You know that, when we are kids or when we're happy or settled, we don't want change. We want to stay exactly as we are. Why risk something new? We're not caterpillars. We don't turn into butterflies. Usually, change is darker; sometimes only just a little, but the shade of change can be much darker for a man when he becomes a man, goes to war or loses a friend or a part of himself. You've read *The Odyssey* right? Everybody's got to read Homer. You can lose yourself when change happens. Like the Kimmerioi, or the Cimmerians, those people on the edge of the world and on the brink of Hades, who were stuck in fog and darkness. You've got to get out of it somehow. Ari's doll is his line back to his other self. I don't blame him. He's had that mist fall on him and held on to a little part of the person he used to know, who he used to be. The unknown is scary, especially when the unknown is your own self. Do you think that, if you come back from the war, you'll recognise the person that you were? Who you are now?"

Massiva looked at Masinissa when the question hit him, and then looked down, shrugged a long, slow breath, and answered the only way he could, "I don't know. I hope so; some, at least."

*

After a while, the kneeling figure of Ari returned to them, and he was more composed than Masinissa had expected: quiet and reflective, but without tears and with some of the humour with which their acquaintance had begun earlier. The three spent the next few hours regathering what they could, and reorganising the camels and the caravan. There was a lot of booty, and it was little wonder that lives were staked on its capture. The griffons soon realised that they had been left more than scraps, and hopped around and into the corpses. It was not pleasant watching their beaks go into soft flesh, the jelly of the eye and the brain in particular, but all of them shared a little battlefield schadenfreude and let the birds act as the agents of their contempt.

Wishing to get back to the city before darkness fell, they retrieved as much as they could, leaving a little for the vultures of human variety who might be lucky enough to stumble on the raggedy end of the train. The most valuable items they abandoned were the weapons of their enemies. Some were well made, but Masinissa's and Massiva's were better. Ari took the best *falcata* from the pile, but the rest they left to the sands. His new blade was lovely, and Masinissa had a slight tug of jealousy when Ari tied it neatly on to his waist, nudging his doll slightly closer to his midriff. The handle had a grip of gold and ivory, and a carved figure of a horse shielding the knuckles of the hand. It also included a wooden sheath wrapped in burgundy leather, and a smaller knife wrapped in another leather pocket protruding from the outside of the sheath. It was a beautiful object, really too nice to stick into the body of another person, but Masinissa knew that it must already have performed that function and, in all probability, would do so again. It definitely had been a spoil of plunder, and he wondered a little about its provenance. *Maybe it's from a rich uncle of one of the bastards I have to take orders from,* he speculated, a little hopefully.

As they left, he gave the pile of metal they were leaving a perfunctory last glance. Maybe the shepherds in the area could better protect their flocks in the future. As the camel train was still quite long, they let Massiva take position at the front, and he and Ari took the rear and flanks, just in case there was a need to bring any of the beasts back in line. They were quite biddable camels, however, and there was little need to harass them. They just trudged forwards in Massiva's wake.

For most of the way back, all three men were separate from each other, although Ari rode closer to Masinissa as they drew closer to the fringes of Carthage and seemed to be hinting that he was keen to be more sociable.

"You don't look it, but I have the impression you're a pretty tough kid, with today being a strong hint at that obviously," Masinissa commented, breaking the silence with a compliment.

Ari revelled a little in the praise, but turned somewhat contemplative. "You know what helps with that? What helps with trying to make it as a tough guy?"

"Nope, help me out. I'm aspirational where that quality is concerned."

"Denying reality. Getting by in this life – or my life, to be more accurate – is all about denying the facts, and forgetting the truths and the things that have happened to you. My friends used to tell me that some of their memories would haunt them in the night and wake them from their sleep. For me, it's different. It's not my memories that haunt me. It's what I have forgotten, am trying to forget or am blanking out as best I can. My shadows and spectres."

"I guess I've got a bit of that to do in the future. I know what I want to keep in my thoughts, anyway. I hope I can keep the painful stuff at bay. Don't beat yourself up."

Masinissa didn't really know what to add, or how to counsel a younger man who must have already seen much more of the brutalities of the world than he had. He let the conversation drop, and they rode the final league to the stables in silence. As they tethered their horses, slaves swarmed over the camel train and started to unload the wares from the animals. Masinissa gave them instructions and even hinted that if a little of it disappeared, he wouldn't notice. He also gave his instructions to Ari, giving him directions to quarters where he could get food and lodgings, and telling him where to report for his new duties. He told Ari to just get his bearings on the following day. He had other matters to attend and he gave a cryptic nod in the direction of Massiva.

As they parted with a warm embrace not befitting of the clear disparities in their social standings, Ari made a final remark. Evidently, he had been reflecting a little on what it took to be a tough guy. "You know another thing that helps with tough-guying your way through life?"

"Feel free to enlighten me further," responded Masinissa.

Ari raised his palms forwards in a gesture that prefaced his comments with a little "hold on, just go with me on this" reassurance. "OK, this may sound a little crazy, and it's not a religious or spiritual belief or anything, although I do believe in the gods, including Tanit and Baal Hammon, but I don't believe in death."

Masinissa gave him a derisory look and said, "Well, we dealt with the fact of that most of today, either making it or clearing up after it."

Ari winced a little. "OK, I need to be clearer. I don't believe in my own death. That's not to say I'm immortal. It's just that, when it happens, I don't think I'll know about it. I might, Tanit willing, go peacefully or I might bleed out in mounting agonies, but, in that final moment, I don't think I'll know. If I emerge in some paradise moments after, then great, but I'll be different. I'll have missed that moment of transition. I don't remember my birth and I don't think my soul is equipped to contemplate its rebirth either. You're not the audience to yourself, right? When you see people die, it kinda helps to believe that you won't know that moment yourself, even if it seems peaceful in some cases."

Masinissa looked at him. He was a traumatised boy trying to work things out on a day when he'd lost so much and dodged something he was declaring so stridently that he was trying to hide from. Masinissa stated, "Sometimes, it's best not to try to work things out or try to convince yourself of stuff. I'm too beat up to open up a line on philosophy or ontology. Get a little wasted, find some tail if you can, and get some rest. Death's as tired as us right now. You might not believe in death, but believe in life, huh? It's the antidote for what's running round in your head right now."

Ari smiled, bowed and let Masinissa give him a little avuncular hug before he headed out into the night to follow Masinissa's advice.

THE CRUCIBLE

After the brush with the Masaesylian bushwhackers, Masinissa realised that perhaps Massiva was still a little raw. He certainly had been spooked by their charge, and, if not for the intervention of Ari's unerring rocks, the enemy riders might have outflanked them and cut them both down. This was a matter that needed attention, even from a purely selfish perspective. Never mind preserving Massiva's life, he needed to preserve his own, and therefore his nephew better have enough about him to be able to have his back a little better than he had demonstrated so far.

His solution was simple. He would toughen Massiva up a little. Horseplay and javelin throwing were all well and good as training exercises, but there needed to be a little more iron and grit in his young protégé, and he needed a few specialists for that. A few years earlier, when Masinissa was in the middle of an only mildly obstreperous adolescence, Gala had assigned a couple of his tougher henchmen to guide his son. They had been perfect for him. They were tough old hands, who had been initially as stern and fierce as drummers on a galley, but had yielded a more affectionate and fraternal side as Masinissa proved himself capable and worthy of the emotional kinks in their armour. Massiva was even more amiable and even-tempered than Masinissa had been at his age, but there was a moment during youth to introduce the crucible, and that time had come for Massiva.

Masinissa had gone into the Numidian barracks the previous day to talk to them and give them their instructions. There would be hours of drills and runs, and the usual trials out in desert ahead, but he felt that it would be useful to break Massiva first. Massiva was an avid equestrian. No doubt, in the future, if he had pause for reflection, he would appreciate Masinissa's imminent behaviour through that prism.

Both of Masinissa's ranking men had colourful pasts, and these were reflected in their names and their attire. The first, the larger and more senior, went by the name of Big Pun. The name had developed as a comical endearment as much as a reflection of his status as the disciplinarian in the barracks. He was a large man, hence the "big", and he would be the person who made the routine decisions in relation to punishments, hence the diminutive "pun". He commanded the respect of all the riders under Masinissa's command, and he was renowned for his fairness as well as his severity. He could be the embodiment of the Numidian concept of *anaia*, and be merciful and compassionate, but he could also be relentlessly demanding of his men, and leave them without a drop of energy or sweat left in their bodies. Those who took a dimmer view of him hadn't survived, but had been shipped back to the mountains or had found service in one of the irregular militias, who survived on a fraction of the pay of Masinissa's elite cavalry. His appearance was three-quarters haughty and one-quarter comical, with a little companionability thrown in. That side of him was chipped away from his haughtiness as you grew to know him a little better and had started to earn his respect, which was only surrendered grudgingly. His most striking idiosyncrasy was the cap he wore, which was distinctive. It was a soft, round and flat-crowned woolly hat of a kind that most of the men surmised was of Etruscan origin. It certainly seemed as if it would be more appropriate on the head of a shepherd rather than that of a large, bowlegged dragoon. It was hard to say if it was an affectation or a practical adaptation to spending long hours on horseback or in the field. It certainly protected his head, and could be yanked to shield his eyes depending on which side of his head the sun was blazing. Even when they were mustering for battle, he was notorious for sticking to it and demurring on the offer of a standard issue helmet. A curio on his cap, which he had attached to a ridge that he had raised on the front of it, was a gift that he had been given from Gala, as a token of gratitude for helping transform his son into a man. It was a silver brooch, which was not as grand or ornate as the ones in the possession of Gala and Masinissa, but it was a fine piece of jewellery for a man not of the nobility and one that added a little patriotic sparkle to his appearance. It depicted the symbols of Numidia and the Massyli – the charging horse set against a palm tree – and served as a warrant for his position and an obvious patriotic totem for his men who had, to a man, turned their resentment of Big Pun into a veneration bordering on devotion.

The other man commanded somewhat less devotion than Pun, but there were patently obvious reasons why. He was the regiment's lasher, and – as much as he could share a joke around the fire – given that it was his bullwhip that would tear into your back for major or minor misdemeanours, most men kept him at arm's length. To get too close would be viewed as a sign of sycophancy amongst the ranks. He was also a veteran of Hannibal's marches, had fought at both Cannae and Lake Trasimene, and carried a few of those ghosts with him. He had done a circuit of the Mediterranean, up through Iberia, past Massalia, across the Cisalpine passes, down the spine of Italy, and back across to Russicada and North Africa, in a small vessel hijacked by a number of the Numidian veterans who had become disillusioned by Hannibal's apparent vacillation before re-enlisting in Gala's cavalry.

The name he had acquired was even more apt than his superior's. He was known as Tigerman, being so called for the stripes he would cut in a man's back. He had no shame in displaying his own either, and it was almost a sign of empathy when he stripped to his waist and showed the weals he had picked up in his years in Hannibal's forces. He had even developed a little song that he would sing in drills, in combat and, occasionally, when thrashing a misfortunate who he had taken a particular dislike to. "I'm the king of the jungle, and they call me Tigerman. If you cross my path, you take your own life in your hands" was a little ditty that one would be best advised not to be too close to overhear.

Oddly, after he had subjected Masinissa to the full rigours of Numidian military training and discipline, he had developed a sort of confessional relationship with him and would occasionally confide some of his troubles and woes in Masinissa. Perhaps it was because of the distance that existed between him and the lower ranks that he was only able to unburden himself with his superiors. Masinissa, in turn, felt a little protective of him, as someone who represented the psychological trauma and damage of the war, which so many of the veterans were forced to try to bury silently, in the same way as they had buried their comrades conscientiously and reverently.

Masinissa remembered one evening at the beach as the dusk gathered around them, after a little wine and barbecued fish, which was a time when the true natures and feelings of many men started to come out with the bats, Tigerman had turned to him and confessed quietly, "You know, sire, there's this box I have in my head that I'm scared to open, because I'm afraid of what will come out. I've sealed it so tightly that I don't even know what's in there anymore, but every once in a while the cover opens, and my dreams are terrifying."

Masinissa remembered looking at him then, and seeing a mist and distance in his eyes that he had never seen before. His heart had swelled with pity and admiration, some of which was reflected back on him, for Tigerman was talking of a place where he was destined to go too. It was one of those rare feelings and moments where you get a hint at your fate through another. The closest thing he could compare it to was the tears that he had shed at the funeral of his grandfather. The tears were for an intolerable loss, but some of them were for himself, for the recognition of his own ultimate destiny and mortality.

As they approached him just then – across the quarry where he and Massiva were waiting, with the latter clearly a little apprehensive – some of that medley of emotions rose up inside him. These were his guys. He could count on them. He greeted them using the titles they had imitated from their enemies. In many ways, the Romans were innovators and their ranking titles held a strange appeal to many of the Numidians. "Hail Optio," he greeted Big Pun, giving him the honorific the legions would give to their senior lieutenant.

"Good morning, Mas," Pun replied, pointedly less formal, almost reversing the figure of authority by his tone and form of address.

"Tesserarius." Masinissa nodded more brusquely to Tigerman, needing to retain a little of the formality for the ceremony of the situation. They would be Tigerman and Pun at the next ride, but just then, for Massiva's sake, he laid it on thick. Massiva knew the terms as well as he did, and Masinissa knew that his use of the Roman term for guard commander had been to let him know that this was an exercise or possibly even a disciplinary matter.

The two men, after the customary and warm handshakes, stood aside, and assumed impassive and stolid expressions.

It was for Masinissa to break the news to his nephew. He turned to Massiva, looking at him intently for signs of his resolve or desperation. He saw a slightly bowed figure, whom he hoped was girding himself for the impending ordeal. He nodded towards the waiting men and spoke solemnly. "This is not a punishment, Seev; this is a rite of passage, and I'm going to take it with you. Today, these men are going to break you. One is going to scream at you, push you and punch you, and the other is going to lash you. You are fortunate that the *tesserarius* has brought his cane today and not his bullwhip. Be thankful for the mercy." He paused to allow Massiva to absorb the nature of his torment.

Massiva was breathing deeply, gulping and exhaling in little whistles, which were not especially bad signs given the circumstances.

Masinissa placed a consolatory hand on his nephew's shoulder and continued, "I won't let you do this alone. What you do, I will do also, and I have asked the officers not to spare me either. See those rocks over there? We are going to pick them up and carry them over there, and, when we have carried them all, we will turn around and carry them back, and we'll do that until we drop. We will not pause and we will not take water, and these men will not let us slack. Go on as long as you can, and we will decide if you stay with us after that. If you do, you will see plenty more of these fine gentleman. Don't take their behaviour today personally, OK?"

Massiva looked at him earnestly, and there seemed to be something imploring in his body language, not for him to be spared the task, but as if he needed some more resolve that Masinissa might be able to offer.

"Give yourself a rhythm," suggested Masinissa. "You know, when you see slave gangs, galley men or captives after long marches, they always sway a little as if they have a drummer in their heads, and sometimes they've worked out little tunes or sayings that they mutter away to themselves repetitively. When you suffer, hold on to a little something that you can work over in your mind. I know you love to run. I always used to see you in the fancy streets of Carthage ducking in between the merchants and idle classes. I'm sure that, when you're at your last ebb, you roll into some kind of a rhythm to keep your stride pattern going."

Massiva gave him a small, winsome smile.

There is so much of the boy left in him, Masinissa thought. *I hope he can hold on to some of that freshness.*

"I do love to run, uncle," Massiva replied. "I think I'm going to have to adapt it a little to these rocks, but I know what you're saying. I hope you don't get bored of my litany. Let me lead."

Massiva turned and walked briskly towards the pile of stones. The game had started, and the waiting men took their cue and took position along the line between the rocks and their destination. Massiva swept down on the first boulder, one of the larger ones Masinissa noted, and he heard the first part of Massiva's chant.

"Roadrunner once!" Massiva exhaled. As he rose and took the full weight of the stone, he said, "Roadrunner twice." And then, as he started to move towards his first beating and berating, he completed the rest, "I'm in love with rocks and rubble, and I can go all night; roadrunner" A few pauses followed in his head as he set up his internal drum beat, and the mantra concluded with a steadfast, "That's right!" as he walked into his first blow from Tigerman, and Big Pun's vitriol left the first line of spittle dribbling down his cheek.

Masinissa hauled his first rock as the chant ended its first recital, and he felt a little pride in his nephew. *Let's hope there's a little magic in that incantation, Seev. Something to soothe you a little through this,* he thought hopefully.

He could do worse than imitate his nephew, and often, as they passed each other between the two stations, one would cry, "Roadrunner once," and the other would return with the corresponding, "Roadrunner twice," and both would be buoyed by the solidarity of the act.

Masinissa knew that his capacity to endure eclipsed his nephew's, but as the day's beasting wore on, the pain and the thirst magnified. His legs were even starting to drag. The rocks were sapping his vitality. His head throbbed, his back ached, his calves were wobbling and his hamstrings were tightening harder at every pause his complicit overseers overlooked. They didn't miss much, though, and certainly trucked no dissent. A few hours in, Masinissa had been hit at the same point repeatedly for a few turns – Tigerman was unerring in his floggings – and Masinissa could take no more, and winced out a fatigued and irrepressible, "Aah! My back!" He knew his folly instantly.

Tigerman tore into the same spot mercilessly.

Masinissa let out no more yelps, but his muscles could not absorb the force and insistence of the strikes for long, and he dropped his boulder and fell to his knees. Tigerman kicked him in his midriff, a prime and easy target as Masinissa, on all fours, struggled for recovery. Big Pun then did the same from the other side and leant in, and for the only point in the day removed his shepherd's beret and smashed his forehead into Masinissa's exposed temple as, foolishly, he had turned to look at his burly lieutenant. Masinissa's bracing right arm gave way, and he fell briefly on his side. He wobbled to his left as well, and both his tormentors turned from him a little triumphantly, realising that they would get no more change from their half-concussed commander.

Pun left a final barb that reverberating in Masinissa's dizzy brain. "Quit faking it as an old person, little prince!" he snorted.

Masinissa hadn't been called that in a while, but he remembered it as being in quite a similar context and by the same persecutor he reflected grimly. For all his woes, as he spat in the dirt and forced himself upright, Massiva was in considerably worse condition and had hit the ground many times already. Even as Masinissa was losing focus on his nephew's fortunes as he concentrated on his own equilibrium, he realised dimly that his companion was taking a pretty severe and callous beating. As he was temporarily spared, he was able to spectate a little as the fog from the headbutt started to lift. It was clear that the ruthlessness of the assault was far from abating and its intensity was rising as the wolves sensed they could not shake the rabbit in their maw for much longer. Massiva was almost foetal at that moment, his forehead was in the dirt, and his hands and arms were trying to summon up some dregs of energy to pull himself up or at least get one of his feet planted.

Masinissa could see that no more could be wrung out of the exercise, and that his nephew would gain no more by being driven unconscious or insensible. He hailed the men and barked, "Enough!"

It was a signal they must have been waiting for, as both men switched their demeanours immediately. They both took big gulps of air themselves as if they had been at the sharp end of the ordeal. *It is a telling moment*, thought Masinissa, *one which has exposed the true decency of my men.* They took to their roles professionally, but without relish, and he could see that the final act had taken its toll on them too. As he rolled on his back and grimaced as he did so, as the hard ground revealed to him the extent of his lumbar pain, he saw Tigerman and Pun tenderly cup Massiva under his armpits and carry him into the shade. They had left blankets and pillows there, and no doubt a few ointments and bottles of wine. Once there, they ministered to him as if they were his mother and aunt, soothing his brow and treating his wounds. His sides were turning a vivid purple with almost a blackness in the epicentres of the bruises. Massiva was relatively fair complexioned too, so the awfulness of his injuries appeared even more appalling than the more camouflaged marks on Masinissa's own body.

Massiva's body barely flickered once it had found the snuggest posture in the furs and cushions, but his jaw and throat moved as he took the bread and wine his erstwhile tormentors were cajoling into him gently. He would sleep soon, no doubt once he had taken enough to knock him out, and his labours would have exhausted him sufficiently to mask the many pains he must be braving, but Masinissa wanted to salute him before he submitted to the temporary oblivion of unconsciousness.

Masinissa gathered himself and traipsed towards the three men with as blasé a gait as he could manage. *I'm going to make those old lags believe I took that in my stride,* he tried optimistically to convince himself. In the recesses of his ego, though, he knew that they realised he was suffering, but they would show him the consideration of allowing him to walk towards them with a little pride intact.

When he reached them, the shade of the awning that was cooling the men underneath it revived him instantly, with the shelter from the sun being an unexpected boon. He made a grasping gesture to Tigerman and pointed to the nearest bottle. "Pass me some of that," he asked.

Tigerman grinned and tossed the bottle over readily. Masinissa uncorked it, slaked his ferocious thirst with two deep glugs, and then sat himself and the bottle down stiffly next to his nephew, whose eyes flickered at the solid presence that had parked itself next to him, but would otherwise have been closed seeking sleep and relief. It was not really the moment for a lengthy encomium. They both wanted out of their present consciousness, and, besides, the whole day had been spartan and brutal, with gestures being usually far more meaningful than words.

It's better to keep it brief, he thought as he nudged Massiva in the shoulder enough to have him draw his face upwards towards Masinissa with the last moment of alertness and responsiveness he knew he was going to get that day, and said laconically, "I'm proud of you boy."

A little moisture appeared in the corner of his nephew's eye. "Me too," he replied with a soft smile, which Masinissa felt held notes of gratitude and pride. "Wake me late and gently OK?" he added with a little humour, and rolled his head away from Masinissa and deeper into his furs.

Masinissa turned to Pun and Tigerman, nodded quietly and whispered to them, "We'll find our proper beds in a few hours. Leave us now and come back in a while. We might need litters, so come back with a few bearers, just in case."

They nodded, and the eyes of both showed a little of their admiration and dedication.

I'm one tough son of a bitch, Masinissa thought to himself as he waved farewell to the two others of similar caste. It amused Masinissa a little to see the departing figures ease back seamlessly into their roles as adjutants after hours as brutal abusers.

"What actors we can be," he murmured and returned his gaze to the already slumbering Massiva, whose body was heaving peacefully, and his snores showed that he had found his dreams quickly and peacefully. He watched his nephew for a while and let his feelings of guilt fade until his body eased itself into its usual sleeping form, with a few adjustments for his fresh injuries. He tipped the rest of the wine into himself with a few slower draughts, and let the combination of exhaustion, agony and alcohol take him away.

A FATHER'S LOVE

The old man sat in his chair. He felt his bones ease as his posture settled. He thought about how, as he had grown older, he found he was increasingly particular regarding the furniture he preferred and his discomfort in those items that his body could no longer adapt to much harder to tolerate. The stools and benches he had spent hours or even days on, during the festivals and banquets of his younger days, were removed from his rooms and chambers, and if they were present in places he visited, he always chose to stand. He felt an antipathy towards these rigid seats in the same way as an infant immediately grows irritable at the prospect of being handed to a person who has treated them roughly or with whom their inchoate awareness had established a negative association.

However, it was not simply a dislike of the austere that prompted his choice of seat. Gala was far from an ascetic in most of his inclinations, but his aches and pains had made him equally as reluctant to recline in the luxurious loungers he had once so enjoyed. He had no need for them any longer. Who would he seduce in them and who would be willing to be prey to his ardour, if he could muster any? How ridiculous he would look draped over the edge of one, trying to look as vital and alluring as his years and back would allow. He preferred to be horizontal only in his bed when he could stretch out and pad himself with as many cushions and pillows as he could, and take his wife as softly and familiarly as he could. In public, lounging had become difficult for him, as it aggravated his pains and reminded him quickly of his age, as he struggled to regain his feet and his dignity. It was not good for a king, whose vigour was meant to represent the virility of the land, to be seen struggling to get up and hobbling around on a dead leg for a few minutes when he did so.

In truth – for matters of state, or anything that required any degree of solemnity or ceremony – he didn't have much choice of throne. It was fortuitous that it offered the merciful compromise of lumbar support and cushioning, and didn't compel him to emulate the postures of youth or even middle age. He could sink his elderly bones into it, and if what was around him was insignificant, he could even let his mind wander and his eyes close into a few moments of sleep, or at least shut down his mind and body sufficiently to feel mildly refreshed.

Needless to say, such dozing was always noticed, but rarely commented upon. For his part, Gala didn't care much. He had been the centre of attention in his own court for most of his life enough to know that, however discreet he may be, he couldn't escape being noticed, even more so when sat at the head of a room or table with all the men around him waiting for instructions. Increasingly, with age, his habits became as calcified as his body, and his retinue became increasingly irrelevant and invisible. He could be amongst a squad of his finest soldiers, hearing the news of war from emissaries, or leaving orders to faithful and brisk retainers, and he might still find his senses and thoughts wandering. He would sometimes even reminisce and think of the men in front of him as the blithe boys of decades earlier. It was disconcerting to look on older men and accept that you had known those adults as infants. Age was always relative, he knew, and he found himself envying the sprightliness of men even only a few years his junior.

As a younger man, perhaps a little younger than his son Masinissa was now, he had yearned for a little privacy and was impatient for it when it wasn't forthcoming. It wasn't exclusively a craving for seclusion, rather it was, for him, more of an urge to not have to pay any attention to others, to be able to sit and think alone, and to explore his own being in silence and solitude. Sometimes, being with others can reveal aspects of yourself to you or even make you chart new territories of your being that you hadn't explored before; naturally, these were most common with women, but these discoveries were often revealed to Gala when he was alone, and could stop the buzzing background of people and noise from keeping his mind and soul from working things out amongst themselves.

Gala realised how sullen his mood had become. *It is a failure of character to mourn yourself*, he chided himself. *Do not look too closely at your decrepitude, king, else you strip yourself back to your wasted nakedness.* He reminded himself that his people still admired him and followed him. They didn't see the stooped frame of the man who struggled to undress himself, and who looked at his body and found tracks of blood and veins pop out across limbs where there had only been sleek flesh before. *Is this what happens when the body's blood cools?* he wondered. *Does it look to show itself to its host more and more, as if begging to be warmed again?*

An aide made the announcement he had been expecting. His son had arrived. His heart gave a little sharp kick. His paternal feelings had much in common with the turmoil of an infatuated adolescent, but with the greater intensity of a man who understood his affections well. He loved his son dearly and took immense pride in him. Masinissa had always honoured him, and done everything he was asked to do and much that he hadn't. He was a boy who rarely had to be told. He knew the next step he should take without direction or prompting.

Gala became nostalgic for a moment and remembered his son in his infancy and how he had refused almost completely to crawl. He had loved nothing better in his early months than to be propped up on the floor holding on to a chair or on his father's knees, being held upright, and surveying the world with his wobbly body and bobbing head. On his tummy, he would cry and refuse to settle. He remembered that they had even fashioned a sling for him which they took from place to place that allowed them to leave him happily upright. It was sweetest when they were able to have picnics in local woodland or olive groves. They would find a limb of a tree, hang Masinissa's sling on it, and then pop him into it whilst they ate. The little baby was a cooing delight, and Gala would talk with him of his many plans and hopes. The first thing he would always tell the boy was that he loved him. The words must have meant nothing to the baby, but it was a soothing sensation for them both. He looked at the man who approached him through the door, and wondered how easily he could say those words now.

The man before him was an imposing sight. Gala had never seen his son exude such self-assurance. He could see the resolve in him. The boy he had played with and chased remained in the smile Masinissa gave him and the warmth of his embrace, but the man he had become filled the room. There was something magnetic about him, which was a bittersweet acknowledgement for the man who had nurtured him and whom he clearly had eclipsed. One glance at his son reassured him that Masinissa would be able to command and that the rigours of campaigns would not break him. Combat could be sudden or attritional, and he could see that his son had the power and resolve to handle both. There was an aspect to him too that hinted at unseen powers: strength, wisdom, charisma and intuition. The prodigious potential of the man he had sired was not merely the false pride of a doting father but the manifest reality before him.

"It's good to see you," Gala said and there was relief and concern in the tone he used. To be reunited was always a blessing and a moment to savour, but the joy was tempered by the reality that this was a council of war rather than a family gathering.

"You too, Father," Masinissa replied. He held the shoulders of Gala as he did so, stretching out the moment of intimacy a little further. It was punctuated by a brief cupping of the back of his father's head, a gesture Gala understood to be as full of devotion as a dagger to an enemy's heart was full of rage. Then the men had to resume their roles as men, and sideline their love and mutual helplessness, as the tides of their lives and the world had to be discussed.

"Come, sit down with me. I don't see you enough and it's with sadness I see you now, as you know I have to send you to war this time."

Masinissa settled himself in the chair adjacent to Gala's and replied with all the resolution of his character and upbringing. "This war was never going to spare me, Dad. I'm ready and I accept what will come, knowing that I have some mastery of the fates, and that my mind, body, horse and sword are as quick as any I will encounter."

Gala smiled at the informality of his son's address. To be simply called "Dad" by a man whom he had rarely seen as an adult was reassuring. It demonstrated that the boy he had guided and loved was still a part of this rugged figure before him, whom he knew had been tutored by the most agile minds, and scolded by the harshest and most disciplined soldiers after he had, with trepidation and reluctance, allowed him to leave with his Carthaginian allies as a guarantee of his fealty to them. His son was a seal on a convenient-but-ambivalent pact that only the marches of Hannibal had given substance to. The tribes and nations of the world were no longer able to enjoy the luxuries of independence. Sides needed to be taken and alliances forged. Relationships – once loose, and marked by occasional gatherings, tributes or marriages had now become almost symbiotic. The choice was uncomfortable alliances or to be easy prey. It was an easy compromise to make.

"OK, we'll talk about women and sports later, and maybe we'll be able to toast our enthusiasms and exploits a little bit, but now we need to talk about the world, as we are the ones that must act in it." Gala confirmed.

Masinissa interjected, "We, Father? Am I in that group now? The active members of the world?"

"Naturally," Gala replied. "You have enough knowledge and insight, and you have always been marked by great curiosity about the things around you. Believe me, it's not such a common virtue as you may suppose. The average man is usually quite content to exert the least effort to maintain his existence. That is why the whip was invented, I'm sure. In contrast, what scholars, generals and leaders do – or are meant to do – is maintain their curiosity, and apply themselves to their own learning and improvement. It is a constant, consuming labour. It gives acuity to your whole being. I know you, my son; you are always mindful of yourself and the moment you inhabit. You've always been a sharp kid. Compare yourself sometimes to the people you meet, especially when they have not been dulled by their toils or their cups. Value them in part by how much of their senses they are directing towards you and how much is simply a basic awareness necessary to avoid offence. Ask yourself how many of your compatriots see you when they look at you, hear the meaning of your words when they are listening to you, or are merely preoccupied with their survival and inner beings."

Masinissa nodded. "I know what you mean. I'm fortunate, though. I believe most of the men I know, and the women I love or associate with have inquisitive and mostly caring natures. I value those qualities as highly as you."

"We'll get to some of that later, I promise," Gala stated, "although use that mindfulness to censor yourself a little if the need arises. There is only so much a man wants to know about his son's bedroom." Clearly, he was a little annoyed by his son's slightly trite agreement. *He understands my meaning,* he assured himself, *but he's exhibiting some of the opacity that I'm counselling him against.* He continued, "Forgive me, Mas, I'm never really going to lose my impulse to guide you and pass on what knowledge of the world I can. It's a father's duty. It's the last muscle he develops, and the strongest one that age leaves him. That is especially so now when whatever sanctuary or immunity my name has provided you will disappear. The javelins that are flung at you or the swords raised against you will pay no account to your rank or name. I'm sure you see this as a time of change, and, hopefully, a beginning and not an end. Carry with you everything you've learnt, though. Remember that any journey, and your journey now may be long and exhausting, doesn't really begin at the moment we start it. Your journey, in the truest sense, started when you opened your eyes or understood my words for the first time, when your senses started to inform you of the world. It won't end when you come home either. The world is a mess, and the victories you may be lucky enough to achieve will only be succeeded by more challenges, be they of arms, men or both! We Numidians are horseman. Stay on the horse and don't let the beast stay still for long. It's the best advice I can give you."

Masinissa smiled, enjoying his father's obliqueness and concern. He cherished it as something precious. Theirs was a unique relationship. Gala was being the father he had always wanted to be, but could not manage through Masinissa's adolescence and young manhood. You cannot entrust messengers with your own feelings after all.

Gala went on, "I have a legacy to preserve and enhance, son, and you are the means for me to progress it and consolidate the country the Numidian and Massylian people deserve. We are not meant to be constantly in the vanguard of the Carthaginian army, or a proxy force for whoever dazzles or bullies us enough. The edges of our world are changing remarkably, but, in reality, it is us who are on the edge of the world. We need to modernise our ways, and take the learning and curiosity of the Greeks and the Romans as our own. Philosophy, science, art, architecture, and, yes, weaponry too: these are occupations that we need to aspire to. We must explore our minds and engage our hands in matters beyond horsehair and knives.

"I see this country as four countries right now. It is divided, firstly, between our forces and those of Syphax. We have our tribal and regional fissure. The Massyli and Masaesyli are enemies, but we are all Numidians. A leader strong enough or charismatic enough can wrest loyalty from both. It will not be me now, and it certainly won't be Syphax, but..." He looked at Masinissa encouragingly. "It could be you."

Masinissa had not heard his father speak so ambitiously of his hopes for him before, and it was daunting as well as flattering to hear Gala speak of him as a unifying force for a notional North African state that, it seemed, could aspire to all the accoutrements of civilisation that the great states of Rome and Greece possessed. To aspire to just the level of the Iberians, Gauls or Phoenicians seemed an enormous leap, and to go further still would take enormous resolve and dedication, from thousands of people with a unified purpose. To see the towns of Cirta, Tebessa and Thugga begin to resemble Gades, Massalia, Capua or Syracuse, let alone Carthage or Rome itself, seemed a quite fanciful idea to Masinissa.

Gala took his son's thoughtfulness to be favourable, and he continued dissecting his theme. "The other division is more north and south, or roughly so. You know how, as you travel, attitudes and behaviour can change with the terrain. The Numidians of the southern desert are very different from the coastal people, and their ways blur with those of the Libyans the further south and east you travel. As this war has demonstrated, and the mercenary war and earlier war with Rome proved too, it is those riders and warriors who are the most fierce and able. Maybe it's the harsher terrain and their struggle for daily survival within it that makes them so. I can't think of a more hostile environment in which to live, and, undoubtedly, this breeds hard men. They are also, in my experience, loyal and honourable to the leaders they trust and believe in. They have been so for me, and are the reason why this kingdom still prevails intact. Fill your ranks with these men, and cultivate them as long as your enemies threaten you. Always be aware of their simplicity, which is a virtue for their leader. They deal with absolutes, for the most part, not conditional things, compromises or expediencies. Whatever their cause, they will hold to it. Their faith in their lands and their tribe is not a transient thing. It is a bond forged by years digging in the same unyielding earth as their brothers for a few grains or roots. Always remember that if a man can teach you a thing or two about survival, he is worth knowing. If you, our cause and our nation survive, then the northern people will become more important. Maybe the number of our sailors will grow and merchant fleets will expand, and we will start plying the trade routes of the world and bring back wealth and knowledge in all its forms. Maybe our merchants and the many different tradesmen in the bazaar will build our cities into enviable destinations, but – for now, though – even though you are venturing north and west, remember that your power and support lie in the south and east."

Masinissa realised that his father was attempting to pass as much of his wisdom as he could to him, ceding to his son some of his own place in the world. He was frail now, and the warrior mantle had to be passed. Gala was offering him his insight into how to preserve his inheritance. He was the king of the Massyli, and he had a paternal understanding and love of it. It was clear to Masinissa that his father's words were shrewd and that he expected him to heed them. In reality, he was experienced and perceptive enough to have adopted much of his advice already. Most of his cavalry and auxiliaries were desert men originally, and he had consolidated strong tribal and family links with the southern Massyli, as well as a significant group of Libyans. As his father had said, the differences between them in any case were quite slight and vague.

"I won't forget, Dad," he replied. "I know how valuable the desert riders are. All the men who trained me or who hold rank under me have been from the nomadic tribes. They even tease me that I am a soft northerner sometimes."

Gala grinned and nodded approvingly. "Good, try to keep it that way as far as possible. You're going to lose many soon, I fear, so send word for others to be prepared to join you. It's always difficult to quantify the numbers of available men in the deeper desert, and those who may cross it from further south in Africa, but our bonds are strong and our family respected by the Libyans, so any calls we make will be answered in time."

With the hint about losses, a glance was exchanged between father and son, and Gala's body language altered imperceptibly. He stuck his thumbnail into his index finger, looked at the indent momentarily, and then brushed it and his middle finger pensively over the bristles of his moustache. It was a gesture almost subconsciously intended to close the mouth or one that suggested the topic on the tip of his tongue was an onerous one.

"We have to do this," he said.

Masinissa took the comment to refer to both the direction of the conversation as well as the imminent battle they were about to discuss.

Gala continued, "Syphax is targeting us. He has no immediate interest in Carthaginian territory, although I suspect Rome views us and them – right now, anyway – as inextricable. They are pouring so many military advisors into his territories."

"How many?" queried Masinissa. "There have been a lot of rumours, and you know this sort of thing can get inflated as it gets spread around."

Gala worked his tongue under his incisors, and appeared to ruminate a little on the question, suggesting to Masinissa that his answer may be a little vague or uncertain. "Troop movements into Masaesyli and Mauretania are hard to ascertain fully. I think most, if not all, of the Roman deployments have come by sea, over possibly at least a year. We believe at least one legion is training and bolstering Syphax's forces, and there may be elements of a second, so, from their point of view, there are over 5,000 men, for sure. When you ally that with the 20,000 Numidians and mercenaries that are mustering for Syphax, it is very substantial force. Most of the Masaesyli, though, are conscripted, and his cavalry is much weaker than ours, and I don't think there is much of an elephant brigade amongst them. He is trying to compensate by utilising the expertise of the Roman contingent to improve the quality of his infantry units. I don't think that, even with the disciplines fostered by the legionaries, they will pose any great threat, and if the terrain is favourable, your men will pick them off and cut them down with the same proficiency that our riders have become renowned for."

"I hope so," Masinissa replied. "There are plenty of veterans in the cavalry, and they are well used to spearing Romans. We need infantry of our own, though. We are badly outnumbered otherwise."

Gala gave his son a slightly feline grin. The sly old man had a little more to offer. "Of course, we will have both the Hasdrubal's as our jaws. Gisco will march with us and direct the eastern forces, and a large cohort of the Iberian army will advance towards us from the west, commanded by Hasdrubal Barca himself. Messengers are informing us that many of his forces are disembarking at Tingi at the moment.

They will march east, and we will look to meet them. There may be elements of heavy Gallic cavalry with him, and if so, all the better. We could integrate them into our flanks, and, when we have weakened and softened their sides enough, they can plough through them with impunity."

Gala was painting a very auspicious picture of the battle ahead, and Masinissa knew his positivity was very much intended to allay the concerns of his son. It was likely that, even with the presence of the illustrious Barcid general, the heavy cavalry his father was describing would be meagre at best. Nevertheless, he had heard and read quite a lot about the heavily armoured lancers used in the eastern Asian armies, and been impressed by how effective they appeared to be. The splintered factions of the Macedonian empire were especially fond of this type of warfare. The Seleucid Empire, in particular, had a reputation for utilising lancers in thundering charges that often dealt decisive and devastating blows against the opposing infantry. It was quite antithetical to the Numidian style of speed and skirmish. Even Masinissa wore only the lightest armour. However, it was a notion that intrigued him, and he could see how potentially complementary a joint light and heavy cavalry might be.

"The war has really come home hasn't it? When our forces engage, this could look like a smaller version of Cannae," offered Masinissa.

"Let's hope so," Gala interjected cheerfully. "The Romans were completely routed there."

"Weren't they! Hannibal, Maharbal and Mago killed about 75,000 that day, as well as taking the surrender of the equivalent of two whole legions. If we could do the same to Syphax's crew, we could march right back up through Iberia. I'll advise Gisco shortly, when he brings his forces to us, that we should lure Syphax onto the plains; keep the ground as unfavourable as we can; try to disrupt their supplies, especially their water; and if Gisco can station enough soldiers in the rear, cut off any secure line of retreat."

Gala made a little leap in his chair and clapped his hands in abrupt delight. "Ah, you're a general already. I'm convinced."

Masinissa let the compliment fall, gave a few shallow nods as gestures of gratitude, looked his father square in the eyes and gave him a pursed smile, which left a little questioning and melancholiness in his eyes.

Gala was intuitive enough to realise that Masinissa's silence heralded an end to their martial theme, or the pragmatic part of it, at least. Before him was his son, after all, and a goodbye that had the prospect of being a final one. His elation ebbed like a retreating wave, and he sagged back in his chair and felt his larynx constrict a little as his body tightened with the emotion of the moment. "I'm proud of you," he said quietly, "and I always will be." His voice faded, but his eyes shone bright as they glistened with the tears that his taut frame held back.

"There is nothing I could cherish higher," Masinissa replied, wavering only slightly less than his father. "And that will be the case forever, regardless of what kudos or fortunes may come my way."

He held his father's arm as he rose, and they held each other with a rare intensity.

As they broke their embrace, Gala said softly, "My sweet boy, only children believe in forever when they say it. We all know the word doesn't mean what it promises. Everyone's forever comes sooner or later. My prayers and hopes are that yours will come later than mine. I'm supposed to watch over you in the heavens, not the other way around, remember."

"Let me watch myself for a while yet," Masinissa replied, squeezing his father's hands tightly. He let one go and held the other as the two men walked together to the courtyard where Capuca was waiting with the horses. They lingered in their farewells, both men wrestling with their emotions.

Finally, Gala bid Masinissa a final farewell and kissed him paternally on his forehead before dipping his skull gently to his offspring's, as if communicating his knowledge and affection as directly as he could, cranium to cranium.

"Bye, my boy," Gala said hoarsely, and, with that, the father and son parted, perhaps forever.

NEMESIS

It wasn't long before the march west began, and the prospect of meeting the rival Masaesyli tribe in open warfare became very real and very imminent. There would be no last-minute diplomacy. It had been drummed into all sides that the fissures between the Numidian tribes were irreconcilable. The relationship had always been more than merely fractious. There could never be acceptance or wary coexistence. One would have to conquer the other and gain hegemony, and that was that.

To Masinissa, for whom the genesis of the separation was obscure and impersonal, the enemy was distant, even though they occupied adjacent territory. There was no sense of kinship either, even though they claimed to be the same state, and possess the same identity and bloodlines. He was sure that he would not find himself in an embrace with the rival king Syphax one day, insisting mutually that the years of hatred and mistrust were just a terrible and unfortunate misunderstanding. The wider world only exacerbated the tensions and the factionalisms. Carthage had Massyli as its proxy. The Romans courted Syphax and the Masaesyli as theirs. They were like gladiators or cornered wolves. They had no choice but to fight each other.

After long years of having the Masaesyli diabolised, and their otherness and wretchedness inculcated in him, Masinissa found himself in their territory, riding west with his army and the Carthaginians to reach Tingi, and from there to sail to the Iberian front. He knew they would be intercepted, or they would be fortunate enough to take the initiative and create their own ambush. However, their numbers were the largest he had ever witnessed, and there were more allied forces coming east who had disembarked at Tingi, and were looking to reunite with them or, even better, catch Syphax's army between them. In any event, the swelling of tribal hatred was about to burst.

His nemesis – the man he had heard condemned from every quarter from the moment he could distinguish between the basic concepts of good and bad, or friend and enemy – was in his way, and he was prepared for him. Certainly, Syphax had taken heart from the encouraging Roman campaigns of Gnaeus and Publius, and was attacking settlements to the east more frequently. The raids were increasingly well orchestrated and savage. Masinissa and the Carthaginians were aware of the Roman mission to Syphax, and of the fact that they had sent three centurions to him to train his men and make assurances to him that he would be well compensated by an indebted Rome if he attacked his neighbours and helped tilt the balance in the field to the Romans favour.

According to Massyli spies, some of the emissaries to Syphax had returned to Rome, but they'd left seasoned soldiers and trainers behind, who were working intensively with Syphax's recruits, and creating a more disciplined and organised force. The effectiveness of his infantry brigades in particular appeared to be benefitting from the tutelage of the expeditionary legions. The Numidians, of all denominations, were renowned as poor infantry soldiers, so if the Romans could upgrade their competence in this area, Syphax would have a much more balanced army to utilise. They would also no doubt be a lot fitter. A typical, and more or less daily exercise of the Roman instructors was to march, in full kit, roughly twenty miles within a five-hour limit. Anyone who trooped in after that time would be beasted. Those boys would be exhausted, but they'd also be a physical proposition.

Masinissa and his fellow soldiers were passing through a vineyard, and Masinissa caught himself feeling a little envious and resentful of the quality of the soil, which would surely produce some excellent wine and vinegar. Whilst Numidian wine lacked the reputation of that of the growers on the other side of the great sea, he could testify to its quality. The harvests could also be abundant. He remembered, as a child, enjoying squashing the fruits in the autumn under the benevolent gaze of his mother, aunts and the local growers. As he reminisced, his *optio* rode up to him. Pun was always good company and had a knack of knowing when to be around. He could read people well, and had a quality of wisdom that could only have germinated from a perfect union of intelligence and experience.

"What's new, BP?" Masinissa asked, affectionately breaking down Big Pun's nickname into its acronym; a form doubly expressing affection and familiarity.

"I'm just seeing how you're doing. Are you doing all right? This thing is going to light up at any time. Have you made your peace?" Big Pun questioned.

"As far as I am able," Masinissa replied, not really very convincingly.

"Did you get any tail before you shipped out? How about that rich piece with the poppin' arse that we've seen you knocking around with?"

Masinissa took the ribald comment in his stride. All airs and graces were gone by then. You lose any contrived formalities fairly quickly when riding into death's guts. "Yup. We left on pretty good terms. Who knows, maybe I left a little bit more than a good time memory with her too."

"Dawg!" Big Pun whistled. "I won't pry any further. Just as long as you've got something fresh to take your mind off stuff. You know, I find a good way of prepping yourself is to remember the time you spent with survivors and the stories they share with you. People do walk away from these things, you know. Some of us are lucky and do get old. I remember a veteran whom I used to spend time with who had fought in the first war for Hasdrubal's father Hamilcar – yeah, the Baraq, the thunderbolt himself."

"Oh man." Masinissa looked at him a little askance. "You like to go back a way, don't ya?"

"Sure do! That's how you learn. Those old boys can teach you plenty, and they always have a juicy anecdote ready to go. Anyway, this old lag's name was Jugurthu. He was being cared for by one of his daughters, but she left him alone for most of the day with only his dog for company. He knew he had only a short time left, and he wanted to share some of his stories. He went right back to when he was a small child for some of them. He was one of those kids who always got into fights. He was destined to end up a soldier. Well, anyway, he was talking one time about being surprised by the enemy. They'd crossed a river somewhere and were in rough country, and thought they were safe from any marauding Romans. They didn't anticipate any trouble. Their runners and outriders had spotted nothing. Out of nowhere, this legion appeared in full battle order and with plenty of cavalry. They had no time to plan, but they were all mounted and armed, and they flew right into the enemy's nearest flank. The speed of the offensive surprised the Romans, and the initiative was reversed quickly.

"Most of their cavalry were caught, and lost their lives or their horse before they could react. Unlike his compatriots, who had flung their javelins and were flailing their *falcatas* at anything in red tunics and greaves, Jugurthu was using his as a lance and was spearing everything that got in his way. He wouldn't take any of them in the midriff as he would lodge his javelin too deep, but he had the strength to hold it in front of him like a sword, and take the impact if it was against the shoulder or the head. They say he took out about twenty Romans that day in that way. See, there's more than one way to skin a goat. You've got that kind of strength, Masinissa. I can see the power in your shoulders. You could force most of a man back at full clip and slide him off your javelin. For his valour, the men called Jugurthu Bloody lance after that battle. Do you fancy that kind of honorific for yourself after we get past Syphax's mob?"

Masinissa smirked and clicked his tongue. "You know, maybe you could have suggested novelty combat tactics some time ago. If I'm plunging into the columns of Roman-trained troops, I don't know how far down the experimental route I want to go. I'd rather have more range of motion, and get those horses stampeding with a few licks of my *falcata* if I can. I'm not on a suicide mission."

"Do what you need to do, sire."

"I do have an innovation I want to try, though. When we have them broken or reduced into smaller pockets, I want to split our riders. Have one group continue the harrying and encirclement, circling the pocket continually, whilst the other better-armed cohort go straight through the middle, looking for the points of least resistance and hacking their way to the end. I'll be in the vanguard of that one. Straight in, straight out… and if there's no blood on the end of your face by the time you make it through, most likely you've joined the dead."

Big Pun looked impressed. His lower lip pinched into approval. "I've ridden similar tactics before. It suits the stronger riders, and the ones with more brawny thighs and calves. If you can hold arms in both hands as you plough through, you are almost like a chariot wheel but harvesting your enemy's blood much higher. The trick is not to take a man's weight on both hands at the same time, or else over you'll go, straight into the gore, and you're done."

"Now that I can try," responded Masinissa almost euphorically. "If you want a sturdy-legged rider, then look no further!"

"One more thing, Mas; well, two more things. Firstly, I know you well and I know your qualities; they shine out of your pores. But you're not a veteran yet. Don't think you know everything or have seen it all before, even after we engage with Syphax. There's always plenty to learn about staying alive. The other thing is that it's OK to be afraid. It really is. You'd be an idiot or a stone otherwise. Feed off it. It's the natural consort of courage and bravery. Keep that fire burning in your pit. Keep it burning hot. It keeps you alert."

"One day I'll ask your real name, Optio. Thank you. I'll take your advice and your boost."

"Save it till your dying hour, sire. You can laugh at it then."

The two men left it at that.

*

A little while later, they received orders to head for the upper end of a ravine a little further into the mountains. The elephants, and there were about forty of them, were driven to the front, followed by auxiliary pikemen with *sarissas*. The slingers and some of the more accurate javelin throwers took considerable amounts of arms, and were given orders to march quickly and fan out at the top of the nearby ridge lines.

They had heard word that Syphax's troops were heading their way and appeared oblivious to the presence of Masinissa's army. They were hurrying, disorderly and seemed to be maintaining a high pace as if being pursued, quite possibly by the disembarked army of Hasdrubal Gisco. They were thousands strong, and combined effective infantry as well as cavalry, but, apparently, Syphax had only a few elephants that could be turned anyway on the terrain they were in. Things were looking promising, and word was being carried through the lines that Syphax's army appeared to be funnelling itself into the maw of the Massylian ambush.

His *tesserarius*, Tigerman, rode up and past them, giving them his signature cry as he did so. It was far more reassuring when sung on the advent of battle than at the start of some form of arduous discipline. He whirled his javelin and bounced heavily on his horse yelling, *"I'm the king of all battles, and they call me Tigerman... If you cross my path, you take your own life in your hands."* He rode up and down the line to the amusement of Masinissa and Pun, but his exclamations were clearly having a galvanising effect. It was an untypical military cadence, but he wanted the soldiers to pick it up and they quickly did.

Soon, the counterpoint chant was being bellowed out from all sides: *"We're the kings of all battles, and they call us Massylians... If you cross our path, you take your own life in your hands."*

Masinissa joined in forcefully, but only with the rhythm initially, "Da da da da da... da da da da..." with another pause and then the correct last phrase, "in your hands," in his deepest, most baritone timbre.

Pun laughed and tried an even more resonant, "in your hands!"

Breathless, Tigerman rode back to them. "This is going to go well. Syphax is going to lose many men today. Unless this is a feint, we're going to squash him."

"I think you're right," Pun replied, endorsing the battlefield assessment, almost fervidly. Their chanting and the apparently auspicious position of their forces had tipped him over the edge.

"What could go wrong, Pun?" Masinissa asked as a genuine enquiry, rather than a triumphalist expression of the inevitable, trying to dampen the warrior's ardour.

"Not much, as long as Gisco can keep funnelling them towards us, if that is what he's doing, and he holds his line if they turn. And if their elephants are being held in reserve, we'll splat 'em. You know when you have a fly on the air and you try to swat it, it hardly ever works." He made a few theatrical clapping motions to demonstrate his point. "But if you have a bug on the wall; smack!" And he cracked his left hand on his right and mashed them together. The physical insinuation was obvious.

"I hope you're right, Pun, The last thing I want to be doing is putting my hand in a big old wasps' nest. We'd never get to Iberia, and I'll have my back to Carthage with the Punic javelins pushing me back."

"The omens are good, don't worry," Pun reassured him. "This sort of battle is unconventional. There are no open fields or flanking positions. The cavalry are not going to do anything other than charge right at broken lines and chase their fleeing counterparts. This one is not going to be like in the storybooks when the two great kings or princes meet in combat. You may not see Syphax at all, unless you're chasing after his fleeing backside. You won't fight your way to each other for an epic duel that all your men will pay attention to whilst saving their own hides. It'll be waves of our men and beasts crashing into them from both sides. By the time your wave crests over them, you might not have much to chew over."

"I wouldn't mind that," Masinissa replied.

The two of them settled onto their horses' backs, and waited for the horns, drums and shouts to give them their signals. He noticed that most of the waiting riders behind him were alert, with postures in which they were pulled up close to the withers of their steeds; the exception being his cousin Capuca, who had flopped forwards and was resting with his groin on the loins of his horse and his head on the shoulder and mane of his mount. Maybe he was talking to it, whispering some soothing words that would echo back at himself.

They didn't have to wait long for the muster, and, after that, time paused for Masinissa as the vanguard of elephants, infantry and auxiliaries pressed forwards, leaving the cavalry in the rear. He found himself relying on his ears for clues about the battle that had erupted in front of him, as distinguishing between cries was impossible. From an auditory point of view, a man's agony doesn't vary between tribe or caste. The only clues he had were trying to identify the epicentre of the commotion, and whether or not that was receding from them. As far as he could discern, the whirlpool of dying was moving further from him.

The soldiers he could see at the top of the ridge lines were also now out of sight, which must have meant that they were either pursuing a retreating enemy, or else they had exhausted their ranged weapons and were entering the melee below. All indications urged Masinissa forwards right then. The enemy may not yet have been a carcass, but, before it had a chance to regather itself or take a larger remnant from the battle, his mounted troops needed to swarm over it. He waved his javelin arm high and twirled it as if it were a ribboned baton that dancers sometimes used to accentuate their movements. The few soldiers who had dismounted remounted speedily, and Capuca was given a quick nudge from his nearest comrade to rouse him from his practically horizontal posture.

Masinissa felt both a thrill and a sense of unease. The familiar Numidian tactics of skirmishing and retreat were to be jettisoned, and he knew he could not rely on haphazard attacks and improvisation to prevail. He would charge and drive right through whatever was in front of him. He told himself, *Empty your mind. Think of nothing else other than cutting your brave foes to pieces.*

Despite the change of strategy, there was still some concession made to convention. He split his riders into left and right wings. Massiva and Capuca would lead with him, along the left flank, whilst Pun, Tigerman and Micipsa, one of his more trusted lieutenants, would lead the right. The ravine wasn't too narrow, but it wasn't too wide either before the rocky slopes started to kick up quite precipitously. They would ride a maximum of two abreast. They couldn't hit a full charge for fear of trampling their own troops, who would be nearest to them, but, once through, they would work to reunite with each other, encircle the pocket and then break into the Masaesylian rear.

"Statorius's drills won't help you now you bastard!" Masinissa yelled to the air, to his men, and to the tribal antagonist who stood or had fallen somewhere close ahead.

They charged and negotiated passage around their own men without too much trouble. In truth, trampling the fallen was more disruptive to the horses than getting past the living. There were already hundreds, maybe thousands, of dead and dying men, and the hooves of the Numidian horses accounted for a few more. There were some grotesque sights amongst them. The charging elephants had already pulped men into mush. Maybe those poor souls had been the most valiant of the lot. Taking the full force of a herd of war elephants takes guts, which is pretty much all that Masinissa could now make out of them. He was jolted a little by the images. It was naive to assume you could still be recognised and mourned on the battlefield. There would be no noble elegy for those men who had, only moments earlier, held their pathetic lances at an enraged line of pachyderms.

As he passed his men, he could see the rumps of the elephants in the distance, still rumbling forwards. They had detached from most of the pursuing infantry, but their forward motion was being maintained. A few of the beasts had howdahs strapped to them, with drivers and slingers, and it was encouraging to see the men still kicking into the elephants' flanks to propel the attack deeper. The standard of Gala and Massyli was visible atop the largest of the elephants, albeit the one that Masinissa knew had already lost one of his tusks. Ivory wasn't everything when it came to elephants on the battlefield. As long as he was big and not too skittish, he could be employed in an attack.

Surveying the intervening distance between himself and the one-tusked behemoth, Masinissa concluded quickly that this chapter of the battle was going well. That he was afforded the time to make such a diagnosis attested to the ascendancy of the Massylians. The condition of the enemy appeared to be approaching ruinous. The Masaesylian infantry lines were collapsing in on themselves, and much of the cavalry that hadn't been stampeded by the elephants had been caught between the lines. Many of these were still offering stout resistance, but there many riderless horses and others that by then had new, clearly Massylian riders attached. Furthermore, parts of his peripheral gaze found isolated men whose desperation had forced them to take their own lives. As he urged Napla towards the nearest extant enemy cavalry, he saw one Masaesyli kill another, and then turn the sword that slew him into his own guts. Masinissa could hear the man's howl as he tried to rip the blade up to his own heart. *At least you gave your friend an easier exit*, Masinissa thought to himself.

The interlude of gruesome theatre was fleeting, as his perspective shortened, and the enemy cavalry he was galloping towards spied him and must have appraised him as a valuable target. There were three of them, and they yelled what must have been curses as they thundered straight at him. He scarcely had time to check if his lieutenants were still close to him, but he had to presume that they were and that they would each take one of the outriders. In all the excitement and commotion, you lose the ability to recognise your friends, or do not have the time to scan for their presence when the point of a sword is racing towards you. You can just see the enemy, and his blades and javelins.

As the distance shortened to nothing, there was just enough room between the first and second riders for him to drive Napla through the gap. As she passed the riders, he crouched and hugged her mane with his free hand. It took his adversary by surprise, and the man swung his weapon uselessly across the air above Masinissa's head. Masinissa was through, and, before his enemy was out of range, the trailing third of his *falcata* hit his adversary's larynx, and tore the voice and life from him. The rider to the right of him had met a similar fate, as Massiva had loosed his javelin into him, and the force of the impact had dislodged the enemy rider from his steed. If he was still alive on the ground, he wouldn't be for long.

The rider to the left, however, presented a much direr problem. Capuca had been interrupted by another rider and, whilst despatching him, may have taken a slight wound, so he was not close enough to throw his javelin with any accuracy. Masinissa was exposed, and the third rider had him unbalanced and in his sights. The microseconds he needed to turn, parry or throw would surely give his enemy sufficient opening to slash at his shoulder or neck. He wheeled Napla, hoping to mitigate the force and depth of the cut he felt certain would rip into him momentarily. He gritted his teeth and balled his fists for the impact, but none came. A scream did, however, and then he saw a youthful infantryman pounding towards him, who must have been the agent of his salvation. His enemy had taken a flying dagger in his sword arm and was reaching for it desperately. The Massylian trooper didn't pause to allow him to rearm, and grabbed his foot and heaved upwards in an effort to dismount him. The effort didn't quite succeed, but it jolted the rider closer to Masinissa, who did the rest and yanked him off the horse by his hair, stabbing upwards under his chin and out the back of his head in the same movement. The youth, having the presence of mind to realise that his prospects of survival increased materially if he was off the ground and on the considerable bulk and elusiveness of the free stallion, leapt onto its empty back and looked at Masinissa, conspiratorially and questioningly. There was no time for introductions, and Masinissa gave him a thumbs up, which turned into an instruction to follow him.

They gave Capuca, who did have a lengthy but shallow looking gash in his thigh, enough time to catch up, and, with Massiva, the quartet formed a small but effective unit. The rest of the cavalry had broken into smaller components too, as the initial charge encountered forceful resistance, but it was still apparent that it was, as an amorphous whole, working steadily towards reuniting with the opposite flank and sealing the doom of the Masaesylian pocket.

There would be no reinforcements either for the battered remnant, and it turned slowly from a contest into butchery, as the jaws tightened and the inevitable ensued. More and more of the enemy could be seen to be taking their own lives, or trying to conceal themselves under the bleeding and the bled out. In most eyes, that was a cowardly act that would invite contempt and a concomitantly harsher fate. It was foolish and self-defeating too, as they would be found at the ebb of the battle when retribution would be at its most raw and fierce.

Masinissa had killed or fatally maimed about six or seven of the enemy when he was hailed by Micipsa and Pun; Tigerman, at that moment, was kicking out at a soldier who had leapt at his belt to try to gain some kind of purchase. The noose was closed, and what had been an attritional stranglehold would mutate quickly into an abattoir. Masinissa had no role or purpose in that kind of denouement, and turned – with the three who had accompanied him, as well as his aide de camp, *optio* and *tesserarius*, who had finished clearing his lower half of the enemy soldier – and rode towards the elephants, which were by then turning aimlessly without the urging of their riders.

He turned to his battlefield saviour and asked the obvious, "What's your name, kid?"

"I'm Hiempsal, but most people call me Yemp, if they know me. I prefer it too."

Masinissa was struck by the boy's diffidence. It was a common trait in country boys. They were taught to be respectful. In Masinissa's experience, they were either that or the complete opposite: intolerably arrogant and conceited idiots. "Thank you, Yemp; you got me out of a situation back there."

"It's OK. I needed the horse." He broke out in a modest grin.

"You know it won't be long until all the enemy back there are dead, and then the scramble for plunder is going to begin in earnest. Do you want a new sword and maybe a little gold?"

"I do, sir," the boy assented eagerly, although Masinissa could detect the hesitation in him, as he had to choose between staying with his chieftain or trying to line his pockets with a rare booty.

"You've done your duty. Maybe you could round up a few horses once you've taken what you can carry." Masinissa hadn't meant for the instruction to be appear dismissive, but Yemp seemed to take it that way, which Masinissa regretted.

In any event, it made up the boy's mind for him, and he wheeled his horse, thanked Masinissa and rode back towards the lottery of the dying. Masinissa waved him off, and Massiva, who had seen Yemp's valour in close proximity, tapped him approvingly on his back as he passed.

Hopefully, he has family close by, Masinissa mused, *so that he can share the spoils with them before we set off for the uncertainties of the Iberian coast.*

Micipsa looked at him a little disapprovingly. He was the most pragmatic of his immediate retinue, and had little regard for sentiment, particularly when it proved a distraction from the stewardship of the battle in hand. "Are we chasing?" came his quite blunt enquiry.

"You're a caustic bugger sometimes, Cips. Of course. I will stay here with some of the cavalry to provide cover, and you see what you can hook with the rest. Don't go too far from here, just in case Syphax has sufficient cavalry remaining to return and pounce on our infantry. They'll be drunk in an hour and would be slaughtered if he had the presence of mind to double back on us. It may be futile, in any case. If Syphax has fled, he would have a few hours lead, and this is his country. My guess is that he's riding hard west as far as he can to the Maurusii, where he will find amity and sanctuary."

"OK, Pun, Tigerman and I will follow whatever trail we can find, take the stragglers, and maybe figure out what strength Syphax has remaining and where he will seek refuge. It would be better to wipe him out completely because, otherwise, he is sure to rally another army and come back at us, and next time his Roman contingents may be embedded deeper, may be drilled a little better and they might even catch us out with an ambush."

"Let's not be so pessimistic, huh? The Romans have to get through Iberia to get to him. He's elusive, and you can't govern all these lands with the men who will be left, but maybe he'll just lick his wounds, lay low and hope the fortunes of his allies come to his rescue. He can be the wolf in the hills that takes a few sheep, but no one is too worried about. I can live with that. Look behind you. All that Masaesylian power is pouring onto the red earth over there."

"All right, let's see how long into the campaign it takes for that optimism of yours to unravel," Micipsa replied, his words suffused with disenchantment.

"I hope I don't exhaust that quality too quickly. Every night is dark, but there are always stars in the sky and most mornings are bright. Suck the air in, and enjoy its freshness and the fruits of the earth. A lot of guys lost their futures today. I didn't, and you didn't. We'll set sentries and track the enemy, and then, when we've cleared the field and secured our lines, we'll celebrate."

Micipsa smiled, acknowledging the mercy of the gods and the consolation of Masinissa in equal measure. "There'd better be at least one intact amphora of wine left for me when I get back, all right? I'm due a two-day check out after this!"

"You've got it," Masinissa assented.

Both men turned, one still looking for the living and the other returning to the carnage, trying not to look too directly at the lost.

ANGELS

There comes a point in a battle where the defeated who can flee have put to flight, and those who are left are abandoned and know their fate. It then becomes a slaughter, and all glory and honour is lost. Killing as an exercise rather than a contest revolted Masinissa, and, for those who have retained their souls and humanity, the act is one suffused with pity and despair. It took all of Masinissa's fortitude to return to the battlefield and observe its final act, as his men looted and ended lives that had started dribbling away a few hours earlier. He felt almost a sense of duty to the vanquished that their ends had some trace of mercy and that the more sadistic men in his ranks didn't have too much sport with the dying. In truth, most didn't. Everyone who walked through the piles of dead and dying men knew that only the mercy of the gods and speed of their reflexes had spared them the same fate.

It is us or them. Thank Tanit it is them, thought Masinissa.

There was no sense of vengeance either. Those helpless men were the same as the Massylians. They were adversaries only in the sense that they had been recruited by force or coin, and had done what they had to. The able-bodied had to fight for someone sooner or later. The war knocked on every door and claimed its due in the end.

The residue of battle offered a paradox of serenity and agony. There was, above the moans and cries of dying men, an area of peace.

The clamour of combat carried noise across great distances, especially when the men or beasts that created them still had all their reserves of vitality. The range of the dying was much more limited and waned as the moments passed. Many of the dying were even furtive; their desperate logic being that they may be mistaken for the dead and ignored. Their chances were slight. The Numidians who roamed the battlefield and cleaned the dead of their possessions could detect even the tiniest respiration and, besides, were rough with the presumptive corpses, which was a brutality that inevitably raised a murmur from any who had some chance of surviving another day.

The serenity was a false one, however. Looking upwards, it was possible to sense the passing of the tumult, but, on casting your eyes back down to the earth, the heaps of life moved the parts of their bodies they could. As this was usually their mouths – and many of these were shrouded by debris, and the limbs and gore of other misfortunates – it was the ears of the observer that had to be sharpest rather than the eyes. He didn't enjoy the comparison with vultures, but that is what it most resembled. The tearing apart of abandoned flesh without ceremony or regard was horrific, made even more so when you yielded to any sense of empathy. Dying in this way was little different from being torn to pieces by dogs.

The bravest men, or the ones who could still prop their upper bodies marginally above the remains of their comrades, offered their necks to the passing enemy. It was a sight well known and common on the battlefield, but to witness it in person raised a shudder. Masinissa nevertheless admired the action, regarding it as the most honourable way to end a ruined life. The gesture, at least in the immediate aftermath of the battle, had a companion too. Allied soldiers would make a very similar gesture for aid or water. The meanings of the gesture contrasted absolutely, though. One was a plea for salvation, and the other a plea for release. Masinissa wondered how many men had been unlucky to have their pleas misinterpreted, with an appeal to a comrade for some nourishment being met with a sword across the throat.

Masinissa thought about the Numidian virtue of *anaia*, which was held in great regard by most of his compatriots, and was a matter of considerable obligation when it was invoked or acknowledged. The Numidian people – and that extended to include the Mauretanians and, to a lesser extent, the Libyans – had a very strong sense of mercy and protection, and the two combined into the amalgam of *anaia*. It was an incongruous place for it to be practised, but, as he watched the victorious soldiers pass amongst the vanquished, he could detect pockets of mercy in the final comforting words that were offered or the pockets of prayers that were given as the swords passed quickly and accurately across the throats of the dying.

He thought of his father and how he had always prioritised safeguarding the weak, be they children, women or anyone vulnerable or at risk of harm. It went beyond pride and duty for his father, though. It was part of his soul and a virtue he had inculcated strongly in his son. He knew he would have to defer to the Carthaginian view in most matters, but, at a personal level, he would always look to find the solution or decision that most conformed to his notion of *anaia*.

He turned from the scene to the hilltop where Hasdrubal's camp was being made, and realised there were matters to attend to. Many of his men had pursued the remnant of the Masaesylian and Roman legions, and there were only a few left with him of his immediate retinue. The fact that they had not led the pursuit was a testimony to the devastating nature of the victory. Syphax had entered the battle a proud warlord and the head of a new, modern army groomed by the finest military advisors in the world, and he had been reduced to a fugitive, who was at that moment riding for his life, with whatever forces he could still muster, to the sanctuary of the west and the neutral Mauretanians.

Masinissa hailed his cousin Capuca, who led two horses to him. Capuca's own had been lost in battle, and the slice in his calf suggested that he himself had been fortunate to escape the same fate. Masinissa's own horse had performed as admirably as he could have hoped, but he had long since dismounted and was in no need of the trusty mare for the moment and accepted the offer of the other beast.

"Don't you wish you were still at the lyceum impressing the Greeks with your language and tactics?" enquired Capuca.

For openers, after the rage of the battle, such a reference to his scholarship jarred with Masinissa a little, but he understood Capuca's good intentions. It was not levity he was searching for, but only an alternative to the horror they had prosecuted and were turning their backs on at that point. He responded, "Definitely. I would happily conjugate verbs for hours rather than have to reflect for a moment on what I have just been part of. We can't, though, can we? Look at our swords and our hands."

Capuca made a motion to do just that and turned his hands over before his eyes. They were as dirt flecked and bloody as Masinissa's. "We'll wash off what we can and live with what we can't." He shrugged. "What you don't want to remember will fade and you'll be left with the lessons and the wisdom."

Masinissa stroked his beard in a gesture of thoughtfulness and acceptance. "I don't think killing is quite the same as retaining my Latin or Greek somehow, but you're right, I guess. I don't remember the bruises and bumps of my childhood too well, only the best ways to avoid them. Maybe this battlefield, the next one and the ones after that will give me the same skills of evasion or attack, perhaps. I'm getting as good at spearing a man or a horse as you are at ducking by me when we play *harpastum*." Masinissa felt that a moment of flattery, even one with a grizzly comparison, was in order to reciprocate Capuca's solicitude. Capuca excelled at *harpastum*, and always seemed to be able to duck out of any tackles or trips Masinissa attempted on him. He hoped he would be as elusive of his enemies swords and javelins in the future as he had been against the futile lunges of his friends on the beaches and fields of North Africa.

"Do you see any angels over there?" Capuca asked in a manner that Masinissa thought was a little ambiguous.

Is he being literal? Masinissa wondered, *Or solemn or frivolous?* The battle had thrown his ordinary sensibilities a little off course. "I think that if I stare hard enough or concentrate, I can see them rescuing those who have pleased the gods. I don't like to stare too long at such a view, though, and I'm not convinced too many of the dead have garnered much favour with the gods. Maybe all the ferrying to the heavens has already happened by now, and the boatmen of Tanit have collected the passengers who have lived worthy lives."

"There will still be a few out there waiting for their end. If you stick around, maybe you'll catch some mysterious zephyrs carrying away a few souls."

Masinissa liked the idea that this rocky, worthless ground wasn't the last sentient moment for so many men. He knew that if he found himself lying in a similar position one day, choking up his own blood and fearing for his next moment, he would clutch onto the thought of an impending angel with everything he had. He smiled a thank you to Capuca for the reinforcement, unsure whether his cousin would recognise the deeper gratitude. He doubted it.

"Who stayed, Cap?" he asked, wondering who of his guard hadn't chased after the fleeing Syphax. He knew his troops showed little restraint with a wounded and beaten foe to pursue. They knew the caprices of battle could put the swords quickly in the opposite hand. The military logic was the fewer hands and the fewer swords, the better.

"Well, there are plenty of Iberians and Carthaginians, but not too many of us lot," Capuca confirmed. "Of the ranking guys, there's just me, Soldier Boy and Juba Tunic. The rest are still flinging their arrows at Syphax. There's a bounty on him, after all."

Masinissa looked skywards, amused by the avarice of his men and the nicknames they gave each other. There were two things you could always rely on amongst soldiers: they would always sniff and chase profit, and would always look to find alternatives to real names. There was something a little childlike, if not necessarily innocent, about both. He wondered about the names his men reserved for him. He was sure a few were only whispered, but he knew he was held in high regard and so he was probably spared the more disparaging ones. He knew a common name for him was Baby Melqart or Baby Hercules, and he didn't think any comment or praise could reassure him of his standing in the army as much as that. So long as his men still made that kind of association, his reputation was intact.

He looked beyond Capuca to Soldier Boy and Juba Tunic, who had found a couple of rocks and had planted themselves against them. They each reclined, leaning slightly forwards, resting the inside of their elbows on their raised knees, and sagging a little but poised to jump at any moment. They were reliable men, who had been part of his entourage and bodyguard as he criss-crossed between Numidia and Carthage, and who had found their ways out of adolescence with him. They were bound together in ways that only really young men who had laughed together, learnt to trust each other, and confided their worries and desires over cups of wine could be. The ties of fresh adulthood bound one tighter than those strung in later, wearier years. Perhaps it was their exposure to one another at a formative age, that lack of guard, their understanding of each other's similarity and the forging of bonds when the fires of kinship burns fiercest that had meant that their fellowship was unbreakable. Many hours joking on their ponies helped a little too.

Some of the fondness related to the men – or boys, in truth – that they used to be, and a sadness that those people were disappearing slowly or retreating. Wisdom and experience were giving all of them plenty, but they took away plenty too. Looking at Soldier Boy, Masinissa remembered the keen young man who had always done exactly what he was told, and acted in ways that he perceived would be correct and exemplary for a soldier. He would always run, ride and train the hardest, and always listened attentively and responded promptly. He wanted to be part of Masinissa's brigade, and everyone could see it. Naturally, he was teased relentlessly for it, but in ways that could be taken as compliments and that, inevitably, led to even greater enthusiasm from the young man. It confirmed his identity to himself, and he readily took to the nickname they gave him. As soon as that happened, his given name was jettisoned completely, and probably no one other than his mother or whichever women he took along with him on the campaigns would call him by his true name. He was remade and his name forgotten, even by his friends.

The two men looked up at Masinissa almost simultaneously. Their exhaustion was plain to see, but so was their affection and triumph. They were not far enough away that their expressions could not be detected either. Juba Tunic sent him a soft smile and a short clenched punch, a bit like a "we did it" gesture for someone who didn't have the energy to exclaim it.

Soldier Boy did something similar. It was always his way to stay in step, and he did so automatically. He scratched through his hair and gave Masinissa a little thumbs up. It was clearly more forced than usual, however, although Masinissa couldn't quite see the cause. There was a coldness and a lack of expression in Soldier Boy's eyes, and he couldn't quite figure out whether that was the result of fatigue, trauma or something breaking at Soldier Boy's core. In any case, the spark had left his eyes, at least for the moment. Juba Tunic was a little older than Soldier Boy, and, as much as Soldier Boy revered Masinissa, he idolised Juba Tunic and took his cues – often almost telepathically – from his senior. This time, it took a little more to muster a reaction from him. Juba Tunic nudged Soldier Boy lightly in the ribs, and the two men rose, although without any eagerness or energy. They both knew they needed to escort their leader off the battlefield and towards the Carthaginian encampment, where the reviews – and, hopefully, the celebrations – would begin. They had just defeated the largest opposing army in Africa, after all. The Roman foothold in the southern Mediterranean coast had been obliterated, and it would take Syphax time to recover, even if he could rally an army of sorts in the west.

The two men separated slightly, nodding at Masinissa and giving him the opportunity to start a conversation if he wanted to. They realised intuitively that it might not be a moment for pleasantries. Words, after what they'd been through, may turn out hollow, pathetic or contrived. It was too much to explain and too hard to express. They were not orators, philosophers or generals, and words often just did not convey thoughts very well at times like this. Fear, relief, exhaustion, satisfying themselves with emotions and conditions, and letting their bodies do the rest was where they were at that moment.

Masinissa caught their mood and responded to the surge in his own being towards his confederates. In battle, your lieutenants are extensions of yourself, and he treated them as such, emotionally and intellectually. He opened his arms, and, in turn, wrapped each of the men in his arms, kissed both and thumped them in the back hard as he let them go. Neither were surprised and each responded in the same way to him. Rank was a category best suited to banquets and ceremonies in Masinissa's view. They had just ridden, wrestled and killed in the same dirt, which were actions that consolidated the egalitarian instincts in all of them.

He had always been impressed with Juba Tunic. Some men lead by their example rather than words or authority, and Juba Tunic exemplified that type of man. His men did not need to rally to the standards like the Romans did. All they needed to do was look for Juba Tunic and be buoyed that the fight was still being carried. Juba Tunic had dignity, kindness and wisdom too, all of which were qualities he had retained even after years of campaigning. He had his stories, and they were better than most, but it was his advice and example that the men played closest attention to. He had become a role model and a leader, and those were qualities that Masinissa attached the highest premium to. Juba Tunic had told everyone of the nickname the Gauls had given him, which he had become fond of. They had called him the Vitesse Africain and it was a pretty fair description. Anyone who observed Juba Tunic on horseback or on foot realised that he was fast. He drove himself and his horses at top speed, and even the Numidians, who were faster than riders from other lands, conceded his superiority.

Even his nickname had a little tradition and solidity about it. Juba was about the most common name for Numidians, and saying "Juba" rarely identified the person you were looking for. "Juba who?" was the most common response to anyone looking for a Juba amongst the Numidian forces. Any Juba who had a distinguishing characteristic invariably had that attached to their names. Of those most familiar to Masinissa there were three. The eldest and the one with the most comical, and perhaps cruel, suffix was Juba Bump. He had served with Hannibal in Italy at the battles of Trebia, Lake Trasimene and Cannae. With that kind of record, he certainly could be regarded as a lucky charm, and most of the men did so. He had taken a few blows for the cause, and his biggest scar had split his skull pretty well. How he had survived was a miracle, but the blow had made him pretty forgetful and unpredictable. He retained his skills in the field, though, and he provided plenty of good morale around the campfires. Originally, the soldiers had started to call him Juba Bump on the Head, and a few still did, but most had settled for the far simpler Juba Bump, and some of his closest friends had even dispensed with the "Juba" part completely and settled for Bump, which somehow seemed oddly affectionate.

The other Juba had also served in the north and east, and had a legacy from it in his name. However, for him, it was a sartorial association rather than a physical scar. This Juba had gone quite native, and cold, in Gaul, and had adopted the local dress a little, especially below the waist. The Gauls were notorious for their trousers or *braccae* as the Romans called them, a little dismissively. He'd brought examples of them back south with him and kept wearing them, even when they were crossing desert areas, or wading through rivers or the ocean. Some of his company wondered whether it was an affectation, but most realised it was a genuine preference. Nevertheless, they began to call him Juba Pants whenever a specific Juba was requested. By default, and simply by way of contrast, Juba Tunic became Juba Tunic because he was the one in the more orthodox form of clothing.

As he returned to walking up the hill towards the main Carthaginian position, Masinissa felt a further surge in his soul. They'd all survived. A battlefield that had swallowed, by the looks of it, 30,000 that day had left them unscathed. "Thank you, Melqart," he murmured to himself. Halfway up the hill, he looked back. The men had not quite become dots, but their identities as dead and dying men had become a little blurred. In the same way that you don't really notice the insects you step on beneath your feet, the distant carnage detached itself a little from his senses. That much was a relief to Masinissa. The worst was over. Soon the dead would be picked clean, and then buried or burnt, and the traces of them would only be left in his soul and memory, and then only sketchily.

Juba Tunic had noticed the movement and the pause it had given in Masinissa's expression if not exactly his stride and offered him a consolatory pat. He said quietly, "You know, Mas, the world I know has taught me that holding on – whether it be to a horse's mane, to a cause, to an angry woman or to whatever it might be – has made me stronger. The act of resilience itself has forged something stronger in me. Sometimes, though, it takes a stronger will just to let go. Looking down there now, the stronger ones are letting go, offering their necks. Let it go. The friends we lost, no one can harm them anymore, and as for the enemies… well, it looks like there will always be more of those, so turn to the new ones and leave the vanquished to the judgement of their gods."

Masinissa nodded and pursed his lips. His friend had found the words he needed but had struggled for and was afraid to experiment with aloud. He had received them purely, and without distortion or any hint of foolishness. "OK," he replied just as softly, "Just be there to counsel me when I'm not sure, all right? My grip can be tight sometimes."

"I will," Juba Tunic assented, thinking it enough to seal the commitment.

The four men walked on, glancing at the Carthaginian sentries, whose dress clearly indicated that their role in the battle had been towards the rear. Their inability to fully meet the eyes of the cavalrymen as they passed confirmed the fact amply.

OPERATION IBERIA FREEDOM

As a counterpoint to the acuity of battle, the senses can dull in its aftermath. Whilst often self-induced and transient, it is also a necessary means of self-preservation of the soul and the mind, as well as the body. Every mournful and healing part of one's being is helped by a little numbness. In dealing with pain and loss, and a reassertion of drudgery, soldiers often embrace more of it.

The next weeks for Masinissa, after the hiatus of a feast day to the warrior aspect of Tanit – she was also a goddess of war, after all – was spent traipsing along the coastal routes heading west, and then crossing the sea at its narrowest, if not calmest point, close to Tingi and the pillars of Melqart. The next phase of the war was about to begin, for him at least, in a new, somewhat alien land, if not a completely alien landscape. It was marginally colder and marginally more verdant, at least close to the rivers, but the people were certainly different. There seemed more diversity in their physical characteristics, and their tribal affiliations seemed looser. The people seemed happier and freer too, if such advantages can be deduced from fleeting impressions and presumptions. The torpidness of long hours on horseback, and days of transit with the senses trying to devour what they could as a distraction were now over.

The cavalry of Masinissa – which numbered over 3,000 at that time, having gathered recruits and a not inconsiderable number of deserters from Syphax's ranks – had camped with the infantry forces of Hasdrubal Gisco, and awaited the arrival of Mago and the other senior figures, including apparently a few of the more notorious local chieftains. However, the prospect of a conference with allies didn't hold a great deal of interest for Masinissa. Quite the contrary, he reserved his keenest antipathy for the usually lengthy dissection of battle plans and strategies. He had a much more intuitive approach to warfare: assess what opposes you, and either retreat or devise a counter to the threat in that moment.

He had grizzled a little with Ari and Capuca about the onerous duty, but there was nothing to be done. There was no way you could elude such things and venture out as a renegade division, however much such a notion might hold quite an appeal. Unfortunately, he was obliged to attend the conference and receive his orders for the coming campaign with as much enthusiasm as he could muster. The fact that most of the major Carthaginian commanders in Iberia were likely to be present would inevitably make the charade more difficult.

The scouts and spies had indicated that the Roman armies were looking to move and intercept one or more of the Carthaginian armies that were then present on the Iberian mainland, and strategies were to be devised and plans drawn up to meet this challenge. In outline, there appeared to be a rough draft of a response whereby the three armies of Hasdrubal Barca, Mago Barca and Hasdrubal Gisco would drift apart from one another and invite an attack by one of the opposing armies. Masinissa and other-local tribal brigades would act as mobile units that could muster quickly and attack the rear of the threatening enemy force.

There were many tiers and layers to his revulsion for this type of congregation, but the most overt was his distaste for the strategising patricians, who blithely moved their little wooden facsimiles of brigades and legions on the tactics table, with not a care that the reality of those movements would be a catastrophic loss of life. The ordinary soldier was held in scant regard and was no better than a numerical unit. They could have been money or coins for all the attention that was paid to their status as living beings. All that mattered was that more of the enemies little pieces were destroyed than your own, and that, preferably, you were left with your army perched on a higher piece of land once the bloodbath had abated.

The most saurian of these – the most cold-blooded, reptilian bastard of the lot – was Mago. All he cared about was conquest, wealth and domination. He had seen plenty of it too, and his marches with Hannibal into Italy had only fed his conceit and sense of invincibility. Masinissa quickly got the impression that Mago viewed his destiny and his campaigns as being divinely sanctioned and protected. If he had wanted to boast of his achievements, he had a long list of successful campaigns and engagements, despite his youth: the crossing of the Arno Marshes, the Battle of Lake Trasimene, and the devastating Battle of Cannae. He had been conspicuous and spectacularly successful at them all.

Amongst the troopers, the most frequent anecdote that referred to him, and one that was usually recited resentfully rather than admiringly, related to his return to the senate in Carthage after the devastating victory at Cannae. Wishing to convince a wavering legislature of Hannibal's military efficacy, he brought with him a large basket, which he threw onto the assembly floor. In the basket were hundreds of gold rings, all of which had been cut from the fingers of dead Roman nobles. It made the dramatic impact it had intended. For the troops, however, it garnered him a reputation for meanness. Under other commanders, a lot of those fingers would have been fair game. It was a campfire lesson that Masinissa swore he would never lose sight of. If someone risked their lives for you and came through the other side, compensation was due.

Since that time, Mago had relocated to the Iberian front, and he had continued his good fortune in the peninsula. He had scored many successes against the twin Roman armies of Gnaeus Cornelius Scipio Calvus and Publius Cornelius Scipio. Why did the Roman praetors insist on such pompous names? Fortunately, the Carthaginians, Iberians and Numidians had no reason to address them so grandly, and abbreviated their titles tersely at all times. Gnaeus and Publius or often just G and P were much simpler and more succinct descriptions. A recent victory against Publius's legions had reaffirmed to others the qualities of Mago's command, and had buffed his swagger and haughtiness. At Akra Leuke, his forces had ambushed and killed nearly 2,000 Roman troops. Mago spared no one and crucified many, including all the commanding officers. His savagery, as much as his victories, convinced many of the wavering local tribes to stay true to the Carthaginian cause. Of course, it wasn't the first time he had demonstrated his facility for ambushes. His flawless attack of the rear of the Roman forces at the Battle of the Trebbia River was an early sign of his prowess in that type of warfare.

He had been given a substantial army to campaign with as well; many of whom were very capable veterans. He had crossed from Tingi with nearly 12,000 infantry; 1,500 cavalry, many of whom were Numidians; and twenty elephants. These numbers had taken barely a dent, even during the period when Hasdrubal had returned to North Africa to help crush Syphax's insurrection. That operation had left him at a significant numerical disadvantage to his Roman enemies in the field, but he had preserved the status quo, the key lines of engagement and territorial possessions.

From a purely martial perspective, there was a lot to gain from Mago's acquaintance. He knew Hannibal's tactics intimately and had learnt a great deal about campaigning during his time with him. Masinissa had paid attention to much of this and much that had come from third parties, notably Gisco, but he struggled to force himself to seek out his company when the chance arose. It was a visceral disdain, and he went with it. Still, he couldn't argue that the youngest son of the mighty Hamilcar, the most junior of the Lion's brood, had more than proven himself. The fact that he had gone about it with excessively bloodthirsty zeal and contempt was the part that Masinissa couldn't quite reconcile himself to. Gala had always told him that you have to have honour to be a hero; it wasn't just victories and conquest. By that measure, Mago would never be a hero, at least not in Masinissa's eyes.

Whilst it was clear that Masinissa and Mago were never going to share a brew or confide in one another anything other than manly resolve to do one's duty, there were some signs of esprit elsewhere in the war room when Masinissa had a moment to turn away from the arid ruthlessness of the Barcid brothers. As much as he loathed much of Hasdrubal Gisco's behaviour, he was much preferable to his namesake Hasdrubal Barca and said namesake's younger brother, the aforementioned Mago. Neither appeared to brook any interference in their planning or paid any heed to suggestions that were offered. At least Gisco could raise a smile. Nevertheless, Gisco still remained in the category of people he would prefer to steer around rather than towards.

The most likely sources of relief from the blithe and hubristic Carthaginian commanders were the colourful local chieftains, whom Masinissa hoped would have an easier outlook and at least shards of a shared language. Two such were the chieftains Indibilis and Mandonius. Relatively young as they were, they could be regarded as veterans of the Iberian campaigns. Masinissa knew that the eldest of these, Indibilis, had a reputation for liveliness. Chieftains weren't always noted for their cleverness or wit, but Indibilis was, and Masinissa could see by the warm greeting Indibilis gave him as he entered the villa that they would get on fine.

Indibilis had commanded the formidable tribal forces of the Llergetes, which had been the most powerful tribe in the north of the peninsula for much of the early part of the Iberian war, and a much more effective army than anything the southern Turdetani, Bastetani or even the Celtiberi of the vast central plateau had managed to field. A lot of traffic had passed through their territories over the years since Hannibal had marched north, and an alliance was more than useful. Indibilis and his men had fought bravely and suffered terrible losses. When they were introduced, Masinissa remembered to acknowledge these sacrifices, and complimented Indibilis on his kinsman's reputation for valour, and it obviously had pleased him immensely. It was a good start!

The personal bravery of Indibilis had been demonstrated amply at the Battle of Cissa, where he had first engaged the forces of Gnaeus. He was defeated and imprisoned, but regained his liberty within the year and resumed offensive manoeuvres quickly against the Romans and the Iberian tribes that had aligned themselves with them. This impudence was met with devastating reprisals by Gnaeus, who employed a combination of slaughter and imprisonment to quell the uprising, or at least take the sting out of it. Indibilis, with Mandonius and support from Hasdrubal Barca, fought on and resisted in a series of battles against the Romans and their Celtiberian allies. The later estimates from that campaign calculated that the Roman forces, whilst suffering comparable losses, killed 15,000 of the Llergetes, and imprisoned and enslaved a further 4,000.

Despite these devastating losses and depredations, the two brothers proved redoubtable and almost preternaturally resolute. Their reputation as field commanders exceeded any aside from Hannibal himself, although they were regarded a little suspiciously by the Carthaginians, particularly by Gisco, who seemed very keen to take the wives of the chieftains to New Carthage as potential hostages to guarantee their fidelity to the alliance. Masinissa was well aware of that sort of conduct, having had the dubious honour of the gilded cage in his own youth, and he felt a certain fellowship with the Llergetes as a result. The Carthaginian vortex sucked in a lot of convenient, rather than sincere, allies, and it appeared that Indibilis and Mandonius were in the same boat as Masinissa, albeit one that had seen most of its crew slaughtered already. Their reputation, though, had clearly influenced recruitment, and at that point they boasted a freshly raised force of over 7,000, mostly from the Suessetani tribe. How these men were likely to be deployed and regarded by the Carthaginian high command was moot, but, in Masinissa's eyes, they had fodder or bait scored right through them. Nevertheless, his greeting to Indibilis was fulsome and warm, as if he were embracing a man who had already trod the path that he was on, rather than someone who may be destined to cross it.

To a bystander, the meeting couldn't have put two more impressive figures together. Indibilis, whilst not as conspicuously athletic as Masinissa, cut an imposing figure. His forearms were so powerful that the individual muscle groups were very obvious, with his brachioradialis pulsing as he gripped Masinissa's hand. Ordinarily, he was quite suspicious towards, even derisive of, people with forceful handshakes, as if they were attempting to project their authority or machismo upon him. Such attempts were rare with someone of Masinissa's size, but it invariably invited his ridicule and scorn. Indibilis's handshake was of a different order. It was simply the greeting of a strong man wishing to make a connection with another. There was no squeeze. He just put his mitt in Masinissa's, and held it like a rope. There was a ragged cicatrix biting into the gap between his forefinger and thumb, suggesting a parried assault of some kind. It was curious, as even a weak swipe into that region with any weapon ought to have sheared the thumb right off. Indibilis must have been rescued at the exact point of losing the digit or else he had managed to take out his adversary's limb only moments before he had his fingers orphaned. He also seemed to be missing a corner of his ear, but his hair was very long, perhaps as a means to conceal the deformation, and the hint of loss Masinissa was given was covered quickly by the forward-sweeping mass of Indibilis's impressive mane.

"How are you finding this?" Masinissa asked, deliberately leaving the remark vague enough for Indibilis to respond in any way he chose.

"The same as ever; nothing changes but the terrain and the numbers. Essentially, we take this many in one direction, you take that many, we meet here, hope to confuse and encircle the Romans, and we all come out of it in one piece, exultant and victorious – though, of course, most of the poor buggers probably won't, even if we're fortunate enough to prevail,"

"Ah, you cynic," Masinissa scoffed approvingly. "This is genius at work. Don't you think you ought to sit back and marvel at the invention and ingenuity of our commanders?" His words saturated with irony.

"I hope you're right, but these guys…" and he motioned mostly towards Mago. "They don't see much of the ends of these young men they've armed and fired up. They shout at them at the beginning of battle, but they don't say prayers over them at the end, and, for each, put enough of their body in one pit to make it look like there's a whole person there. They don't see what all that young pride and enthusiasm is squashed into. Glory is not what it's cracked up to be." He looked at Masinissa with a desolate expression, almost imploring him to fill him with some hope or shred of purpose.

"I guess. In their minds, it's their job merely to kill and conquer. For us too, but our part is also to stay alive and keep our troops alive. The Numidians always fight like that. We know we'll ride for each other, and we'll rescue as soon as kill."

The comment was received like a promise of redemption by the weary Indibilis and sparked in him some of the bonhomie that he was renowned for. He clapped Masinissa on his cheeks, then his shoulders and cried out, "Then you're my guy! If you're going to ride into a Roman storm just for poor old me, then you're my guy!"

Masinissa resisted a little bit, but only out of surprise rather than any objection. "You got me too then?" he replied, as if to ensure that the commitment was reciprocal.

"For sure," came the brisk response. "I'll slice up anyone who gets within a spear's length of you or your horse."

As oral contracts go, that wasn't a bad one. Indibilis was a survivor and had a peerless battlefield pedigree, so if he had one eye out for Masinissa when it mattered, that would count for a lot. At that point, Mandonius – who was just as hirsute as his kinsman in appearance, only slightly less frayed at the edges – stepped in with a few cups of wine that he was just about keeping from spilling, as they were large and full to the brim.

"OK, kids," he said puckishly, "let's get this party started. Make sure someone can tell me in the morning just what we're meant to do."

"It won't be me!" roared Indibilis.

In the background, Mago, who had been pointing at a few charts he had laid out on a table, gave him a withering look as if his deference and attention were mandatory throughout the whole gathering.

"That leaves me then!" said Masinissa with a little mock resignation. He was fortunate that Mago and Hasdrubal were becoming aware that the wilder constituents of their audience were drifting towards revelry, and responded by accelerating their briefing. The plan was relatively basic but mirrored the perceived intentions of Publius and Gnaeus. Scouts had indicated that the Scipios were fielding separate armies, and that Publius's army was the smaller of the two. The estimates were that he had a force of about 20,000, whilst Gnaeus's was considerably bigger at approximately 35,000. Mago would go west, Hasdrubal would go to the east, and the forces of Masinissa and Indibilis would disperse ostensibly, but – being more-mobile units – would be ready to aid whichever of the two armies engaged the enemy. They would go to the coast initially, make camp and appear, to all intents and purposes, to be on furlough. The tactical presumption then would be that they would be overlooked, and either of the armies encountering or skirmishing with the Roman units would look weaker, and stripped of effective cavalry and veteran forces. Of the two, it was more likely that Mago's troops would appear the easier prey, and the agreement was that his troops would agitate more and appear the more bellicose. If the Romans took the bait, they would then rush to their aid collectively, and try to encircle and annihilate them.

That sounded pretty straightforward to Masinissa, and even to Indibilis and Mandonius, who, despite the brisk pace that they were quaffing their wine, were alert enough to imbibe the tactics as well as the alcohol. As they drank, the chieftain's mood altered with their intoxication. Mandonius grew wilder and looser; he was a proper party animal out of his cage, who was clearly looking for more colourful recreation than Masinissa and Indibilis could provide: either a woman or a brawl being the most likely. By his third cup, he had fuelled himself sufficiently for an excursion into the unsuspecting night, and he was gone in a flurry of hugs and exhortations to join him. The wiser, slightly more sober heads knew he was in the mood to cut them adrift the moment he found a prospective partner for the evening, or at least at the point when he lost consciousness, and they left him to it. Indibilis, by contrast, had been slowed by the wine and had become more maudlin and affectionate. There was wisdom, regret and sorrow in the man, which was not uncommon in men renowned for their humour, and Masinissa, almost paradoxically, took some spiritual succour from him as he exhibited those more private traits. He was someone who could look back and was willing to see the trail he had left behind him: the things he had done and the things he had seen. He could dance and make peace with his own demons, and Masinissa watched him conjure them as they wandered into the night air of the gardens.

The air was cooler, and it dimmed the sobriety of both men. Even as he lost reason and function, Indibilis retained his courtesy. They sat under a tree after a while and enjoyed the scent of the orange blossoms, with Indibilis going to the extent of putting his snout right into the fragrant flowers. The trunk anchored them when they felt as if the earth became more turbulent. Masinissa even acknowledged his loss of equilibrium in a joke about the "choppiness" of the ground, and Indibilis responded with a line about an earthy tempest, which was far less funny a comment than he must have hoped for or intended. They were getting hammered, and their wit was getting as knocked out as them. They were tiring too, and it was likely that they'd both had enough wine to ignore the nuisance of the cool evening and the minor privation of a hard ground for a bed. The pair slouched gradually, improving their view of the stars, to the point where they were almost recumbent and ready to close their eyes for a few hours.

As Masinissa's last gentle nudge to rest was almost on him, Indibilis made a small-but-dramatic gesture. He patted the ground between the two men's heads and rubbed the tufty grass between his fingers. "These gardens are lush. This whole region is almost as verdant as the lands of the Astures and Cantabri." He was right, but the comment was unsettling, as it clearly framed a more doleful thought. Maybe he should have left it there, so both men could switch off their worries and cares, but it was only a precursor – as Masinissa suspected – for a brooding remark. "It's fertile ground," Indibilis added cryptically. He made a few more pats and ran his flat palm across the grass. "The soils of Syracuse have the fertility of the volcano to nourish them, but we have to rely on other mulches to enrich our lands. How many proud young men do we have spread over and under our lands, Mas? What will we harvest from all this blood and bone?"

Masinissa looked at his collapsed new acquaintance and presumptive brother-in-arms, and was lost for words. He struggled for a kind of neutral agricultural analogy to take the sting out of Indibilis's smashed nihilism. "One day, we'll bend these swords of ours into ploughs, my friend and what has rotted beneath will nurture us. We'll see the flowers grow and the fruits ripen, and enjoy them as the birth of a new day and a new time." As the words tumbled forth he almost believed them himself, and, as an emotional salve, it did the trick.

Indibilis gave him a gentle nod as if he had mastered his trial and his pains were subsiding. Masinissa had expended his reserves of reason and thought in the comforting words he had managed to offer at the edge of his lucidity. He had scaled the mountain of clarity that wine can often allow you to climb, and by then he was tumbling down the other side of the slope into dreams and insensibility.

Indibilis rolled away, and Masinissa just caught his final words, which retained much of his yearning melancholy. "Oh earth, if I could sleep in your moistness for all eternity like my brothers, I would be at peace. When I am exhausted and defeated, and I trade the elements I inhabit, and give up air for earth for good, roll over me and cherish me. Even as you consume my flesh, liberate my soul."

A portion of Masinissa's mind, which was still attentive enough to approve, hoped to remember the line in the morning. Alas, his thumping, hungover morning brain would have more prosaic matters to preoccupy it, such as which tree trunk to rest his head on whilst he peed the night away.

NOSEJOB

Prior to major engagements, allied militias and stray units often coalesced with the main contingents, and the impending assault around Castulo was quite typical of those preparations and amalgamations. A vetting process was obligatory, primarily to identify any spies or hostile agents but also to make rudimentary assessments of character; the enquiries looking in particular for any taint of cowardice, mental collapse or impairment. It was almost inevitable that most of the troops were neurotic in some respects, and those foibles were largely ignored. You couldn't be in the conflict without picking up a little of that baggage, but, in terms of battlefield discipline, it was important to root out the most damaged individuals who had succumbed to a deep psychotic reality. Of course, both cowards and psychos had their uses, but they were best utilised in certain ways.

The recreants would find their places reserved in the front of the advancing columns. There would be no retreat or opportunity to take flight. There were spears in both directions, and neither ally nor enemy would demonstrate any compunction in using them.

The psychotic were an altogether different proposition. In certain cases, they were deemed as much a danger to friend as to foe, and then were cut loose or redeployed to the rear, out of harm's way. In other cases, where individuals had garnered a certain reputation, perhaps for ferocity or for being steadfast on the battlefield, then their aberrant aspects were overlooked.

One such was Nosejob, a notorious figure who had linked up with Masinissa's force from a small contingent that had fought in the north of the peninsula. A number of men, over a period of a few years, had escaped from Roman enslavement and bonded together into a vengeful fighting unit, and Nosejob was perhaps the most vicious amongst them, which was quite an accolade given the company. As his sobriquet suggested and his appearance manifested, he had suffered more than most. His Roman captors had cut the lower part of his nose off. They had a habit of mutilation, particularly for those who had a haughty or defiant streak. In Nosejob's case, the remedy had proved ineffective. His vanity was cut from him, but he retained an arrogance and a defiant streak. He was pretty much out of control, but retained a usefulness as he extracted full and eager revenge for the loss of his beak.

His notoriety had even extended into the Roman ranks, as observers had seen prisoners become, by turns, hysterical, and ostentatiously craven and cowed as he passed by or showed them any attention. This was understandable. Firstly, his identity was impossible to mistake. The mutilation that had been performed on him was just the first of his idiosyncratic features. He was almost equal parts theatrical and reserved. His coyness was reserved for the big gap in the front of his face, which he concealed with a bandanna that ran to a triangular point at his throat. He would have exhibited the appearance of a bandit if the flat hollowness where the bulge of his nose should have been hadn't revealed that he was concealing deformity and not identity.

The rest of him was gaudy, to say the least. Perhaps in an attempt to restore some symmetry to his face, he had drawn a thick, black line on his forehead, running from the point of his eyebrows to the peak of his hairline. His style of hair extended this symmetry and peculiarity further. He had shaved the sides of his head down to the skull, but left a line of hair at the top to grow long. Sometimes he tied it into a tail and other times, usually in combat, he greased it into spikes and made it into rooster's comb. On such occasions, he also tried to dye his hair with some Tyrian purple dye, with mixed results. It ran on his face a little but he seemed to find that appealing. It gave him another nickname for those who tired of calling him Nosejob; it was equally unflattering. They called him Blood Clot. It was almost a backhanded compliment, as this particular shade of the dye was known to be the most expensive, and piling it onto your cockerel peaks was regarded as obscenely extravagant. He might as well be putting gold in his hair, as some aristocratic Romans were known to do. Where he sourced it from was a mystery, but there were plenty of productive sites where the sea snails and their murex shells were harvested and crushed into dye. He claimed it was sourced from Meninx, but that might have just an idle boast. Meninx was renowned for the superior colour of its dye, which was of far better in quality than that produced in Kerkouane, Zouchis or even Carthage itself.

The gold he did wear, though, was in his ears. He had made holes in them and had loops adorning both lobes. It was a risky thing to do for a soldier, but his reasoning was probably that a man with no nose shouldn't worry too much about someone chopping off parts of one of his other senses. When that happened, he'd likely be a corpse anyway.

As his identity was easy to establish, the reputation associated with it was equally well known. His fondness for savagery was notorious and egregious, even for a war that was already many years old, and had seen its fair share of brutality and criminal abuses. He was brave in the heat of the battle, but sadistic after it, revelling in inflicting maximum pain and humiliation. The main Carthaginian and Numidian units had little time or stomach for him, and only in the larger battles did they consider enlisting him and calling him away from the rampages he tore into the edges of the Roman lines.

His most repugnant retribution, and one that often caused his own comrades to intervene and commit mercy killings, was his predilection to set fire to his captives, either individually or bound together in little bonfires. As others were recovering from the daze of the fighting, he was pulling out unfortunates, lashing them together and pouring oil over them. Before the others knew what he was doing, there was a pyre of dancing flesh, which the more humane would show enough compassion for to throw a few spears into. Of course, some of those who did so had no sympathy for the immolated, but merely wanted to see the appalling dance jerk a little to a different beat. Most wanted to end the cruelty, though, and it was a common practice to see strong and true arms taking men out of their agonies with a final throw. Unsupervised, Nosejob could even add another layer of savagery to his depredations. He was known to douse his own fires early, only to resume them as a means of prolonging the torments and screams of his victims.

It was, in all probability, just savagery, but a myth surrounded him that he was favoured by the gods and his evil actions were intended to gain favour with a tutelary spirit in some way. The accounts of his survival against the odds in several encounters fed that myth. There was even some speculation as to who amongst the celestial pantheon approved of him. Mention was even made of the high gods Melqart and Tanit, although not Baal Hammon himself. This revolted Masinissa and almost put a taint on the reputation of the gods, which he couldn't abide. The sullying of Melqart by association with such a degenerate was unforgivable, and he derided the spreading rumour whenever he heard it. There was also a sense amongst the ranks that he and Nosejob were antithetical figures, specifically in the ways they conducted themselves in respect of warfare. Masinissa, whilst a ferocious warrior and astute tactician, retained qualities of honour and morality, whilst Nosejob was consumed with the most putrid hatred. Naturally, most saw Masinissa as the heroic example to follow, as a true adherent of the legacy of Melqart. However, some – and it was a growing, if small, proportion – succumbed to Nosejob's viewpoint.

On the eve of battle, Nosejob's presence in the Numidian ranks, on his team or even as an auxiliary was beginning to really trouble Masinissa. He'd sought out the views of the wiser ones of his non-commissioned birds – Pun and Juba Tunic, in particular – and both winced a little at Nosejob's name.

Juba Tunic was laconic and simply dismissed him with, "He's a wrong 'un," without offering any remedy or tactic in terms of bringing some discipline – let alone morality – to Nosejob. Presumably, he felt that the odds of survival for someone with that degree of disregard for himself and with the reputation he had already garnered would lead to a reasonably swift and appropriately savage despatch.

From the Roman point of view, Nosejob must have some kind of bounty on him. Maybe if someone could chop his ears off, they could get the reward from that as well as from cashing in on the jewellery. It was surely just a matter of time.

Pun was more circumspect in his views, feeling that such a character needed a tight rein. He felt that Nosejob was an infection who had the potential to contaminate others. There were plenty of sadistic individuals around. They just needed the people with control to look the other way. In this instance, it was clear to Masinissa that he was the person with control, and it was not his intention to look the other way at all. Pun approved. He had seen Nosejob in action previously and had even done his best to end the suffering of his victims. He had considered some kind of discipline, but there were risks attached to cornering a psychotic, and he had taken the prudent action, about which it was clear he was now somewhat abashed.

Masinissa duly summoned Nosejob, and ensured that Pun, Juba Tunic and Capuca remained in his tent with him to project an additional authority, as well as to ensure they had the muscle to restrain Nosejob should the need arise. As the guardsman announced him, Pun – as the one amongst them who was most familiar with his conduct – said a few sober and damning remarks before he came within earshot. He said it in the tone of a man fatigued by violence and evil. Ordinarily, he managed to retain quite a sanguine disposition, but, clearly, the thought of Nosejob put a bleaker aspect on him.

Pun declared, "Trust me on this one; with this madman, there's no trace of decency. Nothing nourishes his soul other than hatred. There is no love, music, laughter, mercy, reflection or sorrow. You only see hatred and the tendrils of that emotion: vengeance, malice, violence.

There is no depth to him; don't even bother looking for it. You'll only find this bloody, swollen, surface rage; everything else has been excised."

"Thanks Pun, I trust your judgement, but I need to see this guy for myself, you know. To try to put some kinda cuff on him," responded Masinissa.

The flap of the tent ruffled slightly as Nosejob made his entrance. He had a certain poise and grace in his movements, which Masinissa was sure most would not have noted, as the impact of his physical appearance would no doubt obliterate any wider consideration of his bearing. The first impressions of the man lay squarely in the appraisal of his face. Curiously, though perhaps not that unexpectedly, it was the man's eyes – not the kerchief below them – that formed the basis of the verdict. His look was intent and raw; it was a gaze that betrayed him for the man his reputation had suggested, who was apparently on the brink of rage constantly. They were red rimmed and dark; crescents that were almost jet cupped them. It was clear that the man knew little rest and relief. His demons no doubt took their revenge on him when he sought any underserved peace. Maybe someone like him entered a different level of consciousness? As the fires he set consumed his victims, maybe their screams and their ghosts goaded him similarly? Some stains don't wash off, and to live with them is to be devoured by them. Masinissa, to his surprise, thought suddenly of rainbows, or, more accurately, drew a metaphor in his mind between a man's normal range of emotions and the colours of the spectrum. He knew he had retained his whole range of emotions, and all the colours he imagined fancifully that they might be represented by. In contrast, he credited Nosejob with only red at best or else completely achromatic. He was dead of light and colour, other than the sizzling anger that poured out of him.

Nosejob spoke first with a simple, "Sire," accompanied by a short bow. The tone was set, brusque and formal, even perhaps a little truculent, as an audience with his senior commander was not really something a renegade such as he had much time for, apparently.

Let's get this over with, Masinissa thought to himself. *I don't have time for vicious bushwackers like you either.* At that point in the audience, he realised a little oversight on his part: he didn't know Nosejob's real name. He was so associated with his *nom de guerre* that any other name by which he had been known had long ceased to be in use. There was nothing to it but to bluff it out. "What's your name, soldier?"

There was a pause. Nosejob tapped his fingers together in a crab like motion as if weighing up his response, which no doubt he was.

Masinissa wondered if the bluff would be called.

"I am Candamius, sire," came the reply, which took Masinissa a little bit unawares.

He had thought that perhaps Nosejob would have found the question sufficiently irritating to have stalled on the answer or otherwise given some kind of recalcitrant mutter. Moreover, the name itself was a surprise. Masinissa took a little pride in knowing the pantheons of many tribes and nations, and knew that Candamius was the name of a much revered sky god for the Iberian people, often conflated with the Roman god Jupiter. Masinissa wondered if the Roman wretches whom this man had immolated had any knowledge that they were being torched by a man equated with a son of Saturn.

Masinissa was not confounded for long. "OK, Candamius. I have only summoned you for one reason, and it's not about the deployment or equipping of forces, or anything of that kind. Your reputation precedes you, and it is one I do not intend you burnishing under my command. Clearly, you have value to this army and you have shown yourself capable. However, your conduct towards captives, and your lack of any battlefield discipline or – let's face it – any remnant of morality is unacceptable. I recognise that the boundaries of propriety are far wider and looser for a soldier than a civilian, but your actions are contemptible and will be punished should you persist in them."

Nosejob was passive throughout his castigation, in both his body and expression. He neither bridled nor protested his innocence. If anything, a trace of a smirk touched the creases of his mouth. He seemed to accept and perhaps even revel in his guilt, a perception only deepened by his response, which was framed entirely pragmatically rather than defensively. "What would be the nature of any punishment?" he asked.

Masinissa had given some consideration to how he would respond to any further violations, and he had concluded that, even given the heinous nature of his offences, he should be disciplined in exactly the same manner as his transgressions. It turned his stomach to think of it, but to deter these kind of breaches required the firmest resolution. Baal Hammon would pardon him he was sure.

He was blunt in his sentencing. "Once you have crossed the line – and, before you start, you know where it's drawn – what you do to others will be done to you. I'll do to you what you've done to them. Even in the chaos, I will have eyes on you, so don't think you can slink away and indulge your repugnant vices out of my sight."

Nosejob, Candamius, exhaled slightly; seemed to unstiffen his shoulder blades a little as if he were about to dive into the sea from some rocks; and nodded his acceptance of the terms. "I understand, sire. Will that be all?"

Masinissa, a little nonplussed by the succinctness of the interview, mirrored it with some terseness of his own. "Yes," was his final word, and he flicked the back of his hand towards the man to dismiss him, wondering to himself whether his probation or pardon might be short lived. The son of a bitch looked too much of a habitual offender. He doubted there were ladders to climb out of that type of depravity.

Nosejob left the tent.

When he was gone, Juba Tunic stepped forwards and put a hand on Masinissa's shoulder. "He may not have horns or talons, but that is a pure demon there, Mas. You may have to honour that vow some time, or I'll do it for you."

Masinissa grimaced at the prospect, but gave his friend a wan smile.

*

There was little time to dwell on the encounter as the various armies were manoeuvring and skirmishing, and the dance between them was about to get a little more intimate. Masinissa was satisfied that his horses and cavalry were rested and prepared. Their numbers were substantial, and they were combat ready enough to cause havoc for whichever flank they charged into. They had swelled to 3,000 in number, but there were few, if any, that he suspected of cowardice, or who might show signs of fear or apprehension when the critical moments came. Those had already been weeded out, in truth. They had either fallen or been dismissed. He had faith that those who remained would be steadfast, or at least be able to throw a javelin or swing a sword with some firmness and accuracy. How they coped with their wounds and the terror was their own business.

They rode out of their encampment to an area where their scouts had indicated was roughly the midpoint between the two armies of Gnaeus and Publius. There was a little pomp and ceremony to the departure. As they realised it might be their final day, many intended to leave the mortal realm in style. For many, going to war was not stripping down to your roughest garments but dressing in your finest. Under the armour that was worn were robes of the finest quality and in the most extravagant dyes. Jewellery was abundant and of all kinds, and the shimmer of gold, silver, pearl and lapis lazuli caught his eye everywhere. Many of the country boys had even tied fetish animals on themselves that had been blessed by shamans or priests. Horses were popular, of course – they were Numidians after all – but he recognised the shapes of wolves, bears and eagles as well. The more urbane or Phoenician amongst the troops preferred the symbols of Tanit, Melqart and Baal Hammon, and many hedged their bets, and turquoise bears and golden ankhs jangled around necks, or were lashed and entwined together around biceps, wrists or thighs. The Romans would have a colourful bounty to loot if it turned out it was their lucky day. There was plenty of earned luck being worn in Masinissa's ranks, so the Romans would have to have propitiated their gods lavishly to match the Numidians heavenly credit.

Their departure and much of the early ride had a tranquil feel, which Masinissa found quite incongruous given the deadly mission on which they had embarked. "*Tranquilo, tranquilo*" was a favourite expression of the Iberians, and – on looking at his troops nodding their heads like donkeys with soft, often peaceful expressions on their faces – he thought they were due a siesta rather than a Roman javelin through their eye socket.

The landscape seemed to have quite a soporific influence on the collective mood. When they rode close to the Baetis River, it showed it's gentler, more meandering aspect. It was much narrower here than in the wide channel close to the sea and a little inland at Tartessus. The land rose in gentle hills around it, and the colour of the water held a more greenish tinge. It seemed bursting with life and ripples on the surface, and the quite common sighting of strutting and satisfied herons suggested abundant fish and amphibian populations. A few ramshackle huts and moorings dotted the river, and it felt as if the war were very distant; this was an illusion that was no doubt soon to be abruptly shattered.

Masinissa envied the elderly suddenly. For them, the news of their friend's diseases and final departures would likely be more remote, and their emptier world will probably fall on them silently and even peacefully. In their own infirmity, they would hear the news, and by then may have even forgotten the bond, the admiration, the fellowship and even kinship that they had held with the newly deceased. If they remembered, they would likely be more accustomed to loss or more numbed by the incessant blows time had dealt them.

Masinissa knew his losses and his wounds would be fresher, rawer and harder to suture. How can you laugh at someone's joke one day and put bits of what remains of his flesh under a pile of earth or stones the next? You go on – he had gone on – but it was a choking grief rather than a sighing one. Maybe he was being unfair. The older you are, the more you have to remember and grieve for. Maybe it was just that the sorrows of the old were harder to spot or to credit behind a mask of forbearance. Their helplessness and their tears may be private; maybe we gather dignity into our souls as we age, and conceal our desolations for the sake of others. How little we know of someone's emotions until we share them. Our interior worlds can be so mysterious. So much goes on in our minds and hearts that leave no traces outside them.

He looked forwards and around him at his men, sure that none of them suspected that he was having a philosophical and existential moment. Big questions were – like the bands of gold, and the prayers and invocations – an intrinsic part of the eve of battle. No doubt those serene gazes were contemplating similar questions in the upper slopes of their beings. Their last fire, their last spark, their last noise before the silence could be close.

As they rode along the scrubby riverbanks and over the gentle hills that turned into almost undulating plains with very long horizons, the riders, envoys and scouts were intercepting them constantly with updates and appraisals of the enemy's strength and deployment. It was confirmed that there were a lot of mercenaries within the Scipios' armies, which was a testimony to the successes they were having in garnering local tribal alliances, as well as their prodigal spending on what it was hoped were unreliable troops. Around 20,000 Iberian mercenaries were swelling the ranks of the 30,000 Roman foot and 3,000 horse. They had split, and Publius was now the closer force, marching with a combined total of 20,000 men. It was a rough estimate, but a hundred here or there wouldn't make much of a difference, particularly if they were not on horseback. He was heading for Mago and the town of Castulo, whilst Gnaeus was heading in the opposite direction towards Hasdrubal Barca's forces, which had mustered near Amtorgis. Most of the mercenaries and one double legion of 10,000 were with Hasdrubal Barca.

Hasdrubal Barca appeared to be the first to act decisively. He, at least in Masinissa's judgement, had concluded that the impending battles were to be fought consecutively and not concurrently, and therefore had bravely despatched the armies of Indibilis and Mandonius to reinforce Mago, and perhaps allow him to encircle the army of Publius if the movement of forces could be properly coordinated. His apparent battlefield perspicacity had also extended to the provision of additional horses. Whilst Masinissa's cavalry composed of 3,000 men, there were nearer 5,000 horses, forming an equine contingent intended to replace those destroyed or exhausted from the first battle. Hasdrubal's tactics also were extending to fortifications, and his sappers and slaves were creating defensive works with the intention of holding his ground whilst the first act was played out. The news cheered Masinissa. They had a plan. No doubt the Scipios had one too, but – assuming the battlefield situation was not too greatly altered (that is, *ceteris paribus*, to borrow a Roman phrase) – the Punic forces seemed to have an edge. To a great extent, he recognised that his forces ability and mobility was that edge.

The harassment of Publius's forces began close to dusk. It was a fortuitous moment. The Roman legionnaires must have been badly fatigued by that point in the evening, and, instead of being able to find some measure of comfort in the damp earth and warm embers of their camp fires, they were fending off javelins hurled by a speedy enemy, who was increasingly indistinct in the gloaming. The pace of the charges and the equally hasty retreats bamboozled the Roman cavalry too. Some made haphazard counter-offences, but they were naive rushes, and those impetuous fools became isolated quickly and were cut down. The Numidians added dozens more spare ponies to their own that night. The defending cavalry mostly resorted to making circuits around their troops, trying to intercept the darting mounted hurlers and prevent them from getting too close to their vulnerable middle. As the night drew on, the moon illuminated a little of the horror, but the sky was thick with clouds and the moon made only an occasional peek from behind them, with its occasional silver glow doing little to brighten the gory scene.

Despite the attrition in the ranks, the Roman forces were considerable, and, come morning, would mount a sterner resistance and press a counterattack with the full weight of their forces on a more visible and, by then, in their turn, exhausted enemy.

When it came, the dawn did appear to vivify the Roman effort. They were no longer chasing phantoms. The Numidians, wisely, saw no gain or honour in being slaughtered by the superior numbers that were far more able to flank them, and beat a temporary retreat.

Masinissa – who had sat out most of the later surges of the harassment, choosing to direct the probes, with his riders making returning loops to his station for their next instructions – was less exhausted than most of his men. A fact he was conscious of when he ordered the dismount beyond the reach of any possible Roman pursuit, if not their reconnaissance.

He convened his closest retinue to a late breakfast in the lee of a hill that they felt comfortable enough to rest in, beyond the site of the Romans, who were no doubt occupied with tallying the extent of their losses and burying them in whatever pathetic form they could manage quickly. Pun, Tigerman, Capuca, Juba Tunic, Massiva and Ari – Masinissa's favourite sextet –had all survived the night with barely a graze between them and sat with him under the shade of a small grove. They all demurred on the wine that was offered, but tucked into the cheese, bread, eggs, meat and olives that were brought by retainers. As they lolled, the tension in their bodies and minds untangled a little with their nourishment and deliverance. Their relief and friendships showed through in the smiles and taps they gave one another. Masinissa sensed that another night of tenebrous warfare lay ahead, which would be inevitably bloodier, more chaotic and certainly liable to have a more definitive outcome. The company, and the opportunity to close his eyes and pause his movements and instincts helped him and the collective daze hung smokily over all of them. One of the thoughts they were probably casting off was the recognition that it was easier to kill or maim a man you weren't able to see properly.

*

A few hours passed, with all of them realising that they should resist any of their usual instincts and conserve their vigour for the next round of darkness. As the sun moved lower, messengers from Mago confirmed that the movements of some of the other rival troop formations were facilitating the prospect of another night attack and another foray into the Roman flank, but this time the bite would have the jaws of the other Punic forces to drive the teeth in deeper and take off a bigger chunk. It appeared that the absence of obvious enemy silhouettes on the horizon reconnoitring their position may have been because Publius's scouts were casting their surveys in the other direction, and had discovered and become increasingly alarmed by the movements behind him. Indibilis's forces had been marching fast, and had reached the outskirts of Castulo. In truth, he had gone beyond the town and was prowling directly behind his line of retreat by then, a fact that was evidently known to Publius. The Roman general then had a dug-in, capable army on one side, and a very well-regarded field commander, with a substantial battalion of his own (a little under 8,000 in total), on the other. It seemed that, in having to pick a lesser foe from this particular pairing of Scylla and Charybdis, Publius had chosen Indibilis.

That is the only call, Masinissa thought.

Overwhelming Mago's position may not have been impossible, but it would certainly be time consuming, and the Carthaginian would be capable enough of resorting to dilatory tactics that were protracted enough to allow both Indibilis and Masinissa to tear into his rear and annihilate him. His choice was to turn towards the Iberian chieftain, and then break through and out. The die was cast. There was no turning back for Publius's army, and so everything else would follow according to the battlefield logic. That logic dictated more of the same for the Numidian cavalrymen.

Capuca was the first to throw off his listlessness and to realise that there was a need for a greater urgency. They had ridden away from Publius and, given the reputed movements of the bulk of the enemy's army subsequently, they had moved further from that enemy army too. They would have quite a long ride to intercept their enemy, and finding them in the remaining daylight would be a challenge. The hills were shallow and undulating, but still rose high enough to offer a little concealment, and they could steer off course and lose time, which would cost Indibilis dearly.

Looking mildly perplexed, Capuca rose and made the case for haste. "Mas, we'd better get moving, as the Iberian troops won't resist for long, and Mago must be a day's ride from where the battle will be.

He won't last without us, and then the Romans will have the claws, and we will be the one's pinched and running."

The words spurred on Masinissa immediately, as if he had been prodded by a knife. Pun had performed that literal action on him often, so he was well aware how sharply it can pull you from your reverie or daydream. He was not punctured or panicked, but he felt riven by guilt at his own complacency and lethargy. What he was thinking? It was OK to rest when danger had passed, but this was a battle that had commenced and in was progress. It may have been only a night-time skirmish up to this point, but time and distance was closing between the different factions, and his troops were a key piece on that board full of movement.

He rose, grabbed his *falcata* and scabbard, and ran towards the horses, practically vaulting onto his own mount. He would have done so if not for the loose weapon he carried. The others followed, mimicking Masinissa's swiftness as closely as they could manage. They set off and rode in a long line for a little while as the stragglers, delayed by various meals and ablutions, caught up. Masinissa scattered the fastest riders ahead to pick up trails or signs. He knew the rough whereabouts of Indibilis, but Indibilis's trail was coming from the other direction, and so he was reliant on his own hunches rather than the precision of visible signs of the recent passage of a large military contingent.

The weather conditions had altered little from the previous night, and, as dusk fell, it was heralded by the greying blur of a sunless evening. He ordered torches lit, including one in a metal frame adorned with the sign of Tanit, which he hoped would, when it was spotted, reveal him to be an ally. Were the detection made by the Romans, he would order the torches to be extinguished and the splitting of the cavalry into an encircling formation, to confuse the Romans and to allow two waves of raiders to storm across the Roman positions. He also ordered a number of the men to dip their javelins in tar, or soak tows in oil and wrap them around their weapons with the intention of lighting them when they came within range of the enemy. He ordered a few of the weaker throwers to relight their torches, and to ride in the middle of the charge when the time came and ignite the projectiles of the others, which would then be launched into the Roman ranks. The adoption of some modest thermal warfare tactics would not do measurably more damage than ordinary javelins, but tracers of incoming fire into your line against a blackened sky could only be damaging to the morale of the men facing the barrage.

The remaining hours of darkness, however, proved long and frustrating for Masinissa and his men, and the chances of heaving burning spears into Publius's army receded as a prospect, with the value of the action being lost with the arrival of the morning. Both the enemy and Indibilis were elusive, and it was only when the night started to hint at the day and to lift light from the edges of the horizon that Indibilis's forces and situation were spotted belatedly.

It would seem that, on this occasion, it was the defenders who had best reaped the benefits of the night's shroud. Publius's cavalry were well matched by Indibilis's mounted troops, and they had sheltered the infantry well from the attrition the Romans had intended for them. That is not to say that a lot of blood had not been spilt. The carcasses of horses and men formed clumps on the edges of both groups of soldiers, often on top of one another and not necessarily with the rider on top of the horse in those cases. Many had been crushed more ignobly. Most likely, being pinned by an equine had not been the end of them either. The torso and head of many of the dead protruded outside of the flank of their dead beast. In many cases, however, with what those parts of the body resembled by then, they might as well have been stampeded by elephants.

The beleaguered Iberians gave out a resounding collective cheer when they saw their allies approach. To be heard at all above the cacophony of the battle – with its screams, charges, incessant screeches of metal on metal, and duller thuds of metal on flesh – was impressive in itself. The morale of the tribal militia was clearly revived by the arrival of the Numidian forces, and they began to hold their ground, aided immeasurably by Masinissa's cavalry launching into and along the Roman flank. The deteriorating prospects for Publius only worsened with the arrival of Mago and Hasdrubal Gisco's fresh and fully intact armies.

Their appearance was pivotal to the outcome of the battle and the momentum of the slaughter. Hemmed in front and back, with a marauding cavalry on their flanks, Publius was doomed. The whoops of the Numidian riders were juxtaposed by the slump in the Roman ranks. Many tried suddenly to break ranks and escape, but the runners only became easy targets for the Numidians, who tore behind the runners, and used their spears and swords to swipe deep into the runners' necks. As their fate became more and more apparent, the Roman horse, almost in unison, ceased their resistance. They broke, often with a fortunate infantryman clambering onto the haunches of a fleeing horse, hanging on to the rider like a drowning man clings to driftwood. It was the last chance any of them had of survival, and many turned on each other in an ignominious scramble for survival. The rump of a horse was the only ticket out just then, and they fought for the berth as ferociously as they had fought the enemy.

Stripped of their mobility and considerably outnumbered at that point, the remaining Romans were fed into the grinder. Having been depleted of men, weaponry, hope and vigour, they were picked off. Firstly, at a greater distance, as the Carthaginians, Numidians and Iberians started to be more mindful of their own survival, and threw their javelins into them. And, secondly, from a closer range, they were like packs of wolves on wounded beasts, as the incentive of loot became more of a spur to fight at closer range. As the last of them were put to their end, the mood changed in two distinctive ways.

For Masinissa, his usual more elegiac mood at the end of combat returned as he surveyed the losses on both sides. His enemies were dead by then and unthreatening, and were restored in his pity. The flurry of battle was over, and he started to feel a more tender sorrow as the adrenaline and instincts of the fight ebbed to nothing. *The glory of victory is a very specious concept*, he thought. Victory only really meant survival, loot and another cohort of demons to contend with.

He cast his eyes around the battlefield for sight of Nosejob, and his distinctive appearance was not hard to spot. He had, as expected, his hands deep in the gruesome epilogue of the battle, but his retributions appeared swift and no more deplorable than those of the others, who were picking pockets and cutting throats. Maybe Masinissa's rebuke had mollified the thug's viciousness. He almost felt a little resentment towards the man for making him monitor his behaviour. He wasn't a school teacher or drill sergeant who had to pay attention to errant boys.

His attention didn't linger long on his most savage soldier, as he was quickly summoned by riders from Mago's army. The attitude of the leading figure was unexpectedly officious, which Masinissa took instant umbrage to. Some jumped-up Carthaginian *tesserarius* wasn't going to patronise him, and, as he rode past the man in the direction of Mago, Masinissa gave him a palm punch straight into middle of his face, which toppled him ignominiously from his horse. His own men, who had rallied close to him by then, in particular Ari and Capuca, found their commander's pique and subsequent jab highly amusing. Naturally, the Carthaginian dragging himself up from the dirt did not, and he just glowered, but at least thought better than to throw any curses or challenges towards the back of the Numidian prince.

As the regular troopers performed their part on the remains of the enemy, so the generals and officers knew their role, and the leading commanders of the three armies found one another quickly. It was quite easy to navigate. Mago had an ostentatious streak, and his banners – depicting the usual Carthaginian menagerie of symbols, most conspicuously depictions of palm trees, stallions, dolphins, and the more orthodox and sacred symbols of Baal Hammon and Tanit – were easy to pick out.

What had possessed the Carthaginians to incorporate dolphins into their battle standards? They are hardly going to strike terror into the enemy. It is better than palm trees as a means of intimidation, though, Masinissa thought to himself a little wryly.

As he rode into the makeshift symposium, Masinissa took a lighter view of the gathering, as Indibilis was there, waving at him enthusiastically and gesturing to the amphora beside him with equal relish. Masinissa could see the stark differences in the senior figures represented. Both Indibilis and Mandonius were splattered with the stains of earth and men, weary but triumphant, with hair streaking wildly across their faces and necks, and their shoulders still pulsing with the efforts of driving other men back, down and under them. Mago, in stark contrast, had clipped hair like a Roman, coiffed to the point where a golden laurel or crown would not have been out of a place. He was also quite pristine in appearance. He had certainly not risked any of his own blood in the recent encounter. His callousness, though, radiated out of him like the sins of the wicked. The impression was only exacerbated by the dripping head of a middle-aged man that he'd lodged next to his camp stool, which he was fiddling with idly with his toes. The sight was repugnant. Masinissa felt a tug of pity for the recently decapitated man, who was presumably the erstwhile Publius Cornelius Scipio.

When Masinissa dismounted, Indibilis embraced him like a pining lover. Masinissa had probably arrived on the scene just quickly enough to spare his life, so the ardour was quite warranted under the circumstances. At that moment, between them, there was no need for communications, except what could be read in the eyes and felt in the body. They were fellow soldiers, but, on the edges of death, their instincts were those of inamoratos.

The little bliss of survival and fellowship was interrupted by an impatient Mago. His tone was as abrupt as ever. "Save your relief and affections for your banquets and your women. We need to chase the other dog now. This one needs its partner." He gave the head of Publius a little jiggle.

The Carthaginian general's curtness brought the Iberian and the Numidian back to their harsher reality. Each gave a sober bow.

"You're right, sire. What is the position now? Do you know the whereabouts of Gnaeus?" Masinissa asked.

"You're to the point, Masinissa; back in the room now, huh? We do… or we think we do. I don't think Gnaeus was waiting for an outcome on this battlefield. He must feel more secure in the north, as he's been spotted scurrying in that direction. He's left the fires in his southernmost camp burning, and seems to be retreating towards the Ebro. If that was meant as a feint to wheel around on us, it will soon become the truth. He will learn soon that he has no axis on which to pivot. We should not wait too long to follow him. I want his head before his brother's starts to rot. So…" He pointed behind them to the battlefield, which was then full of looters scything up their bloody harvest. "They have an hour, that's all, then we march again. I will join my brother's army, and you and Indibilis – well, the mounted part of his group, at least – will find and tie down Gnaeus till we can catch up with you. We won't be long, I promise," he added a little sarcastically.

Hasdrubal Gisco, who was standing to the side of Mago, grinned at this minor condescension.

Typical, thought Masinissa.

"Haughty bastard," muttered Indibilis when they had turned and were out of earshot of the imperious pair. "We're going to have to patch ourselves up on horseback by the looks of it!" Indibilis offered, showing off a gash that he had taken in his shoulder and into which he'd plugged what was by then a very sodden rag.

"That's not too bad, Indy," Masinissa consoled. "It won't tear any worse, and I'll clean it and sew it for you once I put the order in."

Indibilis scoffed, "OK, you're on; do some of your best African tailoring, OK? I want a neat seal on this cut."

"You got it," Masinissa replied, and he rode up to Juba Tunic and Pun to give them their instructions.

Neither grumbled, but both were clearly weary and in need of a spell off horseback. As veteran campaigners, they understood the exigency of the pursuit. A well-matched adversary had turned into prey, and there is no dawdling when the horn blows on a hunt. The rabbit wasn't going to take a rest.

"The only friend the Romans have now is the hills," Pun said grimly, and he was right. The Romans either had to get beyond them and across the Ebro to safer ground, or find an elevation sufficiently high to hold off the enemy. That would probably just prolong their deaths, though, as the Carthaginian forces would starve them out. There would be no relief coming from the north for a while, and not much of a viable force remained from Publius's division to mount a counterattack.

Without any further comment, Pun and Juba Tunic rode into the charnel slime to convey the news of their quick departure, and Masinissa, in the meantime, got to grips with stitching up the chieftain's seeping wound. Indibilis had quite a lot of slices on him, and this battlefield patch appeared quite routine for him. He didn't squeal and barely flinched as Masinissa's needle laced him up. In fact, he was almost a little peaceful and reflective.

Mid-stitch, he looked over towards Masinissa thoughtfully. "Do you think what has just happened will be remembered for long, or what might happen later or even the war itself? Will we be the heroes or villains? Will the sacrifices that have been made be appreciated or even known about? If you never knew those dead men, those young boys and old men who were just a little bit weaker or slower than the men they fought, how much would you really care or think of them? They died for our freedom; for noble causes, didn't they? But what does that mean to the future?"

"Not too much, probably," Masinissa replied just as sceptically. "I'm sure they'll make a fittingly heroic statue of you, though. Life moves on, doesn't it? And the past is confined to smaller and smaller pockets. It's like walking. The further we move away from something, the smaller it gets till, eventually, we can't see it any more beyond the horizon. The endurance of our memories can be like these poor buggers we just killed too, in a way. They stood tall and proud and fresh, and then got reduced to nothing, both suddenly and slowly. I'm sure their mothers and wives will remember them, but their sons will know them only as causes and justifications."

"Have you ever thought about how we'll be viewed if we lose? Our reputations will be torn to shreds then, won't they? Or we'll just be the anonymous bogey men: monsters who were justly defeated and removed from the world. Our losses won't be calculated, measured, or held to be of any note or value. We'll just be anonymous, non-beings, worthy of nothing but destruction, and just accessories to our enemy's glory."

"Ah, you are such a pessimist, Indy," Masinissa chided "We're gonna win, and they'll be the vile savages then. I agree with you, though. History isn't written by the guy being flogged on the galley or the dead children massacred in the final acts of war, excising the last of your enemy's legacy. Anything can be justified. Murders, torture and Nosejob's dancing-men pyres – they never happened. They didn't happen even when they were happening. None of it matters. None of it is of any interest. There's your statue. There's your slave. This is the present, and we got here the way we tell you we got here."

Indibilis snorted, in a sort of cynical agreement. "Maybe Mago is giving us too much time to relax if we're starting to dwell on our own prestige or anonymity."

"Well, yeah, we're the grunts, after all, you know. Killing and philosophising occupy exclusive realms. Let's get back to the one we're good at."

*

The pattern of their days resumed as they got back on their horses and went in pursuit of their enemy. Gnaeus had quite a start, and they ended up hunting in darkness again. Although Masinissa let the horses slack a little that time, they were still travelling faster than infantry, and he let the trotting beasts' rhythm lull him into something just above consciousness but low enough to allow his mind and body to restore themselves slightly. Many of his men were in the same condition as him. They were exhausted, and had bowed heads and closed eyes, albeit with upright backs and postures. Their numbers were slightly reduced, but Masinissa consoled himself with the fact that most of that loss was down to injuries rather than fatalities. The battle had been light on the cavalry so far.

He pulled up the bulk of his force just before the dawn to make the slumber official and allow the men at least an hour before the sun's rays made sleep a trickier and more guilty experience. Scouts were despatched and guards posted, and the Numidians were soon dozing in the spreading twilight, with their bodies gaining ascendancy over their cares. A snoring chorus kept some up, but not many, as most grasped the opportunity to rest. It was inadequately brief, but, nevertheless, Masinissa woke feeling the benefit as the flesh of his eyelids turned lighter, forcing them open, and he started to muzzily nudge the others around him back to awareness. To be fair, Juba Tunic was doing much of that task for him, and, in a brusquer manner, was kicking many slumbering forms sharply, with the deeper sleepers earning a few extra revivers.

As Masinissa drank some water, news came of the location and distribution of Gnaeus's army. They had not got far, and they could be caught and harassed within a few hours. He estimated Mago and the Hasdrubals were half a day further away, and he sent word to them of the coordinates where they hoped to intercept Gnaeus's army. He instructed them to rendezvous at Ilorca.

*

His rough calculations proved precise, as the moderately rested Numidians found them just outside the aforementioned town a few hours later. The numbers of Gnaeus's army had plummeted precipitously. The mercenary army, so lavishly recruited, had abandoned Gnaeus and melted away into the hills, there to wait out this phase of the war. These mercenaries would possibly later be cajoled by the Carthaginians into an equivalent contract with them, with probably just as irresolute a commitment.

The cavalry was by now exceptionally well drilled in their harassing manoeuvres, and deployed without much prompting. The fact that the mobility of Gnaeus's forces was pretty limited, as he had few horses and no elephants, meant that his infantry could do little other than parry the projectile assaults with their shields, and look for higher ground where the physics of gravity imposed a restriction on the Carthaginian range and an extension on their own.

Gnaeus may have thought the move a sage one. The Numidian horse stumbled on the steep slopes that the Romans retreated to, and their javelins made looping arcs that reduced their velocity and made them much more avoidable, if they even managed to get near their intended targets. They were also repurposed avidly by the Romans, who, heedless of the imperative to ration their arms in a position of encirclement, threw them back at the Numidians with relish. The error of their retreat, and their prodigal and wasteful use of their scavenged javelins only dawned on them slowly. Masinissa ordered his men to perform circuits of the hill on the fringes of their projectile range to entice them to throw, but also to pin them down. Gnaeus made no further move, and a stalemate of sorts ensued. Foolishly, Gnaeus had overlooked the fact that the strategic balance would be tipped imminently and in the favour of his enemies.

*

The armies of Hasdrubal Barca, Hasdrubal Gisco and Mago Barca reached the carousel as night fell. Few on either side had been killed by that point. It was almost as if the protagonists were waiting for the other to become exhausted and then settle on a dignified truce. Nothing so noble or merciful was going to happen once the rest arrived. In the manner of a gluttonous child spying a full table, Mago elbowed his troops through the encirclement, and set them off up the hill. The two Hasdrubals did likewise at other points on the hill, and threw their *velite* and *hastati* lines straight at the Romans. Unlike on the previous nights, the moon rose full in the sky this time and gave the death struggles an appropriate pallor as if their blood had already been drained from them.

Masinissa turned his horse and cantered to a point where he could see all means of escape, should Gnaeus's men find a way of breaking out down the slopes. He was joined by Ari, Massiva and Capuca, who knew their role as Masinissa's effective entourage, but also had joined him opportunistically to gain a better view and spectate what promised to be an infantry bloodbath. Their spot allowed for a panoptic appreciation of the carnage, and they watched it half-grimly and half as connoisseurs. Even before the march upwards began and the improvised barricades were assembled, Masinissa had learnt at least one lesson. Higher ground was not always going to provide an advantage. Sometimes it was a trap, especially in Gnaeus's case. If Gnaeus had retained at least some mounted troops, he could have organised some kind of charge or some kind of vanguard. Instead, the few horses he had at his disposal were being slaughtered and used as improvised barricades. It was as good a sign as any that their Roman equerries would be meeting a similar fate in the not too distant future.

The heat was off Masinissa and his comrades, and their sudden detachment from the violence was apparent when Capuca broke the silence, and increasingly obvious as the heart rates of men and horses regained their normal equilibrium. His comment was at quite a tangent, but it was easy to understand the connection he was making. "Romans crucify their victims and their criminals on hills like this one. Maybe they like the silhouettes they make. I've spoken about it to some of the slaves who've seen them do it, and who may have nailed a few of those timbers and flesh together themselves when they were in possession of a more fortunate status. None of them admitted to it, but some of the descriptions were quite vivid. It's a pathetic way to die and a sadistic way to kill."

Masinissa nodded. "The Romans have a flair for the gruesome. Their hilltops are often full of crosses, I've heard. It is amongst their favourite torments. I'm sure the Carthaginians won't bother to prop up the dying and the condemned when they're through with this hill."

They were close enough to the fighting to see it clearly, and the elevation allowed them to observe the tiers of the action. The first lines of the Carthaginian armies were pouring up the slopes, attacking with their swords rather than their javelins, as they would be hurled straight back at them. The reserve line of the Romans was composed of desperate men trying to establish barricades behind their dead animals, and attempting to dig into the ground for some kind of improvised bulwark. The ground was hard and stony, however, and their efforts were fruitless. In truth, the greatest impediment to the Carthaginian assault was the mounting piles of Roman dead, and they were mounting quickly.

Masinissa could see the Roman line retreat incrementally, but, as they fell back onto the crest of the butte, the pressure upon them intensified and their retreat accelerated. It almost reminded Masinissa incongruously of an adolescent pimple about to be popped. The Romans wouldn't burst in quite the same way, but a few were gushing as the Carthaginian swords sliced through arteries with increasing frequency.

His line of sight was obscured finally as his sightlines blurred the opposing forces, and he could only see the backs of the Carthaginian attackers as they devoured the pocket like hunting dogs on a young deer. He heaved a little sigh, a half-hearted sough for the guilty being slaughtered, and turned from the scene. His ears couldn't turn off the denouement, though, and the sounds had become more discernible as the cacophony subsided. The cries became more piteous, the begging more detectable, and the agonies more ripping. It was easier as a blur of numbing sound.

Any threat to them was now past, and, in truth, the moment Mago had started his way up the hill was the end of his and the Numidian cavalry's involvement. He mused a little about how the Carthaginians might commemorate their victory or clear the scene. They may roll the dead down the hill and stick a banner of victory at the top for all to see. It beat crucifixions, at least.

Masinissa realised there were two aspects vying in him at that moment. An overwhelming stupefaction, as his mind and body could not be anything but stunned after the last days of relentless riding and killing, was commingling with an odd profundity. He was thinking about the nature of being, dwelling on his mortality and essence. His numbness and mental acuity rolled in waves into and through him. He became aware of the emptiness of his gaze and the fact that he had lost a sense of time. Around him, the men were finding shady spots and gulping wine, but not in a festive spirit, rather in an impulse to dim or obliterate the moment. He did the same and quaffed from a wineskin that Massiva, who was already a little glazed, had passed to him. He was as greedy with it as if it was his mother's milk, and his sharpness was soon vanquished by his inebriation.

*

He had no idea how long he slept, but it was deep and consoling. The fact that it was interrupted didn't stop him from feeling a little cleansed. It was Pun who woke him. He may not even have slept at all, as the circles under his eyes were dark and defined, and he held the weariness of a man who had not descended out of consciousness for a while.

Pun said solemnly as he shook Masinissa gently, "Sire, sire, I'm sorry, but there is business." And then, less formally, "He's called your bluff boss."

At first, Masinissa didn't quite catch Pun's drift as he put his senses back in order and reached out for an understanding of the oblique reference. "What? Who?" was all he could manage, as his immediate focus was still on recognising that his mouth was fuzzy and his stomach empty.

"Nosejob is the who and the what; well, you know the deal with him."

The mention of the sadistic trooper's name sharpened Masinissa up, and he emitted a long breath of air that exhaled his frustration and disappointment, as well as giving him the time to come to terms with his own promise and his resolve to keep to it. "Bastard. OK, how did it go and where is he now? You'd better have him, Pun."

"I do. I thought he might clear out once he lit his guys up, but he came willingly. Basically, he found a couple of Romans halfway up the hill. They were missing bits, but had enough to be dragged and to still feel fresh pain. So that's what he did. He lashed them, oiled them and torched them. He had some water ready to douse them and start over when we grabbed him. We took their heads straight off, man. A sharp *falcata* was their best friend in the end. Anyway, he's back a way. It's on you now."

"Yeah, I know," Masinissa replied, blowing long into his imaginary horn again. He squeezed his hands together, put his fingers onto his forehead and then ran his thumbs hard outwards from the bridge of his nose across the line of his eyebrows.

Pun read the body language easily. "You don't have to get involved, you know. I can check him out," he offered considerately.

"How would I look then, Pun? Come on. There are places you have to go and things you can't hide from. We don't write them down, and they don't make any sense, but we all know the rules. We know the code. I gotta do it."

Masinissa stood, turned and saw Candamius, Nosejob, looking impassively in his direction. His hands looked tied behind him, and, as Masinissa crossed the dozen or so strides it took to reach Nosejob, he could see that they were. He didn't want to understand him, and didn't want a trial, judgement had been passed already. It was summary justice, with no frills or explanations.

Nosejob's concealing rag had slipped a bit and was not covering his missing cartilage so artfully, so you could see more of the grotesque remains of his nasal bone. It looked like a snout, and so it made him look more like a pig, which Masinissa thought was quite apt. Masinissa sensed Candamius knew what was coming, how could he not? What was it with this man? He was as brave as a lion in battle, but too afraid to kill himself and end his agonies, yet his vile actions would guarantee him the most agonising death. Was it an addiction or thrill? Why speculate? There were no answers. You'd just find more questions.

Masinissa said, "A promise is a promise. I give you no dignity or mercy."

Candamius thrust out his chin, narrowing his jaw, in some form of natural tough-guy defiance. He inhaled and exhaled slowly and snorted softly before replying, "So be it," and looking around him as if there were more things of idle interest in his wider field of vision than the man who had promised to take his life and was about to.

Masinissa felt an odd absence of humanity; this was an automatic reaction, freed of pity or rage, incongruous to him and the nature of the moment. He took the oil, kicked Candamius to bring him to his knees, and doused him with it. Masinissa hesitated, and his humanity and mercy returned to him in that pause.

"I could kill you like a chicken. It would be less," he said in a gesture of mercy.

Candamius's eyes flashed a savage rage. "A promise is a promise."

There was no more to be said. Masinissa gestured to the men to remove themselves to a suitable distance and set him on fire. He saw a moistness at the corner of Candamius's eyes as the first lick scorched him. Masinissa had no wish to imprint the vision in his mind, so he turned, and he rationalised the writhing human torch behind him by imagining it to be simply a pyre of a dead man, which, in many ways, it already was.

WHEN THE WORST
IS YET TO COME

The victory over the Scipios had come at relatively meagre cost to the Carthaginian and Numidian forces. The remnants of the two Roman armies had fled over the Ebro and were, in Masinissa's estimation, ripe for further assault. They were ready to be driven beyond the next great river, the Rhone, and as far as Massalia and into the lands of the Ligurians. There, they would be close to the Roman fringes, and Mago would be emulating his brother in crashing another wave of Carthaginian arms into the Roman north. That shock, that degree of reinforcement and the shift in battlefield momentum may have been decisive in the war. As it was, no second surge over the Alps was forthcoming, and the Romans diversionary tactics, Hannibal's mounting frustration, and perhaps even a seeping listlessness in his campaign and soldiers, robbed him of the critical victories he needed and preserved a still very bloody status quo. The last news Masinissa had heard from the Roman front was that Hannibal had been spending his time chasing the Roman tribune Appius Claudius Pulcher, aiding the defecting and besieged Capuans, and attacking Brundisium. It suggested a campaign that was turning worryingly desultory.

The Barcid brothers in Iberia, though, appeared quite phlegmatic about their sibling chasing shadows behind enemy lines. They seemed more than happy to savour their triumph and enjoy the comfortable safety of the Celtiberian lands that they had supposedly pacified and extirpated of the Roman intruders by then. Maybe there was also an unknown element internal to the Barcids and the Carthaginian armies that Masinissa wasn't privy to. Mago, for sure, was a man susceptible to his own sense of personal grandeur, and his ego and pomposity may have convinced him that he should stay where he was and let Hannibal struggle, then maybe to ride in triumph to Hannibal's rescue at a point of his choosing. Maybe he was just apprehensive of campaigning deeper into the Roman territories without considerable reinforcements. The Romans were still a formidable adversary, and he certainly didn't want to share the fate of the Scipios. They would surely take gleeful vengeance on his body if the fortunes of war turned on him. In any case, he lingered and occupied himself with his own aggrandisement, often at the expense of the local tribes that had fought for him, or at least not fought against him.

Masinissa considered these actions foolish and a betrayal of the indigenous people. How do you win the hearts of minds of the people if you turn on them so quickly? It was a mighty victory, and they had vanquished the Romans from large swathes of the peninsula. Surely the time was right to press their advantage and continue an advance as fast as possible, before the enemy had time to reorganise or reinforce itself. Whilst not as costly in terms of men and beasts, the victory that had been secured in the twin battles of the Upper Baetis reminded him of the hollow victories decades earlier of the king of the Molossians, Pyrrhus of Epirus. This second cousin of Alexander the Great had won only in a certain sense. In the wider context, he had lost. At least he had the grim humour to realise it. Masinissa remembered well the comment he made after the Battle of Asculum: "If we are victorious in one more battle with the Romans, we shall be utterly ruined," he was famously quoted as saying.

Mago's decision to sit on his hands and milk the Iberians struck Masinissa as a similar inversion and one that, unlike Pyrrhus, he was failing to recognise. Masinissa, despite his conviction, knew that making any comment would be pointless, as neither he nor any of the senior Numidian commanders had much influence in the war, which was a source of frustration for many. There was only equality in their sacrifices.

As it was, at least by then he was temporarily idle and largely unemployed. He rode in the mountains with Massiva, Ari and Capuca, and managed to obtain, at a little inconvenience, the thirty-seven volume treatise *On Nature* by Epicurus. Masinissa found his ideas novel and, for the most part, appealing. The notion of minimising harm and maximising happiness was a little pacifist for the times, but, as a credo for ordinary life, there was much to recommend it. He read avidly through his Ethic of Reciprocity, in which rights and duties to one's fellow man were described and recommended. Masinissa was sure that many people would find shocking the concept that people had individual rights to life, liberty and property. Half the world was the property of the other half, who were at liberty, so such an egalitarian view was quite utopian. *One day, maybe,* Masinissa thought.

The lack of conflict, the retreat of the Romans north of the Ebro, and the warm, easy days tricked Masinissa into a sense of tranquillity that was quite in tune with Epicurus's treatise. Of course, he pined for Sophonisba and the imagined future he envisioned with her, but, for that moment, that life was as immaterial and nebulous as the next world. At least it was fun to imagine better times. Epicurus's description of a state he called "ataraxia" – a tranquil, peaceful, fearless existence – seemed idyllic to him, being a man so used to fear that he lived with it like a constant knot of stage fright. The philosopher had described this condition as having a natural consort, which he called "aponia" or the absence of pain, which was to be found in a simple, self-sufficient lifestyle. However, as Masinissa read on, it became apparent that, for all the appeal of such an outlook and lifestyle, Epicurus had a shocking disregard for the gods, be they of the Greek, Roman or Phoenician pantheon. It was an ontological step too far for Masinissa.

His actions – and those of all soldiers, all men and all women – attracted the attention of the gods. His prayers and supplications, be they ignored or granted, were heard. He was acknowledged in some form by the residents of the Empyrean, and his deeds and conduct deemed worthy or otherwise. The idea that the gods paid no attention to mankind, offered neither rewards nor punishments, or perhaps – most outrageously and blasphemously – may not exist at all was absurd. The stories of the gods and their heroes were numerous, with the twelve labours of Melqart being the most famous and valiant, which made such a proposition quite farcical. Death could not simply be the end. He had seen too much of it to believe such a view. The light of life must be transformed, not ended. *Great thinkers are granted their depth of thought due to the narrowness of their field of vision*, Masinissa reassured himself. Epicurus had a great idea about how to live in harmony and peace, but only at the expense of misunderstanding the heavens and the gods. He was sure they would be merciful towards him, nevertheless.

Whilst Masinissa found himself, in his greater periods of inactivity, reading almost voraciously and even recording some of his own thoughts, mostly on governance and the fundamentals of morality, he spliced his contemplative moments with convivial moments with many of his closest companions, and, when their paths intermingled, with Indibilis and Mandonius. Their more intimate and trusted connections with the local communities gave Masinissa an insight into the state of play on the ground, far more so than could be learnt from his own troops, and certainly not from the Carthaginians, who evidently regarded the indigenous communities as little more than vassals, which was a perception that was clearly storing up resentments. When he met with the two veteran warlords, their warmth and affection towards him was as ebulliently expressed as ever. There was something to be said for bear hugs from men in bear skins, as both men favoured soft, warming layers even in the milder days.

They had congregated, as many others had, in the pleasant coastal town of Malaka in the lands of the Bastetani. It was a relaxing region, with good fishing and cooling seas, albeit ones whose shorelines often shelved precipitously. After taking two or three steps into the ocean, you were out of your depth suddenly. Masinissa had made the lazy presumption that all the beaches in the areas were of the same steeply shelving sand, and had dived into the bay at Silniana the previous week, when the water was barely covering his knees. He smashed his face straight into a rocky outcrop, cutting his forehead, chin and nose, causing grazes he was parading for his Llergete friends.

At first, he thought he would try to conceal the truth with a little deception. He was a little embarrassed by the self-inflicted scratches and, taking inspiration from his friends' warm layers, tried to convince them that he had taken a dare to wrestle a small bear and the nicks were from the animal. Though this seemed plausible at first, he was caught out in his lie as he began to stumble in his description of the contest. Indibilis was also of the view that small bears either ran away, or caused much deeper and more parallel scratches in a man's flesh, a point he brought up as Masinissa started to falter. His cause was not helped by the presence of Pun and Tigerman, whose theatrical expressions of mock surprise exposed the ruse for what it was. Even worse, Soldier Boy, whose comic talents were becoming more pronounced after each fresh battle or hardship, almost as if the laughter of others was an analgesic to his own pain and suffering, ran up to Pun, slashed wildly with his arms, and started vocalising very convincing bear sounds. Masinissa was used to men being able to mimic owls or wolves, but Soldier Boy's bearish woofs, grumbles and moans were a fresh talent. It did for Masinissa, anyway, and he had to concede defeat, veering quickly away from a scrambling, "Ah, the thing is…" to, "Ah, OK, I'm talking rubbish; I faceplanted a reef."

"Thanks, Sold, I owe ya a betrayal down the line, or maybe I should just wrestle you in a costume? How about you give him your skins?" he asked Mandonius in an attempt to divert the mockery away from himself.

Mandonius furrowed his chin up and palmed his hands in an impish show of helplessness. "Maybe next time you should make out it's a shark. You can always say you made it swim away when you hurt yourself in the water next time."

"Ah, yeah, I can do that; thanks, funny guy. This really looks like a shark bite, doesn't it?" He pointed to the tiny, brown marks drying on his nose.

"Well, no," Mandonius conceded, "but they sure don't look like bear smacks either." He paused and then went on, stretching out the syllables in a conciliatory tone, "Aaanyyyway, let's get something wet on our lips and warm in our bellies."

"Oh." It was Masinissa's turn to mock up a little surprise. "OK. Yes, indeed. You two have got the perfect pair of shields for a nice, little casserole. I know all about you guys and your little barbeques. I want to sample some of this legendary stuff." He gave them a knowing nod, which raised a smile from the flattered pair.

Aside from the reputations they had carved out in the war, their knives and shields had been put to other, more recreational uses, and their gastronomic talents were well known and highly regarded. If they showed up at a large camp, they often drew a crowd as if they were celebrity chefs rather than battle-weary warlords. They were always, despite this, commendably hospitable, but it was always a bit of a "first come, first served" scenario. As soon as those aromas hit the open air or the word got around, they were overwhelmed with eager prospective diners.

As they were from the northern parts of the peninsula, they had been greatly influenced by the cuisines of the neighbouring cities of Massalia and Barcino. Their seafood dishes and broths were full of flavour, and their prowess also extended to game (boar most notably) when they were foraging further inland, but even horse when times were tough.

Their signature method, which earned them quite a lot of kudos amongst the soldiers, was to use their shields as alternative cooking pots, often sealing their matching pair together to aid the cooking and improve the flavours. It was a practical method that was used widely by the troops, and it was a clear point of approval for them that their commanders shared their practice and didn't have the need to use the normal paraphernalia of the kitchen. The well-worn adage that the army marches on its well-fed stomach was well established to the extent that it was a point of principle or even a pre-battle tactic to get a good feed in whenever possible. However, that provision did not extend to ensuring that all the pots and pans were strapped to your horses or wagons. A true soldier cooked on his weapons.

As they had intercepted the crew of a fishing vessel coming out of the harbour earlier in the day, and bartered for much of the contents of their heavily laden nets, there was an assortment of choices for them. This was a treat for men more familiar with riding with little more than dried bread and hard-boiled eggs. There was nothing as fancy as a menu, but Masinissa was able to make his preferences find the way into the concave shields that were now heating up their contents nicely. There were hunks of John Dory, sliced up octopus and plenty of prawns. The vegetables were of more incidental interest, but Mandonius had thrown in plenty of peas, celery, onions, leeks and quite a few cloves of garlic, the smell of which was now sharpening up their appetites. He also treated them to a little of their stash of precious pepper, so the meal was almost guaranteed to be a delicious one.

When they doled out the food into their bowls, Masinissa soaked his bread into it and savoured his first morsel. It was as delectable as he had surmised, but he gave a melodramatic grimace of disapproval towards the chefs in any case.

It was a convincing show as Mandonius looked at him a little stunned.

"Not good?" he asked bemused, "Not enough salt or have I gone overboard on the garlic?"

Masinissa stifled a reflex to cave in and admit to enjoying the tasty fare, and faked some impromptu tact. "Well… I have to say," he drawled out slowly in a show that was a little amateurish and betrayed by the creases of amusement at the corners of his mouth.

Indibilis was a little more alert than his brother to the compromising micro expression. Before either Masinissa could continue his criticism or Mandonius could become any more affronted, he interjected, "Just hold on now, Mister Full-of-Shit. That's as good a fish stew as we do, and we do a good one. OK, we're missing a few things to turn it into a first-rate bouillabaisse and I'm sure the pros in Massalia will point out a few things we're not quite doing right, but that's good tucker."

Masinissa smiled, "You've got me; I couldn't keep that one going. You guys never miss. Thank you. I can tell straight away that everything in this is going to be just right. Get some of the good wine to go with it, and we're close to paradise."

"Well, I'm sure there are a few other morsels and diversions we can add to get it over that line, but I appreciate the appreciation," Mandonius said just as effusively as Masinissa.

The feast was enough to feed about fifteen of them in total, almost evenly split between the Iberians and Numidians. Pun and Tigerman knew a good thing when they smelt it and were first in the queue; Capuca, Ari, Juba Tunic and Soldier Boy had also sniffed the delights and eagerly got in on the action as Mandonius's ladle started serving it up. Massiva was conspicuously absent, however; the young rake was probably burrowing into a different kind of flesh in another part of town. A few ribald comments acknowledged the absentee and his priority, but the food was too good and the jokes turned into murmurs of pleasure. This was a meal that merited a little focus. Eventually, the last of the bread cleaned up the shields, and the men got to drinking and gassing, from both ends, with some gusto.

The jokes and the taunts started rolling, but the bonhomie, as ever, was interspersed with more maudlin preoccupations, and complaints about the costly delays of savouring victory over pursuit.

Indibilis was first to articulate his frustration. "You know, Mago is screwing up completely the opportunity we had. We had the advantage, Mas. The Romans were in complete disarray, and we could have routed them all the way back to Hannibal's lines. Instead, that remnant of 8,000 or so who managed to cross the Ebro have been reinforced by another 10,000. OK, so their commander – Claudius Nero, right – looks quite inept and lacking in ambition, but that's not the point. He's just holding the fort, so to speak. I've heard that the Roman military have reassigned many of their veteran units to the scion of Publius –

you'll have heard of him, as he's also called Publius or Publius Cornelius – with the instruction to come for us, and come for us hard. These crazy Roman patricians are too proud to give their sons a different name from their own. He already has some of the best men Rome has under his command, mostly vengeful survivors of Cannae; the kid has balls and he has respect too. He's not in your league, Mas, but there are stories, and, from the other side of the game, he's got clout."

Masinissa confirmed, "I've heard some of those stories. He's like their great big hope: young, courageous, and easy to hype up and rally around. He's a hero already. From the stories I've heard, I almost like him. I imagine he's cut a little from the same cloth as us. There was a battle or a skirmish – let's call it that – at Ticinus, where he rescued his father by charging at the encircling Carthaginians, and he got him out of there. The other one was right after Cannae. The consul Lucius Aemilius Paullus was dead, so Publius Cornelius and Appius Claudius Pulcher became tribunes and took charge of their survivors. There was a lot of talk of mutiny, desertion and looking to turn the best of what was left into a foreign mercenary force. He went straight into the heart of the mutineers, Lucius Caecilius Metellus amongst them, and literally compelled them, with sword drawn, to swear fealty to Rome. For a young guy, that's plenty ballsy."

"Yeah, it's a funny one, isn't it? Admiring your enemies more than your allies. It's like the longer the war goes on, the only ones left – at the top, anyway – are the arseholes. The good ones are either killed, repatriated or removed, and you know how that can go down. The officer cadre of the Romans looks much more decent and competent than our guys, from this distant vantage point, anyway."

"Well, they have their share of cowards, Indy. We heard from our infiltrators that when they elected the new proconsul for a new Iberian campaign against us, Publius Cornelius was the only one, literally the only one, to put his name forward. Everyone else must have thought the mission was doomed to failure. He's not scared of us, and he wants to extract his vengeance. We have the blood of his father on our hands, and he wants to dip his hands in ours."

"Let's hope he doesn't, or if he does, that he confines the repayment of the debt to Gisco and the Barcid brothers. I think we're in a 'waiting and seeing' lull in all this, Mas. I am, anyway. My loyalties are coerced and pretty stuck right now, but you know how it goes. The world keeps moving, but, sometimes, you have to change horses to keep up with it, if you know what I mean."

Masinissa understood the crude analogy and the less-than-subtle inference that Indibilis was open to Roman persuasion if the offer was forthcoming and his people were out of harm's way. Maybe Mago and the others were pushing too hard internally and too feebly externally, and had squandered and lost their strong hand. "Well, I probably need something more challenging that these cookouts. I haven't read so much since I was living in Carthage and pestering the Greeks there for all they could give me. I'm becoming more of a scholar than a soldier."

Mandonius scoffed, "I don't see too many of the learned classes with quite your physique, Mas. Your muscles and scars kinda betray you. I'm not knocking your cultural tendencies or aspirations now, OK? Anyway, if you want to blend in with that lot, there are other things beside writings to help you. For instance, your body shows no sign of overindulgence or dissipation... and, on that point, are you full?"

"Ah!" Masinissa replied quickly. "You really worked that angle around, didn't you? You could have just offered me a fresh morsel, and, no, I'm not full. What have you got? I need to work on my tummy!"

Mandonius laughed, reached behind him and brought out a very large, round cake, whose aroma on the air hinted at a delicious end to the feast.

"You made that on the sly!" Masinissa exclaimed delightedly.

"You know me, Mas; some guys find a quiet spot for their standard business, but me, I like to have the odd surprise for meal times. There's a house close to the main square. It's got a nice kitchen and a hot widow. Two birds there." He gave Masinissa a suggestive wink.

What Mandonius had put together when he wasn't kneading elsewhere in the building was one of Masinissa's favourite desserts: a spelt cake. All the guys knew of his fondness for them, and it felt almost like a birthday surprise that Mandonius had made it for the meal. He hadn't spared on the ingredients either. Aside from the *triticum spelta*, as the Romans called it, there were plenty of almonds decorating the top of it, and strong hints of the base flavours of rosemary, cinnamon, honey, wine, milk and pepper.

Masinissa took his knife and sliced a big triangle of the cake for himself. Unable to resist displaying a little of his knowledge, Masinissa questioned the others on the origins of the cake. "Do you know what the Greeks call this cake?"

"Cake, smart boy!" Pun replied from the far side of the fire, his words muffled by a little bit of the food lodged in his mouth.

"Big cake!" Soldier Boy added.

"Big, yummy cake," Ari clarified further, and he threw a morsel of it in Masinissa's direction, continuing the ridicule of his culinary erudition.

"I'm sure they call it all of those things, you cheeky bastards!" Masinissa retorted amiably, "But if you're ever hanging out with a Greek woman – ideally a foxy, pliable one – you might want to have a few words to impress them at hand. For instance, 'Oh darling, that's so sweet; you baked a cake for me,' she may have heard before. However, what might go down a little better is "Oh darling, you made me some *zeia*. (That's their name for it.) May I thank you and Demeter for the lovely, sweet gift,' as their god of harvest apparently came up with the recipe."

"You know what, Mas?" Tigerman broke in, "If I'm ever in such an appealing situation and the said ravishing Hellenic beauty has gone to the trouble of baking me one of these, I think I can probably ease off on the flattery. She's cooked the deal in, and my part of the bargain is about to rise as well."

Masinissa laughed hard, "Nice one, Tigerman, maybe you're at the wrong party, you know. You might be better off catching up with my rake of a nephew to see what he's nibbling on."

"Well, you know what, big guy? I think a few of us may wobble along towards town soon with those kinda intentions. We've got to build bridges and mend broken hearts; it's all part of the job, right?"

"Yeah, for sure; I'm going to stay here, if that's OK with you? And maybe grab some more of the wine and cake till my senses have taken enough. Maybe Indy and I have a few stories or songs left in us to share before we pass out. Take Soldier Boy with you. Look at him, he's the perfect wing man. Put him under there…" He tapped his armpit. "And then later make sure you put something frothy and willing under him." He gave Soldier Boy a wink and the label of being the most callow at the same time, which was a characterisation that he was far from certain he was being fair to ascribe to him.

The beaming grin Soldier Boy gave him and his complete lack of abashment suggested the association probably had little substance to it.

Tigerman took his cue and sprang up with some elan. "Come on then, troopers, let's hit the flesh pots, and leave the husbands and drunks to themselves. There's more fun to be had in town than a little singing and sighing at the beach. Sorry, Mando, there's not much left in the pot, but there's plenty left in the sack if you know what I mean. You guys stretch out, take it easy and make merry, but the wine gets me in a different mood, you know? I'm going to peel off with the younger guys and see what I can get into."

"*Adieu, adieu*, as the northerners say," Masinissa replied, ushering Tigerman and the other gallants, who had taken the same cue, away as fulsomely as his creeping ease would allow. He added a little waved flourish; somehow, the Gallic farewell always merited a little physical embellishment.

The guys offered a few farewells of their own, and a few sandy sprays were kicked up at them, a few grains of which added a little salt to Masinissa's lips.

"Don't let any of those damsels put shackles on you, now. You need to be back in camp by mid-morning at the latest; we've got to work this off," responded Masinissa, and he jiggled his non-existent tummy to clarify his point.

There came various distracted replies along the lines of, "Sure, sure," but none of them were looking back; all their young men's focus was now fixed on seduction and the unwary ladies of the town.

Masinissa watched them as they swayed up the beach, exhorting and teasing each other, with the tough, hard men they'd become abandoned momentarily to reveal a little of a more playful, juvenile aspect. *Thank Baal Hammon that he leaves a little of the boy in us, however far apart from him we stray*, Masinissa thought to himself.

He turned back to the small group remaining, each of whom had either a few too many years or a few too many cups, and met Indibilis's gaze. His friend must have been watching him, as there was a soft affection playing around his mouth and eyes, as if he had been caught in a reflective moment. The two men smiled, both a little ruefully and both for more than one reason. Each of them had reached a point in their own personal evolution when they had acquired a little insight and wisdom, and they'd both had enough to drink to let it show without embarrassment or self-consciousness – not that either of them had much of a reservoir left of either of those qualities.

A song broke out, and, inevitably, it was of home. Juba Tunic let his sonorous bellows soothe them, and the shoreline cooperated with its rhythmic, gentle lapping of waves. They all joined in or hummed along, and the Numidians all felt a tug of yearning for the far, far shore of their other lives. It was the sort of song that made you smile and cry at the same time, and many of them did. It didn't lead into any others, though. It was the sort of sentimental ode that finishes a show rather than serves as an overture for one. They turned slowly into themselves, tucking themselves in, or staring at the heavens or the sparkles on the ocean. Some found their most natural comrades for their final moments of consciousness. For the most part, they were at peace with each other and themselves, and they knew better than to squander the feeling.

Indibilis shuffled closer to Masinissa, moving a little like a turtle by not raising himself too much off the ground but putting in more effort than he would have if he'd just stood up and walked over. Masinissa thought it was a little comical to witness. A little short of breath from his minor exertion, Indibilis rolled onto his back and wrapped his blanket around him, up to his throat. Masinissa gave his profile a glance and noticed his reflective expression. Looking at the dots of the cosmos can turn a man's thoughts to more profound contemplations. It was often that way for Masinissa, and Indibilis did the same. They were two men staring at the heavens, one gulp of wine away from losing their lucidity but right at the point where they had a temporary tighter grip of it, or at least it always seemed that way.

After a few moments, perhaps after trying to trace the lines of the constellations or maybe just letting the right thoughts bubble into the right words, Indibilis said softly, as if speaking to the gods above him as much as Masinissa, "Do you ever wonder how much of everything's already been spent? How much is left? Where are you in your life? Not many of us live to be old. It's easy to kid yourself that you're in the morning of your life, and that your life is an eternity —refreshing and invigorating itself continually – when, at best, you decay and, at worst, you get chopped up in the morning like the guy you rode out with the previous day. You could even say the same for your liberties. How much of those are left? How many days do you have as a free man? How much more would you savour them if you knew that, the following morning, you might have your wrists and ankles bound, and your tongue and balls cut?"

"I wonder about it," Masinissa replied. "I submerge it most of the time. We all do, right? When we lose guys or when they get messed up so badly that they're useless, then I turn their suffering or their demise on to me. I put my head on their shoulders, so to speak. You mourn them and then you mourn yourself for the time when the same thing will happen to you."

Indibilis put his palms over his eyes and traced his fingers down from his forehead to the corners of his mouth, making a little pout that eased out a sigh full of wobbly uncertainty as he pinched his lower lip. "Yeah, you're right. You can't help wondering when your luck is going end, and you're that guy who made plans and thought about tomorrow and is now staring vacantly straight at the sun, waiting for someone to have the time and care to close his eyes and make a bed for him under the earth. I need more of this…" He sploshed his wine in the air and took a big slug from his skin. "When my mind isn't too tired or dazed to think, it can take me down paths I don't want to travel, and make me look at futures I don't want to see, or worst of all, futures without me at all."

"Ah, my friend, I can't offer you comfort for your worries or your fears," Masinissa commiserated. "Savour what you can, find peace where you can, and find comfort and meaning wherever it may be. Take every moment as a blessing. Loss and pain will happen when it will. Don't let it shroud your present. It's funny; we all climb up and down our emotional hills and mountains, fighting internal battles no one else has any knowledge about. Finding friends, and sharing our worries, good times, warm fires and warmer smiles. I've had a good night, I'll remember it, and it'll cause its own little glow in me when I recall it, I'll try to bring the memory out in a bleak moment." He gave his friend a little fraternal pat.

"I know I'm drifting a little now and that can make me a little maudlin. You're a wise bird these days, Mas, and a mate." This was a point he reaffirmed with a reciprocal touch to his friends bicep, before going on, "You know, we should make a thing of this. Good times aren't supposed to last, especially these days, but if we have ones to look forward to, it helps the bits in between to be endured more easily. The days I laughed without a reason are long gone."

Masinissa sparked a little at the vague proposal. "That's sounds good. A regular get-together at the beach. We'll work it into our busy schedules, shall we? We earn our little furloughs, and we can come here from time to time, or a little bit further down towards Mons Calpe or even round the southern coast, but it's a bit windy down that way."

"Oh, yeah, it is for sure; there have been quite a few journeys down that way where I've swallowed a little more sand than is healthy. It stings, especially if you're riding right into the teeth of it."

"OK, Indy, I know this makes us sound like schoolchildren, but let's make this a thing every couple of months. I know it's likely to drift, but at least let's do it this time next year, OK? And definitely bring your head chef."

"I never go anywhere without Mando; you know that, Mas."
Indibilis laughed. "We're a double act. I see more of him than my wife."
The thought of the painful truth of that struck him as soon as he said
it, although it only checked him momentarily, as if it was a fact he was
becoming more reconciled to.

"Hopefully, that'll switch around soon enough," Masinissa
consoled. His chest heaved deeply, but he managed to stifle a yawn.

Those two were the only ones of the group who were not obviously
attempting or finding sleep by then.

Masinissa grabbed a small, disc-shaped pebble, raised himself
and skimmed it over the ebbing tide, counting the bounces. The stone
eluded immersion till its fourth drop. "Three months, buddy; trust me,
you'll be back in her arms by then."

"I'm not sure I have much faith in a stone-skimming shaman, but
I'll keep you informed." With that, Indibilis gave Masinissa's shoulder
a double tap; turned on his side, showing his back to Masinissa; and
let the drink and the food swirl him into a temporary, satiated oblivion.
Masinissa looked at his friend and then out to sea, letting his own
thoughts and the tide rise together, waiting for anything to fall into
his consciousness, and focussing just on the motions of the sea and
the breathing of his buddy. It was an empty and serene moment; his
overriding thought as sleep claimed him was that of spending more
such pleasant days.

*

Little did Masinissa realise that the knot that held this band of
brothers together was about to be untied by the younger Scipio,
whose arrival on the peninsula would detonate the status quo of
skirmishing and haphazard raiding that had grown to define the
conflict, as a result of Carthaginian hesitation and inaction. With
Scipio's additional 10,000 men bolstering the forces already in place,
he quickly recognised the fractious relationship between the three
senior Carthaginian commanders, as well as, crucially, the significant

physical distances between their respective armies. He made a lunge at the most vulnerable and tactically significant target: Carthago Nova, as the Romans referred to it, or Qart Hadasht as it was called by the Carthaginians.

The lack of coordination between Mago, Hasdrubal and Hasdrubal Gisco, and the fact that Mago, as the commander of the city, was complacently three days' march away when it was attacked made the capture and occupation of the city much more straightforward than it ought to have been. Its defenders comprised merely around 1,000 Carthaginians, bolstered by a local militia of about 2,000 men charged with defending the city's gates. Scipio initially blockaded the town from the sea, with the aid of a powerful expeditionary force of the Roman fleet commanded by Gaius Laelius, and then attacked across the isthmus. Whilst rebuffed initially, he attacked again, this time with a contingent striking unexpectedly across the sparsely defended northern side across the lagoon. A fierce gale aided his advance from this direction considerably, as it drained much of the lagoon temporarily, facilitating a quite rapid crossing for his men, who scaled the northern wall barely opposed, and attacked the Carthaginian forces from the rear.

Once the naval forces broke the resistance in the south, and stormed past the bastions, the Carthaginians were condemned to a grizzly fate. Scipio, according to well-established Roman practice, gave orders to spare none of the defenders, which was an order received with much gusto by those of his army who had survived the battles of the Upper Baetis. Chroniclers of the massacre that ensued took care to note that the looting of the town was postponed for some time whilst its men, women, children and beasts were butchered. It was an act of revenge, but also a cold-blooded and deliberate act intended to sow terror in the enemy and doubt in their allies. This doubt was further cajoled by the liberation of the captive allies of Mago and Hasdrubal Gisco, the wives and daughters of the Celtiberian nobility.

It was an astute manoeuvre on Scipio's part, and it quickly reaped a partial dividend. Many of the local warlords and chieftains abandoned

Carthage and switched their allegiance to Scipio, including Indibilis and Mandonius, who – on the return of their daughters and spouses, and a promise of a much more lenient suzerain – concluded it was very clearly in their vested interests to switch patrons. With their choice made, a ripple effect drew most of the locally administered tribal territories into the Roman cause, with only the major cities of the south remaining under Carthaginian control; the main base of operations moved to the Phoenician stronghold of Gades. The happy coastline of the east was lost, and with it the preferred venue for the alfresco feasts Masinissa had begun to look forward to. In any case, the guest list would have been unrecognisable, and it was certain he would no longer be on it, regardless of the bonhomie and personal affinity between him and the local warlords.

Worse for the Carthaginian cause, if not specifically for Masinissa himself, was Scipio's subsequent strategic thrust, which fully utilised his new local auxiliaries. Once his position was consolidated and the very lucrative silver mines of the region firmly under his control, Scipio launched a further campaign against the Carthaginians, who had learnt no lessons from Carthago Novo and were just as refractory in their own stubborn interests at the cost of the common cause as they were before that calamity. He marched west towards the army of Hasdrubal Barca, which was wintering at Baecula on the upper reaches of the Baetis River. Hasdrubal's scouts caught sight of the advancing Romans quite early, and, in response, his army was able to adopt a very strong defensive position on a plateau south of the town, with their flanks shielded by ravines and a meandering river to the front and rear, respectively. It took Scipio two days to devise a strategy, which, for the most part, was a pincer movement, with Gaius Laelius leading an attack to the left of the enemy and Scipio himself attacking the right.

Whilst surprised that the attack was more than a mere skirmish, Hasdrubal evaded being enveloped, and was able to retreat with the bulk of his forces and his elephants. The Romans, fortuitously for Hasdrubal, chose to loot the Carthaginian camp once their victory seemed assured and allowed the Carthaginian army to escape with nothing more than a desultory chase pursuing them.

Whether it was motivated by the defeat itself or the attendant humiliation that may have beset him as a consequence of it, Hasdrubal's next move was to march over the Pyrenees. This was ostensibly to join up with Hannibal, who was campaigning in Lucania, but perhaps also to try to lure a more earnest pursuit by Scipio, which may have led, in turn, to his ruin, with the other two Carthaginian armies ready to follow them both north. If it was a ruse, Scipio didn't take the bait, but instead moved the bulk of his forces to Tarraco where he continued his beguiling of the local tribes.

For Masinissa, it was the first hint of things to come. Of course, he had regarded the Romans as a formidable force, but one that could be as tactically inept as some of the Carthaginians generals. When news reached him of Hasdrubal's defeat and the defections of the Iberian tribes to Scipio, Masinissa felt the change in the air like a gale rather than a zephyr. Mago and Gisco would charge him, as the most capable and strongest mobile force at their disposal, to wage a guerrilla campaign in the mountains, whilst they busied themselves with recruitment in North Africa and Lusitania.

It was with resignation rather than any vigour that he accepted this mission, wondering often whether he might find Indibilis and the others over the next ridge, and what he might do at such an encounter. He wasn't used to trusted friends becoming his enemies. The paradoxes of the war were never starker than when he thought of the prospect of drawing swords with former allies and trying to kill men whom he regarded as friends, even brothers, by then. *Do you pause at the absurdity of it at the decisive moment?* he wondered. *Will I think of their smiles and their affection? Do I have the time even for that moment of tension or hesitation? Could I turn a friend into an object, merely the muscles and sinews wielding the sword?* It was a test he wasn't sure of, nor was he even sure what action would be regarding as passing it, and he hoped it was an examination of his morality and humanity that would never come. The balance of probabilities suggested it would.

Even worse for Masinissa, amongst the captured or slain at Baecula was Massiva, who had ignored his uncle's orders defiantly and had ridden with the more impetuous elements of the Numidian cavalry that had rushed to the aid of Hasdrubal.

THE ART OF PERSUASION

The defeat at Baecula was a shocking reversal for the Carthaginian forces, but one that perhaps Masinissa could have forecast given the ebbing of their fortunes on the peninsula since the advent of Publius Cornelius Scipio and his astute manoeuvring, both on the battlefield, and within the local tribes and communities that he was wooing relentlessly.

The involvement of the bulk of the Numidian forces had been slight, as a small contingent attached to the armies of Mago and Gisco, but their reprieve from the disaster was tempered by the loss of at least two of Masinissa's closest comrades. Micipsa, who had ridden with Massiva as a surrogate guardian at the insistence of Masinissa, had been declared killed at the battle by the few survivors who had returned to the southern and eastern armies. His loss tore at Masinissa, but the uncertain fate of Massiva bit much deeper chunks of guilt into his being. With Massiva it was different; it was a blood bond, and Masinissa would rather have swapped places with him and be strung up in whatever fetid, horrific dungeon he was in, rather than imagine his nephew enduring such a torment. In his imagination, he constructed the worst scenarios and humiliations, and upbraided himself for his failure to save him. It was a long way down from a nobleman's horse to the wetter corners of an overcrowded cell, and Masinissa punished himself relentlessly by speculating how far and in what fashion Massiva was being dragged down.

All that spared him the agonies of his thoughts were the imperatives of the moment and the pragmatic evaluation of their circumstances. It was grim to say the least, but it was better to distract yourself with that than dwell on the hideousness of your ward's captivity.

Concluding that the Carthaginian war effort lay in ruins was a premature and largely inaccurate assessment, but, at the very least, it was a catastrophe. They had taken a pounding that would take some time to recover from. How many more men could they recruit from amongst the Numidians? They had bled long for the cause already. Could the Mauretanians and Lusitanians be entreated to ally themselves in greater numbers? Could the musterers go deep into the southern mountains and deserts, and bring more Libyans, Gaetuli and other nomads up to pad the ranks? Masinissa was sceptical. Those tribes were scornful of the institutions and laws of civilisation and the "sea people", as they were often derided. They would not find common cause unless they were promised plenty of booty or were roped into service.

He doubted that either coercion or exaggerated tall tales of riches would be adequate to persuade many of the simpler folk. If you were happy in your tents and huts, why risk that for shiny baubles? Taking men from those tribes by force was also fraught with dangers. You had a long way to go and a few nights in the open before you reached the safety of your boats, and the prospect of plenty of able trackers eager to cut your throat, or worse, in the darkness.

Perhaps even more damaging than the loss on the battlefield was the perception of vulnerability it instilled, or – more accurately – reaffirmed, after a string of Roman victories over the recent period. The loyalties of the allied tribal forces had vacillated, but the loss at Baecula would likely be decisive in terms of any wavering local support. The local population was going to be pragmatic in the end, and their paramount considerations were how likely they were to live and what quality of life would be granted to them after that survival. With Scipio ascendant, and apparently indulgent towards the local tribes, that loyalty was unlikely to swerve back towards the Carthaginians.

The scales looked to be tipping in the Romans' favour. Even worse, amongst the Numidians, morale was low and questions were being raised, sometimes in the corners of the campfires or tavernas after a few cups, sometimes only in the recesses of their own minds, but often in more careless, open ways, as if the doubter knew their view was shared by everyone else in earshot, and there would be no reprisals or discipline for the loose, or occasionally even seditious, talk.

Certainly, Masinissa took care not to articulate his own doubts too freely, but they were there, and they were sawing deeper into him every time he paused to speculate on Massiva's whereabouts and condition. In a cock fight, you'd be a fool to back the bird carrying a limp, and he was coming around slowly to the realisation that this metaphoric status applied to the present predicament of the Punic forces. He dwelt on his losses too, be they intimate, casual or even just numerical. In previous triumphs, he was part of the army that had retained control of the fought-over ground, the arena into which men poured, and only the victorious would have a proper idea who had made it through. Even in those triumphs, the accounting of lives was far from neat. Identifying pulpy remains was heartbreaking, and there were times when soldiers were not even sure that the soaked corpse they presumed was their best friend or brother was actually them. Many times, it was the clothes or the ornaments that gave decisive confirmation of identity.

Fleeing the battlefield and abandoning comrades to their fate – to the savageries, sport and slavery that their enemies would inflict upon them inevitably – was a materially different experience. It was certain that their enemy's ranks would have as many sadistic psychotics like Nosejob as their own army did, and it was only chance and luck whether they would fall into the custody of those who retained some regard for honour and mercy. You had no way of knowing what type of man your soldiers had surrendered to or been captured by.

"Tanit watch over him, I beg you," Masinissa had murmured to himself reflexively every time he thought of his nephew.

His knowledge of the degradations of the war – the wisdom of battlefield survival, so to speak – nourished a different kind of grief and mourning, one that was fed by his memories of Carthaginian victories at the Upper Baetis and elsewhere, as much as his rampant and fearful imagination. Sometimes, his visions were vivid, and it was hard for him to not put Massiva's face on the victim of his nightmare. One of the flashes of half-recall, half-invention that often assailed him was of a man, often with familiar features, falling with a spear to his side. Masinissa would find himself made impotent by being dragged away from his fallen comrade's aid, and his mind would snap its vision and he would be left to wonder horribly about the man's prospects. Would this nebulous victim bleed out and go as mercifully as they could have prayed for, as no doubt many of the soldiers had at Baecula, or would they be used as an enfeebled target practice or dragged off in chains to some dreadful subjugation? His imaginary brother's fate was piteous, but the pity Masinissa felt in his heart for him and all the others on the real battlefield at Baecula was impotent. He was left without any consolation, clinging to childish hopes that had little chance of coming true, and feebly praying that the calamity could be swept away by wishful thinking or sorcerous rescue by one of the powerful, concerned gods, who would come to Masinissa's aid if he only prayed hard enough, or offered other pacts or promises to the deity.

Of course, the futility of his supplications and promises had been revealed to him many times in the past. You can't bring back the dead, heal the devastated or liberate the enslaved, but, even in that certainty, you had to continue to believe in it. There was no other way to smother the loss. In the past, over time, some of those tugs of guilt and concern had faded, but those that related to his closest relationships, and blood ties especially, would cling on like a stain that couldn't be erased however hard you rubbed away at it. It was only a short time since the defeat at Baecula, and the emotions were high and fresh, but it seemed to Masinissa that his grief and guilt would never fade. In fact, the opposite might happen, and it would only deepen and become more painful. The stain of the loss spread more over his being each day and burnt into every part of him. It lit up questions for which he had no answers, but only more questions. He thought that if it had been anyone else, even Ari or Capuca, he might have been able to reconcile himself to the loss, and the questions might release their grip on him slowly. However, Massiva was his dependant, and regarded Masinissa as a hero, a brother and a role model, and it was a combination of his devotion and Masinissa's sense of his own errant responsibility to him that fused into a relentless scraping at Masinissa's heart.

There were at least wiser heads to offer advice, if not anything that could be regarded as a salve. Both Pun and Tigerman urged him back into the fight to numb himself that way, although the war seemed to be in a momentary respite as everyone licked their wounds, consolidating their gains or planning their counters. Having yielded territory in the loss at Baecula and having mostly detached from the main armies to resume skirmishing, news was hard to come by, and Masinissa dwelt miserably for weeks on the probable wretchedness of his nephew.

This miserable spell was broken suddenly when an emissary of Scipio, bearing his seal, arrived at Masinissa's camp. The emissary declared very tentatively and hesitantly that Massiva was alive and in good health, and – even more remarkably – that Scipio, as a gesture of goodwill between honourable and esteemed foes, wished to repatriate Massiva without any compensation, assurance or commitment from Masinissa in return.

Masinissa, regularly having witnessed and heard of the torments of captivity, regarded the envoy with astonishment and, at first, as if it were some kind of trick. Following a detailed interrogation, however, the envoy's story seemed more and more plausible, to the point where the matter that most made Masinissa uneasy was how he had found Masinissa's troop in the first place. On this issue, the Roman was coy, but it was plain that he wasn't the only party bearing this message, and there were a few others roaming the hills looking to find Masinissa and present him with the news.

Despite his conviction that the man was to be trusted, Masinissa was still conscious that he was perhaps being lured into a trap with Massiva as the juicy, hooked bait. As such, he arranged a rendezvous for two days' time in the middle of a wide, cultivated valley that was free of any woodland and a short ride away. There were vineyards close by, so that, in the event that there was cause for celebration, there would be libations nearby. The Roman assented and left without any escort.

*

For the next two days, Masinissa's mood swung between pillars of doubt and euphoria. It was almost as if the messenger had resuscitated someone and brought them back from the dead. It was barely credible, and the longer he thought about it, the more preposterous a notion it sounded to him.

Nevertheless, he rode out two days later with a large detachment of about thirty riders, including Cap, Ari and Juba Tunic, which he figured ought to provide sufficient muscle to match any Roman unit or evade any Roman platoon if things took a turn for the worse. As they crested the hill overlooking the valley and the bushy, orderly clusters of grapevines that were strung out in long lines along much of it, he could see the Roman party waiting for him. As they rode closer, he could start to discern more of Massiva's features, whom it certainly was, amongst the Roman cavalry escort who waited for them, relatively impassively, aside from the snorts of their horses. Incongruously, his nephew had never looked better. There was a composure in him and a sanguine bearing that was out of step with the situation in which he found himself. Masinissa even felt a flush of pride at the nobility of the scene. It was clear that the Romans had treated Massiva well. He was certainly not in the least cowed or subdued in their presence. He hadn't taken any fists to the face or knives to his flanks, that was for sure.

As Masinissa drew up to the waiting enemy cavalry, his vigilance still on high alert, he nevertheless went through the protocols he presumed were appropriate for such a rendezvous. He was uncertain whether there was some expectation from him as far as the exchange was concerned, and, on the presumption that there was an element of barter to the matter, he signalled for his men to release five Roman prisoners whom he had brought with them as their side of their bargain. None were high-ranking centurions, although that might have been a deliberate misrepresentation of their true ranks. They were, according to their own statements, a pair of *optios*, another pair of standard bearers and a *tesserarius*, whom Masinissa had found quite reminiscent of Pun in his bearing and manner. For that alone, he was quite pleased with the fact of their release. He hoped all five would be given some kind of extended leave, although the probability that they would be engaged in hostile actions almost immediately was far more likely. In any event, one of the *optios* at least managed a smile and a wave as they rode back into their own troopers, where they were received heartily.

As Masinissa was about to make a formal address to the supposed senior figure of the escort, a figure, whom he hadn't previously noticed, rode up from behind him. The man was helmetless, revealing a very round and bald dome. Aside from his striking and quite shiny pate, Masinissa's eyes were drawn to the cuirass he wore across his chest and torso, which was gold and embossed with a wolf at the cleavage of his pectoral muscles, and sported heavily accentuated abdominals lower down.

Golden rectus abdominis *to die for,* Masinissa thought to himself a little wryly. The Roman nobility, and the Greeks for that matter, and their obsession with their auric abs struck Masinissa as a little suggestive of inadequacy. Maybe underneath, most of them were concealing torsos that were a little less sharply defined. The nobility really liked to fetishise their midriffs in their armour.

Underneath the cuirass, the man was wearing a typical Roman tunic of deep burgundy, although the matching scarf around his throat had a few filigrees of gold embroidered into it. The rest of his attire was indistinguishable from the rest of the troop, although the *gladius* at his side appeared, at first glance, to be richly detailed with a highly ornate hilt.

The palpable deference, even awe, shown to him by the entourage as he emerged put Masinissa on edge and made him uncertain of his next move. This figure clearly held some seniority and purpose. Masinissa was rarely intimidated, but the man's bearing made him hesitate. He gave him a deferential bow, but made no other motion or comment. In turn, the man bestowed him with a barely discernible smile. For the next few moments, the man was clearly making judgements. He had allowed himself an interval in which he could weigh up his subject and establish a first impression with a little leisure. Masinissa got the distinct impression that this man, roughly his own age, was missing nothing about him, and not the tiniest stain, fray or scar was slipping by him.

The impression was made more acute by Masinissa's own inability to read the man in turn. In a quite random association, in his mind, he suddenly conflated the Roman commander with a young woman who dresses too immodestly or revealingly. With such types, it was almost impossible to decipher if they know lots about men or absolutely nothing. That mystery was resolved quickly on closer inspection, but that avenue of clarification was not open to Masinissa just then.

In terms of the man's features, the most distinctive to Masinissa appeared to be his mouth. His lips were full, and he almost had the zigzag pout of a woman, accented by a very broad and deep philtrum. It was so noticeable that Masinissa wondered whether or not his appearance might benefit from a short moustache to conceal his medial cleft. Masinissa's drifting thoughts were abruptly broken as those lips parted and the man spoke.

"I've heard much about you, Prince, and you are even more impressive than how you were described. It is good that we meet with our hands empty and our minds clear. I only tend to meet my enemies when they are dead or grovelling at my feet. I'm not used to a dignified meeting of equals," the man explained.

"Nor am I," Masinissa concurred. "May I ask who you are? Forgive me for my ignorance."

"Not at all," the man responded genially. "I shouldn't make any presumptions of familiarity. You are easy to identify from your physique, and, besides, I was expecting you. You, on the other hand, were expecting an anonymous party. I was too curious about you to let the opportunity pass. Your nephew is an impressive person, and certainly one too beautiful to be degraded, so how much more so would you be in the flesh? I am, by that criteria, not disappointed. I have seen some impressive specimens – Spartans and Thracians mostly – but you look as if you would be the champion over them. The gladiator schools would pay a sackful of *denarii* or, more likely, a sackful of *denarius aureus* for you if you showed up in their auctions. I am Publius, Publius Cornelius Scipio, proconsul of Rome and commander of the republican armies west of the Cisalpine passes."

He extended his hand to Masinissa, and they gripped one another close to the crook of their arms, after the fashion of veterans who enjoyed greeting each other with a clap on each other's bracers; it was a spontaneous gesture that surprised them both.

"I am honoured. You're the first proconsul I've met; who knows, you may be the only one I ever will," Masinissa stated.

"There's a strong possibility that will be the case, certainly if you stay true to your present course," Scipio declared.

The hint at betrayal was clear, but Masinissa felt it would be prudent to not pass comment on the inference.

"You're not taking the hook on that one, huh?" Scipio asked as the pause became a little awkward. "You know, one of the only things I've learnt is to value strength where I find it. The weak don't survive or are preyed on. The weak slaves, the weak gladiators and the weak soldiers don't last; they don't survive, but those who do get stronger and stronger, are forged harder and harder, and then you have to watch them. That's you, Numidian. You are stronger than even you realise, and this conflict – on these lands, anyway – would be resolved far more quickly without you and yours. The Carthaginians do not value you but I know what you bring. My soldiers fear your riders, not the Phoenicians or their mercenaries."

Masinissa tried to be impassive in the face of the flattery, but gave at least a hint of gratitude, couched in a quip. "Thank you. It's not always such a great thing to be feared, but, in the way you mean it, I recognise the compliment and perhaps the offer."

Scipio jumped at the admission. "I'm not making formal treaties or proposals here, you know. I'm figuring things out as I go and weighing things up. If I can be a little crude with you, you're one of the fruits I'm sticking my thumb into to see how ripe you are."

"Well, how ripe am I then, in your opinion? I've got a few bruises, so maybe you'd be better off casting your eyes around other stalls in the market."

Scipio looked at him a little flintily and let his gaze become close to a stare. "You're ripe, I'd say; not perfect, not yet, but ready for the bowl." He looked away towards his own men, perhaps as a persuasive nudge, and then turned back and changed tack. "I hear you're a bit of a scholar on the quiet."

"Not a scholar, just a reader," Masinissa qualified.

"Well, you start with the latter and end up as the former; that's my understanding of it, anyway." Scipio replied. "As long as you read then, I take it you've managed to get around to Herodotus. He's a pretty famous guy. If you read enough of his writing, I'm sure you'll start to question your affiliations. He had a very scornful view of your allies."

"I must have missed that one in class. I skipped a few, you know, or maybe my teachers were a little circumspect with my exposure to certain views. I wasn't the only one who could get caned after all."

"No doubt." Scipio winced for comic effect. "Well, it was Herodotus's view that all the conflicts in the world could be traced back to the Phoenicians, and he justified the accusation very simply. They could be blamed as they were the first people to start kidnapping women when they sailed into Argos and took the king's daughter back to Egypt. Soon, everybody followed suit, and Homer's having a fine time writing about Helen's abduction in the *Iliad*."

"Don't you think that's a little unlikely?" Masinissa replied a little sceptically. "I'm sure hostage taking has a much longer history than that. You can't just pin it on the guys with the best boats. Besides, I'm not basing my view of international relations – nor what flag I ride under, for that matter – on who raided what shore back in the day. I'm sure you Romans have done your fair share of trawling around foreign shores for women in your time and infuriating the locals when you've sailed away with the hottest mamas."

Scipio smiled at the remark and scratched his jawline. "Well, you have a point there. There are a lot of hot mamas in Rome, and I would attribute a lot of that to…" He paused. "Various forms of immigration; let's call it that."

"I'm sure they are as dazzling as your arguments," Masinissa countered; this was a witticism that seemed to please Scipio, to the point where it brought him back to his purpose.

"They are dazzling; well, the women are, anyway. I recommend you pay us a visit sometime; just stay away from being part of one of the tributes or games is my advice. Anyway, taking the tangent, as I like shiny things and I'm sure you do too, I've brought a few with me. Call it a fee for the loan of your nephew. We took the silver mines from the Carthaginians, but that doesn't mean you shouldn't have a little of their ore."

He ushered a couple of bearers forwards with a chest, which they, rather extravagantly, opened to reveal a pretty substantial pile of silver and lapis lazuli; this was a combination of precious stones and metal that couldn't be more complimentary.

Masinissa loved the purity of silver and the intense blue, somewhere between cobalt and indigo, of lapis lazuli. He even had a few bangles of his own that featured both, and he regarded them as having beneficial properties for his mind, body and fortunes. Some of the wilder mystics even claimed that lapis lazuli made you a better orator or blessed you with greater insight, which was a claim that Masinissa considered dubious but did not discount completely.

Whether Scipio was aware of this fondness was highly unlikely, but the gift was very well received, and the Roman proconsul couldn't help but notice the delight on Masinissa's face, to the point where he added a little further information about the stone's provenance. "I hope you like the lapis lazuli. I came across it fairly easily, but the men from whom I obtained it – or from whom my intermediaries obtained it, I should say – went to much effort to acquire it. I'm assured it comes from the finest known source of it, deep in the mountains of Badakshan. Those mountains are as large as those in the Alpis range, and some are even higher I believe than Mons Albus. I've been over the Alpis passes, and it made me appreciate how tough it must have been to retrieve this stuff. Can you imagine digging it out at such an altitude and then transporting it down what must be some pretty treacherous ravines?"

Masinissa whistled. "It must have been some task. The pursuit of treasure, though, will put a man in some pretty inhospitable places. For something this valuable, I'm sure many prospectors would traverse the most forbidding wastelands. I've heard a few stories about the men who come from that region – the Kamboja, that's their name, isn't it? Pretty tough customers and pretty merciless too, I've been told."

Scipio nodded quite vigorously at the reputation such a distant tribe had garnered. "I think I must have heard the same stories. I've come across a few of the Kamboja myself. They have quite fluid loyalties, and if they stray west, then they can be recruited. We must have a hundred or so in our legions in various pockets, and they have acquired a mostly impressive reputation. I doubt you'll find any around here, though."

"You're right; I doubt it. I've not come across anyone who lays claim to that ethnicity. There must be plenty of clients for able swordsmen like them, including Rome by the sounds of it, between the Badakshan and here. I'm sure it would be even closer for them to go find a patron amongst the Seres in the far east than come this far in the other direction."

"You may have a point there. The situation in Serica is always a little mysterious, but the few traders who bring news from the distant lands talk of a new dynasty and a unification of power. The old rulers have been replaced by a new one who has called himself emperor. An emperor! Such an anathema to a staunch republican like me. It's probably of no interest to you, but they call him Shi Huang Qin. I don't even know how to pronounce such a peculiar name properly. The latest news I've heard mentions another name, another Qin: Qin

Ershi. It's a little easier to say. Maybe we'll hear more about him, but such news is rare and really only of idle interest. These lands might as well be as distant as Elysium or Tartarus. Anyway, I digress. Your boy must be itching to get back to his gang."

"Well, he might have more of a yearning for a reunion than his gang. Their itch may not be quite so urgent," Masinissa wisecracked. "I do really need to thank you. Not only have you shown me such a kindness as to return my nephew, you even seem to be paying me his ransom. I owe you. I'm not sure how I can square this debt, but I will try."

"You know the obvious way. Switch. Think about it. The door is open... for now," Scipio added ominously, but without too much theatrical menace.

"I will think about it. If it were just me, I would this second. I've seen enough of the Carthaginians to turn on them. They've detained me as a youngster. They dismiss me as a commander. They use me as they would their beasts or elephants, as if I am somehow less than them. I am not enlisted in a meritocratic army, that's for sure. These pompous sons of bitches will wring every last drop out of me and then cast me aside without a trace of gratitude. It's not me who I need to consider when making a move like that, though. My lands and my tribe form a contiguous border with Carthage. Massyli is a buffer state and vulnerable to reprisals if weak. My sovereignty is tenuous. Most of the fighting-age men are enlisted and on foreign soil. Even worse, if Carthage attacked from the east, no doubt Syphax would start encroaching from the west, and we'd be trapped and, most likely, massacred from both sides. Right now, they have me by the balls. I can't defend Massyli from any direction if I'm many, many days ride and a chunk of ocean away. Cirta and Russicada could be overrun in a day. It's gratifying and a great compliment to me that you believe in me and desire my allegiance, but, ultimately, I have to believe in you. I have to believe in your victory, and one on the most hostile and furthest shores. You are strong, but can you march your men all the way down to Carthage and put your foot on the Barcid throat down there?"

"I understand that," Scipios replied, fully apprehending the predicament. "You are a bit like the man who dances before the bull. The animal is stronger, but you are smarter. I'll take away his horns and then you can show the knife behind your cape."

Masinissa snorted, a little like the metaphorical steer. "That's an interesting way of putting it. It's a double game, then, for me. It's doesn't feel so honourable to have treachery in the forefront of my mind, but having options is comforting."

Scipio gave him another of his lingering, penetrating gazes, as if he could tell that the fissure he was looking to tease open between Masinissa and Carthage had just split, and it was for him to tear it wider with his military offensive. "It's a matter of time. I can endow you with far more than silver and stones, you know. Right now, I have nothing to be grateful for. Be assured that my gratitude would be far more lavish than my appeal." His eyes seemed to hold an extra gleam in them when he spoke, holding sparks that seemed to Masinissa something more than simply a play of light. "We understand each other now. It's good that men like us meet, and it's even better if we can ally with each other. Our causes could correlate very well." To emphasise the point, he linked his hands and fingers together in a clutch. He then offered his sword arm to Masinissa again in a gesture of farewell, and perhaps of a mutual understanding or tentative complicity. "Goodbye. One day I hope we will ride in the same direction."

"So do I," Masinissa replied quietly and with a little solemn fellowship. "Thank you," he concluded, not knowing what else to add and opting for simplicity as the safest indication of sincerity.

He waited, self-consciously deferential, for Scipio and his party to ride past, and there were a few random cries and salutations as they did so, as if the pact were already sealed and the enemy soldiers moving away had become, in all but name, their allies and confederates.

Masinissa himself could not resist a final wave as Scipio turned at a distance before kicking his stallion out of a trot and into a gallop. He looked at the receding patrician with a degree of affection that he recognised as improper and potentially even dangerous. *You're not meant to be so beguiled by your mortal enemy,* he thought to himself sardonically.

His reflections on the charms of Scipio were abruptly suspended, however, as Massiva rode up to him and Masinissa almost fell off his horse in the embrace Massiva gave him. Massiva roared and whooped as they broke apart, and his youthful yelps brought cheers all round of relief, liberation and reunion.

"You're a lucky, lucky boy," Masinissa admonished him when his gusto had receded enough for him to get a meaningful reprimand in.

"Yeah, I know," Massiva replied in a manner that blended a bashful shame with a callow cockiness in an odd-but-quite-appealing way. It struck the right tone, anyway, in terms of appealing to the more lenient tendencies of Masinissa. His nephew, still quite euphoric about his emancipation, continued impishly, "Did you miss me? Or get lonely?"

Masinissa did all he could to restrain a grin and looked at his nephew with as grave an expression as he could manage. "I knew you were gone," he conceded with a little dose of reproof.

"Then you missed me!" Massiva concluded victoriously, taking Masinissa's taciturn neutrality as an admission.

In turn, Masinissa relented his sternness and clasped Massiva by the back of the neck with rough affection and kissed him on the top of the head. "Yeah, I did," Masinissa admitted, sparing the rescued boy the additional thought that it was best to excuse him further discipline at the hands of Pun and Tigerman. They'd been down that route before. He was going to gain no more from going through the same ordeals, and, besides, a period of uncertain captivity, however gilded it may have been, was a salutary lesson in itself.

GUERRILLA

The morning was fresh, and the crisp mountain air revived Masinissa quickly. The icy peaks of Iberia were a far quicker means of restoring alertness, if not affability, than the parched desert terrains back home, where Masinissa's instincts were always to linger for a little while in the warmth of his blankets; that is, if blankets were even necessary. The luxury of a tent in a desert where your safety was assured by the empty horizons and you were shielded from the harsh light of the dawn by the canvas felt like a distant memory at that moment. The brisk chill of the Iberian interior forced you out of your languor far too quickly. It was impossible to spread yourself idly once the lids of consciousness were raised even slightly. Lassitude was a treat reserved for warmer climes and lower altitudes.

Masinissa sipped at his bowl of milk and looked covetously down the mountain passes towards the coast and beaches where he had enjoyed barbecuing goats and fresh catches with his men so recently. *Pulpo*, which the Iberians insisted on calling octopus, was a particular recent favourite. He missed drifting away, sated and peaceful, to the gentle murmurs of the Mediterranean. The defeats at Carthago Nova and Baecula, and the losses of the wealth of the silver mines and a large portion of the military stores of the Carthaginian forces had altered the military and strategic landscape completely. The entire eastern coastline of Iberia had been surrendered temporarily, and was crawling with Scipio's forces and Iberians who had peeled off from the Carthaginian alliance, either spooked by the defeats or no longer in receipt of the silver Hasdrubal had lost access to. Scipio was proving quite a diplomat with some of the Iberian tribes, and their loyalties were becoming questionable. Mons Calpe was still a redoubt of Mago, and all the lands west to Gades were firmly in Carthaginian hands, but Mago and Gisco had gone south to procure fresh forces, and Hasdrubal Barca had broken north with the remnant of his forces to try to reunite with Hannibal in Italy.

The hinterland of Iberia was, for the moment, Masinissa's dominion. He had been ordered by the Barcids to take charge of the Carthaginian forces in Iberia. Gades and Ilipa were still garrisoned with Carthaginian infantry, but the Numidian, Iberian and Carthaginian cavalry forces were ceded entirely to Masinissa's command, with instructions to prosecute a guerrilla campaign against the Romans until fortunes turned and fresh levies were brought up from the south. This was the sort of warfare Numidians relished and were suited to. Lightning raids on Roman encampments were the tactics to be deployed for the time being, and Masinissa had become adept at harassing Scipio's forces whenever they strayed too far into the mountains.

That day, though, he had a bolder and more symbolic assault in mind. Over the last few days, he and his forces had crossed north and east through the Sierra Nevada, his intention being to mount a raid of some kind against the citadel at Xativa. The fortress there had become quite a source of bitterness for the Carthaginian forces. It had become emblematic of the changing tides of the war. It had been a Carthaginian possession prior to Scipio's invasion. Hannibal himself had rested and watered his elephants there on his way north, and the gateway into the outer bastion had become known as the door of Hannibal. Scipio was probably well aware of this description when he targeted, occupied and garrisoned the town on his own march south.

There was also a little mystery attached to the target as well. Masinissa had word from Gades that he would be met by a young Carthaginian noble, Hanno, who was particularly keen to attack

Xativa. Masinissa knew very well, merely from the name, that he had little choice in the matter. Although not someone he had known from his long exile in Carthage, Hanno was the direct descendant of his namesake, Hanno the Navigator, and was from as eminent a lineage as the Barcids.

During his studies, Masinissa had always enjoyed reading and hearing about the travels of the original Hanno. Accounts differed, but the view was that he had embarked from Carthage, with at least sixty ships and about 5,000 men, on a mission to secure the gold trade with the wild peoples and establish what, at the time, were referred to as Libyo-Phoenician colonies along the coast south of Tingi. He had travelled far, collected a lot of gold, and even the skins of wild men or beasts that he referred to as *gorillai*, three hides of which were exhibited in the Temple of Tanit.

As he thought about those colossal hides and the beasts they once dressed, he spied dust trails in the valley below, and suspected immediately that it might be Hanno's detachment. Who else could it be at that time? They were due at this hour, and Carthaginians had a reputation for punctuality, even if it was a quality often derided by Numidians and Iberians. He cast his bowl aside and mounted Napla, admiring how the frosty air made her great flanks and curves shimmer. He knew he must be an impressive sight on her back; two better specimens of man and horse would be hard to find, and ones in such perfect harmony were sure to mesmerise any onlooker. He smirked a little at the reputation the Numidian riders, which he, especially, had garnered since the Battle of Castulo. The Iberians, the women not the men, would tell the cavalry – and, occasionally, the more brazen ones even told Masinissa himself – that his forces had the whole of the country running, but in different directions. The women would flock towards them like moths to a flame, and the men would flee in the other direction, either fleeing conscription or attack.

Napla snorted as they wheeled together to face the approaching riders, and feathers of steam shot briskly from her nostrils. They fell into a trot, neither horse nor rider warm or eager enough to break into anything swifter. They both needed to put some warmth into their extremities before they could muster a gallop.

There were no more than a dozen riders making their way up the pass, zigzagging a little here and there as the inclines and natural obstacles dictated. All appeared to lunge eagerly, almost appearing to fight with their mounts, which was a sure sign that they couldn't have been on horseback all that long. They may have only been riding for a few hours. They were probably unfamiliar with the terrain, and had used the stars and the light of a fullish moon to guide them closer. The dying fires of Masinissa's camp may have stood out a little for them too, as they got nearer. As their shapes gained definition, Masinissa could see that they were a mix of Numidians, Libyans and Carthaginians, as four of the riders had no bridles or saddles, and gripped their horses' manes in rough fists. Masinissa always liked seeing a smattering of his own people in a party, be they emissaries or reinforcements, and his mood was enlivened by the presence of his compatriots in Hanno's ranks.

Their riding style identified them as Numidian as much as the absence of any bridles. They were far more at ease on their mounts than the other riders, particularly when compared with the two burlier riders who were flanking Hanno. They held, both rather awkwardly and vertically, the long spears associated with the Libyan heavy infantry, with their round shields bouncing against their thighs with the rhythm of their steeds. It all looked quite cumbersome and formal, if an approach of allied riders could be deemed as such.

At least get suitable personnel for any errand, Masinissa thought, *unless Hanno has anticipated a need for foot soldiers for the errand or mission he has in mind.*

As Hanno approached, it seemed clear that he had no desire to dismount and would exchange initial pleasantries from on horseback. Masinissa was accustomed to this from senior Carthaginians. Dismounting and staring upwards at the imposing Herculean physique of the Numidian commander could leave most, regardless of their status or rank, feeling somewhat physically diminished. As Masinissa surveyed his Carthaginian guest, he considered that such an abrupt inadequacy would likely have been even more probable. Hanno was rather pale for a Phoenician, and quite slight, to the point of appearing effete. His clothing was layered and suited to the climate, so Masinissa could not quite determine at first glance whether his robes concealed a wiry athleticism or a decadent softness.

It won't do to make such premature assessments, Masinissa thought, *and, even though it looks like Hanno would be better suited to a temple than a battlefield, I feel I ought to give him the benefit of the doubt.* Masinissa tugged Napla's mane, who pulled up alongside Hanno with a slight snort and shake of her muzzle.

"Good morning, commander," the youth greeted him. "I am Hanno. I hope our messenger informed you of our arrival."

The comment struck Masinissa as superfluous and suggested somewhat that Hanno may have been a rather banal conversationalist. Maybe he was a little intimidated? "He did, and I guess you know my name, kid, so let's get down to business," replied Masinissa, dispensing with formalities a little cockily.

It was apparent that Hanno knew exactly who Masinissa was without requiring any confirmation. His initial comportment suggested his normal manner was a little compromised by the encounter, and Masinissa realised that it may take a little while for him to take the paralysis out of his throat and the stiffness out of his limbs.

Masinissa glanced around at his escort, and caught the eye of the Numidians in the group as he did so, and their slouched manner and contained smiles showed plainly that the boy lacked the experience and authority to command them adequately. There was a little condescension in their expressions, which faded quickly when their eyes met Masinissa's, and they regained some of their composure and alertness. He smiled back at them slightly complicitly, half-expecting a wink that wasn't forthcoming.

Masinissa thought the moment demanded he be a little more avuncular and reassuring than normal. The war often brought fresh faces to lead weary and cynical ones, and he remembered the times when he himself was in a similar position as an inexperienced commander. It was not entirely comparable, as his schooling had been tougher, but he remembered the slight uncertainties and hesitations he felt when barking orders to veteran cavalrymen. He had only to look at the deep scars many bore to realise they had more knowledge of how to survive on the battlefield than he did.

"Do you and your men need to freshen up, or are you ready to ride to Xativa? I'll leave most of the troops here and take a small company to ride with you," explained Masinissa.

Ari, Capuca, Juba Tunic and Soldier Boy were already mounted behind him, with another dozen riders anticipating that Hanno's response would be to ride into the morning.

"Let's ride. Our journey here has been quick, and our horses are still fresh. Let's take advantage of the coolness of the morning to make good time to the castle our enemies occupy," confirmed Hanno.

"Spoken like a man too used to riding in the heat of midday. Wise. Come on then, let's go." With that, Masinissa kicked hard into Napla's flanks, and they set forth for Xativa.

*

For the Romans, such a journey would have been fraught with danger. The landscape was beautiful, and the mountains eased the spirits, but it was perfect ambush country, and the Carthaginian forces and local tribes pounced regularly on unwary Roman detachments. Both sides did, in truth, but the better marauders were those who knew the country best and who held the advantage of mobility.

Hanno rode alongside Masinissa, and, quickly, his ingenuous ways and surprising exuberance, rather than proving an irritation, began to endear him to the Numidian, who had seen little of either quality for some time. Besides, it was easy to notice that he was, at heart, a simple and decent boy. Hanno's anxiety slipped from him quickly, and it seemed to Masinissa, without conceit, that the earlier tension in the lad was simply due to him meeting someone he held in high esteem. The questions that poured out of him once he had lost his apprehension resembled the fervid chatter that young boys pester winning athletes with at games or the idiotic questions adolescents pose to drowsy philosophers.

Hanno was clearly an avid consumer of military tactics and history, and pressed Masinissa several times about his views on Alexander of Macedon. He was on relatively secure ground responding to those, but when Hanno veered into mathematics and astronomy, which the boy appeared equally as enthusiastic about, he caught himself glazing over a little. Hanno appeared to have a particular fondness for Eratosthenes. Regrettably, or perhaps mercifully, Masinissa had to concede that he had never read any of his works, especially *Hermes*, which it was clear Hanno loved. The fundamentals of astronomy were of limited interest to Masinissa. Obviously, he needed sufficient knowledge of the constellations to get about in the dark, but, beyond that, he was indifferent. The fact that, apparently, Eratosthenes, by comparing the shadow of the sun at noon on the summer solstice at both Alexandria and Syene, had been able to calculate the circumference of the earth as 250,000 stadia was of interest, but really only as a casual remark that Masinissa could share around a campfire when he had exhausted more interesting themes. He felt himself biting back irreverent remarks that he knew would offend Hanno, as he wittered on about geometry, mathematics and astronomy.

"You know, sometimes, it is as important to look down as well as up," Masinissa chided his companion mildly. "I admire scholars highly, but they don't charge with me into enemy lines, and the war is not a place to get too distracted by higher-minded things. Pay attention to your weapons, your horses, your soldiers and yourself. For instance, looking at your horse's hooves now, it would seem they are due a trim and a sturdier wrap of hide. This is hard country we're going through."

"You're right. We have to keep all our equipment in order in the field. I'll take more care," responded Hanno.

Masinissa nodded approvingly and allowed the young rider to

continue his prattle if he wished to, or to take the hint and either be quiet or take a detour in his topic of conversation.

Hanno had the insight to notice Masinissa's boredom and rode silently for a while. As they drew closer to the castle he asked, "Do you know the importance of Xativa?"

"Only vaguely," Masinissa replied. "I'm aware that Hannibal passed through there."

"His association is a little more personal. His wife Imelce is from this area, and when he left for the Cisalpine regions and beyond, he left her and his son here. They even, quite sentimentally, left the top room – Hannibal's bedroom – empty. They have since crossed to Africa from Gades."

"Ah OK; I see now why you might take a particular interest. You know I was going to attack it anyway, or at least raid any parties or camps in its vicinity. Horses don't scale ramparts all that well, after all!"

"I'm sure we'll notice a few plumes of Roman smoke pretty soon. Their sentries will be easy pickings for you."

*

As they rode over the crest of the next hill, their destination loomed before them. A small village appeared at the foot of the hill, and the fortification stood above it as the land rose. There was an outer gatehouse and curtain wall, and the inner battlements traced a line up to the higher keep, which was perched at the apex of a neat pyramid hillock. There were some scrubby trees to one side, but on the others was bare rock. Another interior wall ringed this hill, about halfway up the slope. Appraising the fortifications with a military eye, Masinissa thought that it would be quite a tough task to attack it, but that it was an easy place to besiege. He couldn't see where any wells may have been situated, but he doubted that the higher fort had any water supply of its own, and sustenance amounted to a gnarled, bare olive tree digging obstinately into the dirt fractures of the rock.

Regarding Hanno, Masinissa noticed that some of the boy's earlier unease had returned, that his jaw and shoulders had become more set and rigid, and the grip with which he held his horse was tighter. Masinissa asked him quietly, "What's the matter? The way you are squeezing that leather bridle has got me worried."

"I'm that easy to read, huh?" Hanno admitted. "I should explain my interest to you. I can do it simply enough, but it's painful for me, so my apologies if I have not chosen to allude to it already. If you're going to support my attack on this castle, then you should know the full extent of my motivation. It has dual origins: one personal and one spiritual. My family name is Brega, and my father, Kanmi Brega, was one of the few senior members of the Sacred Band to campaign with Hannibal. When Hannibal continued north with his army, he left my father here to garrison Xativa. It was an important assignment and not the sinecure you may suppose, certainly not in hindsight. Part of his obligation was to ensure the safety of Imelce, which he did at the cost of his life, as he fought the Roman legionnaires sufficiently long to allow her small party to escape south. He was also the custodian of a most important artefact that Hannibal had entrusted to him."

Masinissa leant forwards a little and was clearly intrigued.

"This artefact," Hanno continued, "was one of a pair of chalices that had been kept at the Temple of Melqart, and were the last cups used by Melqart before he died. They were, fittingly, both decorated ornately and cast in gold. When Hannibal received his vision of conquest there, the priests entrusted him with one of them as a means to show the tribes that he had Melqart's blessing. The Turdetani are practically Phoenician themselves and are our brothers, and the Llergetes further north, commanded by Indibilis and Mandonius, fight with us, but the Oretani, Bastetani and Contestani were felt to be more ambivalent. Being in possession of one of the cups, it was supposed, would rally these tribes decisively to our banner, and this is what transpired. However, whilst Imelce eluded capture, the cup of Melqart was left at Xativa, and I must retrieve it, and return it to the lands of the Turdetani and to its sacred home. Besides that, I intend to kill the Roman centurion, Atilius Metellus, who killed my father and who still commands this outpost. I have heard word of the nature of my father's death, and I wish I had not, for the circumstances are as brutal and savage as you could imagine. They captured him alive, and, after brutalising him for their amusement, Metellus hurled him to the camp dogs, who tore him limb from limb. Furthermore, the animal proceeded to boil alive the captives he had taken. The Numidian detachment escorted Imelce and escaped, but many Carthaginians, Libyans and Contestani perished horribly."

Masinissa furrowed his brow, sighed, reached over the haunches of Hanno's mount and offered him a silent pat. The poor lad was carrying a greater burden than he had suspected after all. "I will aid your vengeance as best I can. That part is assured, but how do you intend to retrieve Melqart's cup?"

Hanno paused mischievously and raised a finger to emphasise the moment, made a big comical circle with his mouth and then gave Masinissa some good news. "Well, the reason that the cup of Melqart is still at Xativa is because the Romans don't know it's there. I'm sure they knew that it was taken there from the chatter of the local tribes, but they must have assumed that Imelce would have taken it with her when she fled or that perhaps it was still in Hannibal's possession. In reality, it is buried beneath the ramparts close to where that old olive tree is. Thank Tanit it is still there! I'm going to need that old stump for my bearings."

Hanno glanced quickly at his companion and then took the moment to lionise Masinissa, perhaps with the subliminal intention of ingratiating himself further. From his effusiveness, it was plain he wasn't yet sure to what extent Masinissa would be willing to support him. Attacking enemies in open country was Masinissa's forte, but storming a fortress was something he was less well renowned for. "Thank Tanit too that I am so fortunate to be in the company of our army's most illustrious soldier. All my way through North Africa and Iberia, your name is always the talk of the fires, and always in association with intrepid and indomitable actions. I've seen men visibly take courage hearing about your exploits, and if they know you are to join them in any raid or battle, their spirits revive."

Masinissa was not always at ease with such flattery, especially with those comments that strayed into sycophancy. Women and those closest to him could flatter him as wildly as they wished, but strangers or juniors were another matter altogether. They were more likely to cause irritation rather than amusement or approval. "Enough, now; it is sufficient that I know the reasons that lie behind this mission. Let's hope Melqart is listening to the petitions of his thirsty Turdetani supplicants in Gades."

Since Hanno had mentioned the true motivation for his approach to Xativa, Masinissa had been reassessing the situation slowly. A frontal assault on such a citadel could be prolonged and costly. The numbers and quality of the defenders of the castle were also uncertain. The last thing he needed was to be confronted by capable slingers who could deliver rocks to the jaws of his riders and the eyes of his horses. Fortunately, they were still sufficiently distant to not have drawn attention to themselves. There were agricultural plains around most of the castle and the village, but the presence of some uninterrupted woodland gave him optimism that a small party might approach the castle unnoticed with a little stealth and with the blessing of a cloudy night. Once in the village, it should be easy enough to pass unnoticed or despatch anyone who crossed their path. He resolved to take that approach initially. It was very risky to be so exposed, massively outnumbered and immobile, and to approach the castle undetected would necessitate approaching it on foot – or on his stomach for some parts, by the looks of the terrain – but it seemed the better course. With any luck, he could slaughter the livestock if they could get into the inner courtyards and accelerate any siege if that was deemed a possibility. It seemed unlikely. The Carthaginian armies were still busy reinforcing, and attacking a provincial outpost would surely be considered a waste of manpower. The strategy was to stick to raids until enough men had crossed from North Africa or until enough funds had been found to convince the mercenary tribes of the peninsula to rally for Carthage.

Hanno responded encouragingly to Masinissa's suggestion, albeit with a little trepidation. It was decided that Ari and Capuca would join them: Ari to take out any sentries from distance, and Capuca as the most agile of the party and the one best equipped to infiltrate the castle.

As night fell and they were blessed with the clouds they had hoped for, the four departed, leaving the remaining detachment beyond the furthest ridge to the west. They entered the woods quickly, but stayed on its fringes, and were not enveloped completely by the darkness of the trees. The dim fires of the village, and the muffled noises of livestock and men kept them pointed in the right direction, and they, for the most part, only needed to skirt the small grove as the looming shadow of the Xativa fortress always remained in their murky vision. Swiftly, they gained the stony path that snaked through the village. Ari looked at the walls of the castle, closed his fingers around his stone pouch and then flashed them forwards, indicating to the others that anyone on its parapet was by then in the range of his sling. It appeared larger to Masinissa than he'd assumed from their earlier vantage point, and its turrets more foreboding. It was eerily quiet too. The hour was late, and both village and castle seemed sound asleep. Hanno's eyes shone eagerly as he surveyed the battlements.

"What shall we do now?" Capuca asked the others. They had ropes, but they looked inadequate and a pretty cumbersome form of entry.

"We have time," replied Masinissa. "We can wait until someone comes through the main gates. It might be that we'll have to return tomorrow if it gets to gets too close to the dawn, but my guess is that there will be movement. This does not seem the most vigilant of citadels! We might even be bold and fake our identities to the sentry. How's your Latin, Cap?"

"Not as good as yours, Mas. How about we give it a few hours and then trust to your mimicry?"

"All right, but if they don't buy my fancy voice, it's going to get a whole lot harder to pilfer this chalice. I'm hoping that a late night tryst might come to our aid."

"You've got the call of the drongo, boss. You'll convince them," interjected Ari.

Both Capuca and Hanno turned to him, looking a little puzzled, compelling the young Libyan to explain that a drongo was a small passerine bird that lived south of the desert, and that mimicked other birds and would make hoax calls of other species in order to fool them.

"You got it, Ari; Masinissa the drongo will fool these Romans easily," agreed Capuca.

The men all smiled at the silliness of the moment. They smiled again when they heard the bellowing laugh of an approaching figure, oblivious to their lurking presence. It quickly transpired, from the cooing response to the outburst, that it was a couple, and both seemed to have enjoyed a few libations, by their tone and the irregular pattern of their footsteps.

They passed them in a grapey haze and knocked on the thick, iron-framed door of the outer bastion. A gaunt face appeared at the slots in the window, who recognised them with a little morose nod. A clanking of keys and irons followed, and the door lurched. The amorous couple did the same, and fell forwards as their support yielded inwards.

As the couple stumbled clumsily, the four waiting men offered their antithesis and pounced nimbly, almost in a choreographed wave. Masinissa led and kicked the man forwards. In truth, he needed little to assist his collapse, and, as he did so, Masinissa used his back as a springboard, leapt into the saturnine sentry and drove his knife into his throat. Simultaneously, Masinissa's companions selected their targets and attended to them. Ari smashed his fist into the unfortunate courtesan, and she barely yelped as she hit the floor. Capuca finished off what Masinissa had started, and stabbed his blade into the exposed neck of the prostrated centurion. Ari, for his part, had spied the large dog that accompanied the sentry and was clearly useless as a scent hound, and had broken its neck before it could have barked an alarm.

As their victims crumpled, the four checked the courtyard quietly and realised quickly that their good fortune had continued, as the area appeared deserted, and no fires were lit.

"It looks like Metellus will be receiving guests at this late hour after all," Hanno whispered, although his elation was easy to note despite his murmuring.

Masinissa scowled a little at his exuberance, grabbed him by his tunic and hissed into his ear, "This has only begun. This is not the time for a celebration." He brought the men into a huddle and gave them instructions. "Cap, take the stables, ready four horses and kill as many of the others as you can when you see me next. Ari, secure the walls and find an elevation overlooking the barracks. If anyone approaches or emerges, take them quietly. Hanno, you and I will take the keep, meet justice upon Metellus and get this cup."

The men all nodded in unison and it struck him momentarily how effortless his decision-making could be under such extreme conditions. *I've been doing this too long!* he thought to himself a little ruefully. He had learnt the trick that, sometimes, all you need to do is appear decisive or certain when everyone around you is not and is looking for exactly those characteristics to follow.

The four separated quickly, and he felt confident that they would do as he had commanded. He couldn't be certain that they would not be detected, but, even in that event, he was sure that, as long as they could get to the horses, they had the wit to evade capture, if not injury. Hanno tucked in beside him, and they padded as softly as they could along the walls to the keep. Hanno shivered a little, and Masinissa shot him a glance.

"It's OK to be cold, but don't get scared on me now," he warned the young Carthaginian.

The entrance was as carelessly patrolled as the gatehouse.

"Looks like this Metellus likes a little privacy," Masinissa offered, as much to buoy the spirits of his confederate as to reassure himself.

They mounted the stairway and crept around, with their *falcatas* drawn, each of them hugging the wall and wondering whether, at any moment, an enemy would spring down upon them with their own sabres. Advantage would certainly be with any prospective assailant. At least they were blessed with a few olive oil *lucerna* dotted into crevices to light their way. They were spared the Stygian gloom they could easily have encountered within a less well-maintained staircase.

As he saw the edge of the upper floor, Masinissa sped up his measured pace and burst out of the stairway. The confined spiral had started to trigger a little of the giddiness and claustrophobia that nomadic people feel in such places, and, besides, if anyone was at the top, he wanted to be going as quickly as he could when they noticed him. For a soldier who was braced for the lunge of iron or fist or skull, what met his gaze at the top of the flight was quite vapid and underwhelming. He still held tight to his sword and his posture, but what lay in front of him posed no immediate threat.

For the presumed former suite of Hannibal and Imelce, it was quite a small and drab space, lit only slightly less dimly than the stairway had been. It is easy to assume that someone's renown and station in life will automatically translate to opulence in all their dwellings, but this one was markedly humble, an impression only aggravated by the obvious absence of a female touch, even of an occasional maid. The room was fusty, to say the least, with the sourness of an oblivious man.

The furnishings, such as they were, were spartan and dirty, indicating long months of neglect. There was a recess in the furthest wall, indicating a further chamber, presumably a bedroom, and Masinissa motioned Hanno to investigate, although no sound or motion was apparent from there. Before him, lay a classic triclinium, although one that had certainly seen better days. A low table abutted the couches, and it consolidated the sense of disorderliness. Dishes and detritus lay haphazardly all over it and represented the remains of several meals. A few deflated-looking goatskins lay close by, and their edges were stained crimson, indicating that the party was long over and the participants were pretty uncoordinated when they tipped wine out of the end of the skin. No cup or goblet was in view.

This survey was done as an ancillary to Masinissa's main focus, which was to keep to a cautious eye on the occupant of the furthest couch, who faced him with a swaying attentiveness that suggested the wine from the skins had not long been consumed and his sensibilities were quite impaired.

Never underestimate a drunk man, though, Masinissa cautioned himself.

The injunction seemed quite wise, given the appearance of the man. He was enormous, larger than Masinissa but clearly more dissolute, and with a brutish aspect that he seemed to exude like a poisonous odour. The glare with which he fixed his intruder was chilling, despite his woozy state, and it was clearly one that he'd fixed on many of his prior victims. This was a cold-blooded, merciless killer. The stains on his lips may have been blood rather than wine, for all the look suited him. His eyes were tiny and scrunched in hatred, and he needed to work the muscles around his lenses harder than usual to retain focus. He was dishevelled, with matted hair and beard, but there was something of a cornered animal's readiness in him, despite his obvious dissipation. His hackles were raised, and it struck Masinissa that he looked a little like the hyena Masinissa had seen once in an arena in Carthage before they had let the dogs loose on it. That ugly, condemned beast had taken quite a few of those snarling mutts with him, he recalled.

The man's head rocked in a short semicircle into the nape of his neck, a motion that would be intended to loosen the muscles ordinarily, but clearly had the opposite intention in this case. When he snapped his head back into its usual cradle, his gaze had lost a little of its vagueness. "I don't need a uniform or a herald to know you, Numidian. I'm honoured," he declared.

The words and their lucidity corroborated Masinissa's sense that Metellus's inebriation (for indeed it was him) was at this stage mostly theatrical.

Metellus continued, "Have you come with news of your armies' rout or surrender? There can't be too many able-bodied men left in Africa by now. Why are you even fighting for that cause? Carthage has as much kinship with you as Rome has with the Gauls." He added a little hiccup.

Masinissa bought only the spitefulness and not the deception. Masinissa just looked at him, mirroring his antagonists' contempt. He knew Hanno must have his moment and be given the opportunity to confront his father's murderer. He arrived on cue, with their exchange of looks confirming that it was only the three of them in the chambers.

"Atilius Metellus," Hanno said as he drew in front of the Numidian's sword.

Metellus's response was only to turn and look at him, almost dismissively, with an expression so empty it almost made him appear like a giant grotesque doll.

"Atilius Metellus." Hanno's inflection even more agitated and urgent.

"Do I need to write my name on my forehead for you, idiot? Who else would I be?"

The confirmation visibly eased the tension in the vengeful boy. "Good, I don't want to be groping around another corner of this fort tonight. I am Hanno Brega, and finding and killing you is all I've wanted to do for some time."

Metellus laughed contemptuously. "Funny, I don't seem to have paid you any mind." There was no fear in his eyes at the revelation that one of his many sins had come back to revisit him. "These are the fortunes of war. Your father fell here at my hands. It could have been anywhere. Killing isn't something you schedule or plan. It's anonymous. People have simply two categories: enemies or allies."

"You think you can sanitise your evil so easily?" Hanno responded, outraged and enraged by the fact that his father's killer had explained his torture as almost a humdrum, everyday matter. "What kind of beast are you that you can regard feeding a fellow officer to dogs as a customary undertaking?"

"Even the mutts gotta eat, boy."

Both intruders shook at the insult. There appeared to be no depths to Metellus's effrontery.

Hanno had heard enough. This pig could have eviscerated his father and would have shown more mercy, and he appeared to not have a shred of remorse, nor even the guile to plead for his life. "You invite your own death. Trust that I will show you greater mercy than you have ever granted."

Metellus exhaled a mix of exasperation and relief. "About time!" he rebuked, and with that he pushed the table upwards and towards them.

A mix of crashing plates, bowls and food debris shot towards them, and both men leapt back as the turning table threatened their shins. Hanno's reflexes were a little slow, and the table caught him just above his ankle, sufficient to make him lose balance but not fall.

The Roman had given himself an edge, had armed himself with his *gladius*, and swung it with all his force at the stumbling Hanno. As much as Masinissa knew that this was a fight for the boy, at the same time, the force and direction of Metellus's lunge was about to tear through Hanno's throat, and if the blade was sharp, would most likely decapitate him. He parried the thrust and took the *gladius* in the meat of his *falcata*. The swords resounded on contact, and Metellus's *gladius* scraped like chalk on stone down the convex edge of Masinissa's sickle-like blade.

This kind of commotion shouldn't last long, thought Masinissa a little anxiously, as it would surely alert others in the slumbering fortress.

As their swords met, Masinissa sensed his adversary's power, and despite Metellus's bulk and the considerable force he wielded in his arms, the test was enough for Masinissa to realise he was the stronger. He pushed back with his sword arm as his opponent's blade got close to his grip and the heave checked Metellus and gave Masinissa enough room to crash his open hand straight into the nose of his foe.

The punch rocked Metellus and diverted into empty air the strike his own free hand was aiming at Masinissa's chin. It also had given Hanno enough time to regain his equilibrium, and, for as much as he evidently wanted to revel in the moment, this was not a duel for honour but a savage fight to the death, and he responded accordingly.

As the knuckles of Masinissa's hand plastered his enemy's nasal bone and cartilage, he yelled at Hanno, "*Stick him.*"

His associate appeared to be of similar mind, and as Metellus's head pitched upwards, exposing his throat, Hanno yelled, "*Duck!*"

As Masinissa did as he was bid, he almost immediately heard a set of reassuring sounds: a rip of flesh, the whoosh of air as Hanno's blade passed close to his skull, and the gurgling noise Metellus's larynx tried to make as it was turned into a fountain of blood.

He rose, and his eyes confirmed the message his ears had already received. Metellus had been sliced open from the edge of his jaw to his clavicle. Only one of his arms seemed to be functioning, and that arm's hand was reaching into the pulp at his neck in a vain attempt to stem his ebbing life force. His eyes were no longer scowling at either Masinissa or his nemesis, but were frozen as terror finally found its way into his expression. Masinissa had seen this type of death many times before, men who choked out their lives looking like fish that had just been landed on a boat, and as much as the man deserved to suffocate for a little longer there was business to attend to. He urged his companion, who seemed a little incapacitated in his own way, "Take the rest off."

The adjuration seemed to revive Hanno, who shook both of his arms in tandem by his sides, hesitated for a second as if searching for an appropriate comment, thought better of it and grabbed the hair of the dying man, whose focus on his enemy was restored suddenly. Their eyes locked onto one another and lingered in a macabre antithesis of the gaze of lovers. Hanno broke the spell by expectorating into the wound he had made, drew himself and his sword backwards, and, with his full strength, sheared Metellus head off his shoulders.

Hanno looked at the corpse and then upwards to the heavens, and said solemnly, "Father, my duty is paid. Rest now."

Masinissa approved the simplicity and sincerity of the comment, but he needed to be brought back to his senses. His vengeance may have been satiated, but the cup of Melqart still had to be retrieved, and they needed to do it quickly.

"That's for him, not for you," Masinissa reprimanded, but with a hint of levity and relief.

Fortunately, Hanno showed no inclination to savour the moment and gave Masinissa a nod. "We're in luck in these chambers. The window at the rear lies directly over the tree. Imelce told us that the cup is buried shallowly close to the trunk on the south side, close to a hollow in its base."

"Easy!" Masinissa exclaimed. He threw Hanno the rope he had with them. "Fetch! I hope this is long enough for the drop."

"Don't you want the honour?" Hanno replied, a little surprised.

"I'd rather be the one handing it over to the priests, if it's all the same to you. If I could be blessed with a sense of communion with my favourite god, I would rather it be at his home. Frankly, we haven't got time for prayer and meditation right now, and you seem a little more lithe on the rope than me."

"Fair point," Hanno conceded as he quickly tied the rope to the closest anchor to the window.

He was over the parapet just as briskly, and, for a few minutes, Masinissa was forced to piece together his movements from the tenebrous digging shape he could barely discern, and the sounds of the stabbing and probing of the earth that carried up just within his earshot. He could make out that Hanno had begun the exploration with his sword, but, when the unmistakable clank of metal revealed the location of the goblet, he switched to his shorter knife and scraped around it avidly. He freed it quickly and, as he did so, he let out a short whistle of admiration. It might have been considered a little imprudent, but it was unlikely anyone in the castle would be so vigilant as to notice such a minor expression of triumph.

Having retrieved the cup, Hanno ascended the rope. As he climbed back into the window of the keep, Masinissa could not help but admire the glittering object tucked into his belt. As the Carthaginian regained solid ground, he presented it to Masinissa, and – even though it needed cleaning and the light was poor – its detail and quality was obvious to both men. It was a very ornate skyphos, which is a two-handled, mostly silver cup that had its design origins in Corinth and Athens. In the case of the cup of Melqart, parts of the handles and base were highlighted in gold leaf, but it was the delicacy and detail of the repousse art that the craftsmen had hammered out from the other side that took the eye and was simply breathtaking.

Masinissa himself had heard and seen a few of these before, mostly of males in quite intimate poses, a Greek custom he thought might benefit from the inclusion of some female figures, even ones that were chastely covered, but this one held no sensual elements whatsoever and instead used the large surfaces of the cup to intertwine elements of the first six of the labours of Melqart. It was a little cramped in places, but the artist or artists were clearly skilled in the most precise work and had pulled off quite a *tour de force*. As Masinissa turned the cup in his hands, in turn, representations of the Nemean Lion, the Lernean Hydra, the Hind of Ceryneia, the Erymanthean Boar, the Augean Stables and the Stymphalian Birds appeared, all depicted with the most distinct detailing, captivating him.

In truth, for all the plunders of the war and all the treasures held in Carthage, Illipa and Gades, Masinissa had never seen an object so exquisite in his life.

Hanno nudged him to break him free of his appreciative stupor. "Makes you want to see the other one doesn't it?"

"For sure!" Masinissa smiled back. "I wonder if the depictions of Geryon and Cerberus are as good as the creatures here."

"No doubt they are. I'm sure the commissioner of the pair would have insisted upon it. When you are making tableware for a god, I'm pretty certain you'd do your best work."

"Let's reunite them, shall we? Before these Romans find us and turn our skulls into a pair of vessels like the Boii made out of the praetor Lucius Postumius Albinus."

Hanno agreed their missions were complete, and it would be ill advised to linger too long in the fortress of their decapitated host. "Do you think we have disturbed any Romans?" the young Carthaginian asked, his tone raising the spectre that there may be a tide of their enemies vaulting up the steps of the keep at that very moment.

"These walls are thick, even though the night is still, and, besides, I'm sure Capuca and Ari can despatch any light sleepers. At the window, when you were digging all I heard was the breeze. There were no hints of our interrupted enemies rallying for an assault. They don't have the same need to be furtive as us. Let's go!"

The two men left the room and retraced their steps. As they

reached the courtyard of the castle, the first thing that assailed them was the evidence that they were not the only members of their small infiltration party to have encountered and eliminated one of their enemies. They almost stumbled over the corpse of a young soldier. Even in the gloom, Masinissa could see easily that he had all the innocence of a fresh *hastati*, a raw trooper without any of the scars of battle worn by more experienced troopers; that is, aside from the gaping wound in his forehead that was no doubt caused by one of Ari's pinpoint stones.

"Good sign," he whispered to Hanno.

If this fort was garrisoned with such youths, extricating themselves would appear to be quite a routine matter. He reflected on how suitable Ari had been for this venture. He had been the perfect choice. No one he could think of could perform the role of assassin as well. The thought was reinforced as he felt a gentle hand on his shoulder and his stealthy confederate emerged. After the momentary shock of being surprised so easily passed, Masinissa asked for a quick review of the events outside of the keep.

Ari reassured him, "Aside from this poor soul, another pair at the gate, and a few of their hounds, who took a dislike to my desert odours, it seems they are still oblivious to us."

"Excellent! Thank Melqart," Masinissa exclaimed. To him, as for the others, their good fortune thus far could have no other explanation than it had been divinely sanctioned. The retrieval of the cup had somehow given them all a sense of invulnerability, an impression only consolidated by the night's events, which had left none of them with even the slightest graze.

The three emboldened men moved quickly to the stables, taking the same precautions as they had earlier, but with a greater certainty that they would all still see the encroaching dawn. Their time was short by then, and the cooks and maids of this castle would soon be the first to revive. The discovery of slain men and dogs would send shrieks of alarm throughout the citadel. Masinissa felt a slight tinge of sadness at the prospect that would await him at the stables. They could not risk stampeding the horses, as many would return to the castle and allow a pursuit to be mobilised, and so, apart from the four most fortunate steeds, the rest would be hobbled or killed. For a horseman like Masinissa, that was a tragic fate.

As they approached the stables, which lay close to the gates, he could see that the grizzly duty he had presumed he was to perform had, for the most part, been spared him, or at least Capuca's ingenuity had come up with an alternative no less repugnant. It would seem as if his cousin had the foresight to realise that slaughtering horses in the middle of the night would cause a bit of a commotion and his solution appeared to have been to create something that resembled a cross between an enclosure and a bonfire. He had taken wooden stockades and corralled most of the horses, but had broken up straw and any combustible material he could lay his hands on and incorporated that into his fence. He held a lit torch in his hand that he was poised to ignite the pyre with. Masinissa supposed that a few of the horses may, in their desperate panic, jump the improvised fences he had erected, but most would be consumed.

It will be enough, he thought sadly to himself.

Suddenly, and in close proximity, a throaty, lupine howl broke forth from the nearest doorway, and a man emerged and charged towards him, with a sword raised high above his head and incoherent curses spewing from his mouth. Quickly, it became apparent that the brave fool was alone, but his yell would have the whole castle upon them in no time.

"Mount up!" Masinissa cried to Hanno and Ari, confident that – despite the ferocity and wildness of the berserker charging towards them – he wouldn't need their assistance to check his attack. His two companions disappeared rapidly from his peripheral awareness, and his senses sharpened, focussing upon the approaching swordsman. He sensed a flash of heat against his cheek as Capuca set fire to the stockade, drew his *falcata* across his body and ran at his enemy's unarmed side. It was a move that Masinissa had practised in many close-quarter engagements. You let your opponent lunge, then, when he commits and over extends himself, strike at whichever vulnerable point presents itself.

"Die African," the maddened Roman snarled as he readied his blow.

For a second, Masinissa caught his eyes, which blazed blue with bloodshot edges. *This is an easier prey than usual*, Masinissa thought as his attacker drew his sword over his head and threw his blade at full pelt in a wild arc, which Masinissa easily eluded. *You only get one shot when you fence like that*, Masinissa thought to himself, maligning the rather pathetic effort to take his life.

He caught the man's eyes a second time, and the expression he read was more familiar. The man knew he had sealed his own doom, and his roar of attack had been choked back in his throat to a panicked rasp, which left any longer would have changed into a cry or a pitiful plea. Masinissa didn't give the man the opportunity to forfeit his dignity, and, as he saw death in his eyes, he sent him briskly on his way to the afterlife. There was no time or need for a second strike. The man crumpled to the ground and was no longer a threat. That was as far as Masinissa's immediate cares stretched. He glanced upwards at the blur that had passed him seconds earlier, and saw that Hanno and his mount, not unexpectedly, were already almost at the gates. His opinion of him slipped at the fractional desertion, but he knew Hanno's loyalties to him were slight and he had the cup in his possession after all, which stood as a slight mitigation of his flight.

Capuca and Ari were their reliable selves, though, and had pulled up their horses and the one intended for Masinissa just behind him. The horses were extremely agitated, but Masinissa was quick to gain the back of his stallion before it broke free of Capuca's fist. He winked at the steadfast Numidian and Libyan, and the three charged out of the fortress of Xativa, as the cries of alarmed men and the screams of burning horses gave greater urgency to the digs they drove into the flanks of their terrified mounts.

The village was awake from the raised alarm, but no one made any attempt to impede them as they passed by. They were mostly local Iberian civilians who had, until recently, served the castle when it was in the possession of the Carthaginian forces and may yet again if the territory changed hands once more. They knew the tides of war ebbed and flowed, and that there was nothing to be gained from trying to impede the riders. Those who were bold enough to make the doorways of their dwellings merely crouched there and stared warily at the fleeing men.

For Masinissa, his perception of time slowed even further, as his heartbeat raced as fast as his mount's, and they put a great distance between themselves and the citadel in what seemed only minutes. They had crossed the wood and made the peak of the furthest hill, beyond which awaited the Numidian cavalry. There they could rein in their horses and lay an ambush, should the Romans salvage enough horses to come after them. That prospect, however, was improbable, as it would take them days to acquire fresh steeds, and, once the dead Metellus was discovered, appoint a fresh legionnaire.

Masinissa turned to the others as they gained a vantage point of the valley beyond, and saw, with relief, that his men were busy with their early morning affairs. He hailed them with his deepest baritone holler, like an exultant Norseman returning to his native fjord, and, almost in unison, the men below let out an echoing roar as Masinissa's returning presence was detected. For the exhausted Numidian and his three companions, the energy of the salute restored a little vitality, and they sat more poised and erect on their stolen horses. The certainty of safety and success coursed through them. The smell of camp breakfast – frying strips of meat, garlic and eggs – also began to reach their ravenous senses, and added a little extra impetus to the gallop down the leeward side of the hill.

Inhaling deeply of the cooking smells, Capuca broke their hungry trance. "We made breakfast, boys!" He chuckled with a little mock nonchalance in his tone.

In response, Ari grinned and rubbed his stomach. Hanno, not willing to be excluded from the companionable moment, mimicked Ari's gesture, rolling his hand around his torso like he was a little boy amusing his mother with an eager, pantomime appetite.

"You hungry too, Sacred Band?" Masinissa smirked.

"I sure am!" came Hanno's affable-but-terse reply.

"Well, you earned a good feed; let's get down there before we faint."

The three others goaded their steeds a little harder at the prompt.

Ari chipped in a famished, "I'm going to eat like we're at a feast day to Tanit. My stomach thinks my throat's been cut."

The men laughed at the banal observation they'd all heard so many times before, as if it was suddenly the freshest, most ingenious pleasantry.

Letting his animal follow its kind at a circumspect pace, something of a slow canter, Masinissa let his thoughts elevate their preoccupations from his stomach to his soul. They had just killed in cold blood both men and animals – some guilty and deserving, others just unlucky and almost innocent – and they had ridden out of Xativa with the prize of a cup. It was, he consoled himself, an extraordinary cup and an object imbued with even more value for its association with the god of Tyre, his god, the one he had beseeched for protection frequently and sincerely ever since his tutors had taught him knowledge of and reverence for the gods of the Phoenician people. However, the mundanity of the trinket, despite all its craftsmanship and beauty, bothered him.

The absurdity twisted a defiance out of him, as if he was down to his last couple of dogs in an outmatched game of *latrunculi*, where his opponent was circling him with a mostly intact pack. They had done these things for Melqart, and Melqart was his god too. He had a right to this transplanted diety's protection just as much as Queen Dido had when she had pleaded, with deceitful intent, for the Byrsa. He could and he would drink from it at the temple near Gades when they returned it there, and imbibe greedily all of the mercy the goblet channelled.

He wondered if the gods, as they roamed the planet and made new conquests, retained their vitality or whether their powers withered as they distanced themselves from their origins. Maybe that was why temples were made. Tyre and Gades were at the opposite ends of civilisation, but they honoured the same divinity. He wondered a little about the existence of any native and supplanted deities. What had people worshiped before Baal Hammon, Tanit and Melqart? He didn't know. No one had told him of any ancient myths or celestial beings. Maybe the Troglodytae in their desert caves and primitive understandings preserved a memory of them somehow. *Maybe,* he wondered with an idle heresy, *there may be layers of gods, which time laid like clay bricks, one on top of another, burying false promises and residues of hope with each fresh gloop of supernatural mortar. No one would submerge the powers of Melqart, though. His power was irrepressible.*

What was important was not what was real, and what he could touch or taste. It wasn't the wine in the cup or the designs on it. It was the faith you had in its consecration. In what could not be understood or felt. This was not an ordinary day, the cup was not an ordinary cup, and its journey back to where it belonged would be his most solemn duty.

He closed his eyes and imagined Melqart, with his colossal strength and nobility, and his implausibly exaggerated musculature. He said a silent prayer, thinking out the rhythmic words he often had incantated in sanctified cloisters. His imagination stimulated and sharpened the image, but, when he opened his eyes again, all traces of his god disappeared.

He closed them again, this time summoning Sophonisba, his love, from the phosphene darkness. His memory came to his aid, and he remembered their halcyon summer idylls, curled together, looking for the right words and their hearts finding them. He held his lids tight, clinging to a long-lost moment, but when he opened them again she too, like his celestial patron, fled instantaneously.

"Bless you, sweetheart," he whispered into the emptiness, within and without.